# Holding Out for a Hero

## Amy Andrews

First published by Momentum in 2013
This edition published in 2014 by Momentum
Pan Macmillan Australia Pty Ltd
1 Market Street, Sydney 2000

A CIP record for this book is available at the National Library of Australia

Holding Out for a Hero

EPUB format: 9781760080327
Mobi format: 9781760080334
POD format: 9781760082079

Cover design by Carrie Kabak
Edited by Kylie Mason
Proofread by Hayley Crandell

Macmillan Digital Australia: www.macmillandigital.com.au

To report a typographical error, please visit momentumbooks.com.au/contact/

Visit www.momentumbooks.com.au to read more about all our books and to buy
books online. You will also find features, author interviews and news of any
author events.

Amy Andrews is an award-winning author with 30+ contemporary romance novels to her name. She's sold over a million books worldwide as well as being translated into a dozen different languages including Manga!

She loves her kids, her husband, her dogs, men in tool belts and happily ever afters. Do not mess with the HEA! Also good books, fab food, great wine and frequent travel – preferably all four together.

She lives on acreage on the outskirts of Brisbane with a gorgeous mountain view but secretly wishes it was the hillsides of Tuscany.

For my very own hero, Mark, who has never slayed a dragon, leapt a tall building in a single bound or caught a bullet in his teeth, but would if I asked him.

# CHAPTER ONE

It had been two years, eight months and twenty-three days since Ella Lucas had last done the horizontal rumba. And even then it hadn't been very good.

With the powerful Harley throbbing between her legs, she was acutely aware of every asexual minute. The machine pulsed against her, taunting barren places, reminding Ella of her depressingly sexless existence. Was it possible to orgasm on the seat of a Harley?

Alone?

She revved the engine. *Lock up your husbands, Huntley, Rachel's daughter is back in town.*

Her red lips twisted in a bitter smile. Nearly two decades since she'd been in her hometown and it was still driving her nuts. Seventeen years she'd spent in this speck on the map trying to do the right thing, trying to be her mother's opposite, playing the good girl. Until she'd cracked under the pressure of it all and just walked away. And still they tarred her with the same brush. It had taken them all of forty-eight hours to make her feel like that powerless and frustrated teenager again.

So today she was determined to give them what they'd always wanted. Proof. Real proof. Something sound to gossip about once she'd hightailed it out of this one-horse town. Something to truly damn her. Something for them all to nod sagely over and say, *See, we were right, the apple never falls too far from the tree.*

And she intended having a damn fine time doing so too.

Ella thundered into Huntley's main street. Remnants of some teenage sixth sense alerted her to the twitching of curtains as she flashed by. No doubt their owners were staring open-mouthed, their disapproving frowns mirroring their judgmental minds. The sun beat down, heavy on her shoulders, and the black tar of the main street shimmered in her wake. It could have been any of a hundred main streets in outback Australia—wide, with a strip of central parking down the middle. Evenly spaced pepperina trees cast much needed shade over the sweltering vehicles.

A monument to the fallen from the Great War took pride of place in the center of the street. Her great-grandfather's name was engraved on the white marble. Her mother, who had never known her grandfather, had taken particular pride in that. Ella had been chosen to lay the wreath there the Anzac Day she was in seventh grade and her great-grandfather's name had jumped out at her as she'd placed the wreath of red poppies at the base. How she had envied Grandpa Lucas his fleeting freedom from mediocrity that day.

Four pubs dominated the corners of the main intersection, their corrugated roofs and wide verandahs complete with fancy wrought-iron lacework unchanged in over a century. The bank, the chemist, the beige austerity of S.J. Levy's law practice, the drapers and the Huntley café—complete with the same blue-and-white striped awning from her childhood—stood exactly as they'd always been.

It was like entering a time warp. Not even the advent of two-dollar shops had infected the Huntley streetscape.

People stopped dead on the footpath as she passed, their heads turning to track the path of the noisy motorcycle. Business owners stared askance through their shop windows, craning their necks to see if a marauding biker gang had moved into town.

Ella ignored them all. She was on a mission. She was a successful career woman who had long ago cast off the shackles of Huntley. Her blood thrummed through her veins as she parked the bike and dismounted, her reckless mood ratcheting even further.

The townsfolk still hadn't moved as Ella took off her helmet and hung the sleek black dome on the handle bars. She shook out her untethered hair. It fell in careless disorder around her shoulders, just like in a shampoo commercial, and she smiled to herself. She'd always wanted to do that. Sadly, biker moll was as far removed from her ponytailed school marm persona as was possible—she was as nerdy today as she'd always been.

But Huntley didn't know that.

She heard the scandalised whispers of two familiar old biddies, who were drinking lemonade on the rickety wooden church pew that had sat outside the Crown for as long as anyone could remember. Ella wondered if the good citizens of Huntley had ever stopped to ponder the irony of religion and sin so intertwined.

The town was so quiet she could have heard a bee flap its wings in the next state. Good. She had their attention.

She heard the rasp of her denim clad thighs as she turned resolutely toward her target, squared her shoulders and strode past the women on the pew. "Afternoon, Miss Simmons, Miss Aberfoyle," she said, not bothering to wait for an acknowledgment. She pushed the pub door open and for a second wished it was one of those swinging doors she'd seen in a hundred Wild West movies. She'd ridden into town for a showdown, hadn't she?

It took a few seconds for her eyes to adjust from the bright spring day to the dim interior of Huntley's oldest liquor establishment. The patrons inside the pub stopped mid-conversation to stare at Ella. The only sound was Smokie crooning about living next door to Alice from the jukebox in the corner.

Ella didn't bother to look around. She knew he was in town and exactly where he'd be. She'd seen him at the funeral yesterday, standing in the distance under the lilac canopy of a blooming jacaranda. Like his father before him, Jake Prince was behind the bar.

She approached the bar, coming to a halt beside Mrs. Coleman, Huntley's librarian, decked out in her twin set and pearls and perched primly on a stool sipping a lemon, lime and bitters.

"Jake."

Jake regarded Ella Lucas for a moment. She'd changed. Matured. He guessed twenty years would do that to you.

*God knew these days he felt ancient.*

He'd seen her quiet dignity at the funeral yesterday in the face of Huntley's glaring hypocrisy and admired the hell out of her for it. The townsfolk had been there in full force, their ghoulish delight at Rachel finally being put asunder barely disguised. She had weathered it all with a mellow poise that had called every faux mourner to account.

But time, it seemed, hadn't erased her troubled blue gaze. Or the way it still clawed at his gut in some form of primal recognition. How often in the years they'd all but silently co-existed had he related to her torment? Understood the caged misery of her gaze?

Her eyes were still telling him the same old story. She wanted out.

*Oh, Lady, you're preaching to the choir.*

He picked up a hot glass from the rack and casually dried it off. "Ella."

A beat or two passed. Neither of them said anything and everyone in the pub inched slightly closer.

"I'm so sorry about your mother's passing."

Ella nodded, swallowing a sudden lump in her throat. He'd be about the only one who was—she wasn't entirely sure she was sorry herself. The harshness of the concession almost sucked her breath away. What kind of a daughter was she? What kind of human being?

Disgust with herself intensified her grief, strengthening her purpose. "You still the bad boy around here, Jake?" She was proud of the way it came out. Her voice was steady. Clear.

"No way, ma'am," he drawled, channeling his best country yokel. "Model citizen these days."

*So* not what she wanted to hear. Her stomach fluttered as her bravado wavered, her gaze flicking to Mrs. Coleman. How the hell was she going to pull this off in front of the elegant octogenarian who had taught her how to use the Dewey Decimal System? Her plan had seemed so simple when she'd come up with it back in her mother's house, with its memories and a hostile teenage brother goading her.

She took a deep, fortifying breath, determined to show them all. "Your dad still keep rooms in this establishment?"

Jake stopped his ministration with the glasses to look at her carefully. *What the fuck?* She was in jeans and a cute little gingham shirt that didn't even show any cleavage but there was a directness in her gaze that left him in no doubt what she wanted. Desire slammed into his groin and he gripped the glass a little harder.

"Sure."

"What do you say? Wanna give everyone round here something real to talk about?"

Ella ignored the gasp from a rapt Mrs. Coleman. Her heartbeat thundered through her head. She felt thirteen years old again, as awkward beneath his scrutiny now as she'd been the night he'd picked her to slow dance with him at the only school disco she'd ever attended.

She couldn't tell what he was thinking. His rugged face—still screaming "bad boy" despite his protestations—was completely impassive. Why didn't he say something?

Jake regarded her for a few more seconds, the desperation in her gaze compelling. He glanced around at his patrons, all waiting with bated breath on his next move. He knew not a single one of them understood the demons that drove her. But he did.

He put the tea towel down and reached behind him to remove a key from the board. "Mind the bar, Kel," he said to the peroxide blond staring at them.

The irritating noise of the barmaid's gum chewing was suddenly silenced and Jake knew that Huntley was judging him. Them.

But when hadn't they?

He turned back to Ella. "Ladies first." He gestured.

Ella's legs were shaking as she passed the gobsmacked spectators, ducking through the archway near the jukebox and turning left to head up the stairs. She could feel Jake's gaze on her ass and Huntley's reaction vaporized into nothingness. She wished she'd used the flab-buster Rosie had bought her last year for body sculpting instead of alternative art for her office.

Jake overtook her at the top of the stairs, striding down the corridor to room seven. He inserted the key in the lock, pushed the door open and strode inside.

"What's this about, Ella?" he asked, turning.

Ella kicked the door shut after her and launched herself at the wall of his chest. She heard the intake of his breath at her impact and ignored it. The man was a star footballer—had been for years—he could certainly hold his own with a girl.

"Ella."

She raised herself on her tippy toes, awkwardly mashing her lips into his, stopping his protest. Her hands dragged his neck down, her fingers moving to the back of his head, delighting in the charcoal spikiness of his buzz cut.

Jake wrestled her hands from his neck and pulled his mouth away with difficulty – mostly because he didn't want to. Hell, Ella Lucas had certainly graduated with honors in the kissing stakes. She'd come a long way since the sweet innocence of the brief shy press of lips she'd granted him at the end of that particularly memorable dance at the Huntley High disco.

There was nothing sweet about Ella Lucas's kiss now. It was hot and hungry. Intense. Greedy. He could taste her desperation and a yearning that struck him straight in the solar plexus. He held her at arm's length, the sound of his breathing falling harshly between them. "Ella, don't let them get to you. You were always too classy for this town."

Ella growled in frustration, struggling against his hands, straining to get closer. "Damn it, Jake. I'm not a kid. I know what I want."

"No, you don't."

Jesus Christ! Why did this town always think it knew what was best for her? She pushed against his bonds. "Yes, I bloody do. I'm thirty-four, Jake. I've been making up my mind for a lot of years."

"This isn't about you and me. And you know it."

Ella almost laughed in his face. "I want to have sex with you, Jake. Since when did you give a shit about a woman's motivation?"

Good point. But Ella was different. He didn't know why. She just was. She always had been. The only girl in his fifteen miserable years in this town that had barely looked at him.

And he wasn't foolish enough to believe this was about sex either. It was about hate and frustration and grief and they both knew it. He felt her muscles flexing, straining against his hands and her caged lust surged towards him on a waft of pheromones that almost bought him to his knees. But someone had to be mature here.

It was a shock to realize it was going to have to be him. "It's okay. No one has to know it didn't happen," he said in his very best placatory voice. "We'll just hang here for a bit then go on down."

Ella could see he was determined to be honorable Jake and couldn't believe he'd choose to develop a conscience on the one day she needed him to be the screw-anything-that-moved Jake of tabloid fame. She gritted her teeth.

"I don't want to hang." His gentle restraint on her arms was way more exciting than it should have been and she was over his whole protesting-too-much bit. Time to step it up. "I want you to fuck me. Quick and hard. And when you're done with that, I want it long and slow."

Jake swallowed. Her crude request had a predictable effect. Little Ella Lucas—science geek, math nerd, teacher's pet—who had barely said boo to him all those years they'd weathered Huntley's gossip, could speak dirty with the best of them.

"What's the matter?" she taunted. "Is your *injury* more extensive than first thought? Can you not *perform*?"

Ella had heard talk yesterday that Jake was back in Huntley resting up his "groin". For a man whose groin, according to the tabloids, seemed to rest very little, it must be a frustrating experience. She could help him with that.

Jake shot her a sardonic half smile. "I can perform just fine."

Ella smiled. "Excellent."

"You'll hate yourself for it later," Jake sighed.

Ella stopped struggling. Of course she would—she just didn't do casual sex. But this was bigger than her.

"Jake Prince, in the last twenty-four hours, I've buried my mother, inherited a teenage brother I never knew existed and discovered that the entire town thinks I ran off with the school principal at the age of seventeen. If I'm going to be damned for my loose ways then you better believe I want to at least reap the benefits."

Jake, feeling the resistance in her muscles ebb, let her go warily, relieved when she stood placidly, making no attempt to move closer. He'd been long gone when the scandal had rocked Huntley but he'd heard the rumours over the years on his brief sojourns home. "You're angry."

"No, Jake—I'm furious."

He shrugged. "I guess you have a right to be."

"You guess?" Ella felt her anger surge inside her again, swelling to tsunami-like proportions. "They knew me, Jake. This town. They knew me better than that."

She took a step toward him, feeling a very unreasonable urge to pummel her fists against the solid wall of his chest. What did he know about how difficult it had been for her? Jake, who'd been given a get-out-of-jail-free card by a big city football club. Kick a pointy ball around a piece of grass and the world was your oyster; work your butt off at school and people accused you of sleeping with the principal. She lifted her hands and then clenched them, shocked that she'd almost followed the violent impulse. They came to rest against his shirt and she bunched the fabric tight, rage still simmering beneath her skin.

His top button was at her eye level and suddenly her frustration found a more constructive outlet. She fingered the plastic disk. Jake placed a hand against hers and she batted it away.

"I was a valedictorian," she muttered. A red mist lashed her insides and fogged her vision, making dexterity impossible. All her pent-up hostility was now concentrated on a little piece of plastic.

"I won the academic medal for five years straight," she growled, feeling like a two-year-old who hadn't yet learnt the art of undressing. Her badly shaking fingers fumbled with the button. It finally popped and she made a triumphant noise in the back of her throat.

"I tutored kids for free," she told the next button, having as much trouble as the first.

"Ella." He placed his hand on hers again.

She shook it off and took a deep, steadying breath, the mist lifting a little. "I volunteered at the old folks' home." The button popped. "I sponsored a child in Africa." Another disk fell victim to her steadier fingers. "I still do."

She looked him square in the eye. "I was a girl guide."

Jake watched her, bemused, struggling with his buttons and her emotions. He knew better than anyone how hard it was to grow up in a place that ostracized you for the sins of a parent. How unfair it was. How crazy it could make you.

And he was trying really hard to do the right thing but Ella's mood was heady with seething sexuality. Her anger and frustration, and no doubt her grief, had morphed into a raw, sexual cocktail. She needed to burn off some heat. And he was her explosive of choice.

After years of avoiding his gaze she was looking right at him.

The last button gave way and she pushed the shirt off his shoulders. She pressed her nose to his sternum and inhaled. It seemed like such an innocent thing to do in the middle of her seduction and it took him back a lot of years.

To the high school dance.

To how he'd lain awake later that night running his tongue over his lips, savouring the taste of her.

"It doesn't matter what they think," he said, his resolve to do the right thing weakening by the second.

Ella knew he was right. Jesus! She had three university degrees in *right*. She wasn't here for his Dr. Phil advice. She was here for the sex. And from what she heard, Jake had more than a few degrees in that.

His chest was smooth and she touched it tentatively, the beat of his heart pulsing against her hand. He had a tattoo of some kind of demonic superhero, the Phantom meets Wolverine, on his left pec and she traced it with her finger.

"It matters to me."

"Ella," he murmured. "It won't help."

"Wanna bet?" She put her mouth where her finger had been and licked the length of the tattoo as she reached for the button of his jeans.

"Whoa there." He shifted, covering her hand with his, holding her away from him. "This is wrong."

Ella almost screamed in frustration as she dropped her hand from his waistband. She'd come here for one thing and she was damned if she was leaving without it. "We're two consenting adults, Jake. This has right written all over it."

"I think doing this the day after you buried your mother is maybe not the wisest way to cope."

Ella looked at him. Since when had he become so damn smart? "Why don't you let me decide what's the healthiest way to cope with my grief?"

Jake was running out of reasons why he shouldn't just throw caution to the wind like she obviously had. He wasn't even certain why he was putting up such a fight. "I don't have any condoms."

Ella quirked an eyebrow. That she found hard to believe. Not that it mattered.

She reached into her back pocket and pulled out a strip of five, her gaze never leaving his. They concertinaed down like a pack of magic cards. She threw them at him and they bounced off his chest and fell to the floor. "That should do us."

Jake looked down at the little foil packets of temptation. Five? He swallowed as his gaze returned to hers. "Kel's off shift in an hour."

"Then why are you wasting time pretending you don't want to do this?"

His gaze flicked briefly to the condoms again and he shut his eyes against their lure.

Ella gave a frustrated growl low in her throat at his continued reticence. "You know, Jake, this wasn't how I pictured it."

Jake laughed. "How'd you picture it?"

Ella glared at him. She needed a plan B. Thinking quickly, she grasped the knot at her navel where the edges of her checkered shirt had been tied firmly together and undid it. Then she ripped the shirt open, sending buttons flying, and stripped it off, flinging it to the ground at his feet beside the condoms.

"You weren't talking, for a start."

Jake felt his laughter die on his lips. A gentleman may not have looked but there wasn't one person in Huntley who would ever have accused Jake of being a gentleman. So he looked. In fact, he barely stopped himself from licking his lips.

He'd seen a bra like that hanging on the Lucas clothes line when he'd been fifteen. Red lace. D cup. He'd known it was Ella's—Rachel had never been big on underwear. He felt all his good intentions slowly melt away and he swallowed. There was a point at which resistance becomes futile. And God help him, he'd reached that point. In fact, suddenly, he was way beyond it.

"I can do mute."

It was Ella's turn to laugh, knowing she had him as she reached behind and unclipped the bra, throwing it on the ground too.

"I can do deaf and blind also."

"Well, what are you waiting for?" she demanded as she tugged on the waistband of his jeans and dragged him forward.

# CHAPTER TWO

*Two years later*

Ella groped her way through the crowd to meet Rosie at their usual booth. Except it wasn't their usual booth. Nothing about their local family-owned pub was usual anymore. It had been destroyed, the new owner making no attempt at retaining any of the olde worlde charm.

The death knell had sounded a few months ago when Ernie and Cheryl, owners of the Spring Hill pub for the last forty years, had announced to their regulars they were selling up, buying an RV and becoming grey nomads.

Ella's fears had been compounded when it had been rumored that some dreadful sports star had bought the pub. And the entire time it had been shut down for refurbishment, she'd had an awful feeling in her stomach. Then the sign had gone up, heralding a new era, forever erasing any traces of Ernie and Cheryl.

But this travesty, the Hero Bar, was far beyond Ella's worst nightmare. Gone were the slightly shabby, chipped linoleum tables and worn red leather bench seats and the endearing faux flaming torches that balanced on the walls, throwing a comforting blanket of warm yellow light. In their place was a horrible sports bar with retina-detaching neon and big-screen TVs that further distorted the already flattened noses and cauliflower ears of the men silently running around in tight shorts chasing a stupid little ball. Bloody footballers. The display of beer cans from around the world had been sacrificed as well. As had the comfortable, wide wooden bar stools that actually supported her ass, replaced instead by trendy metallic structures that looked like they'd crumple beneath Kate Moss's weight.

The cheesy Coolidge prints of dogs playing poker and snooker above the pool table were gone, too. In their place were framed footy jerseys and other sporting paraphernalia.

It was dark, black-hole dark. The neon may have been bright enough to induce epilepsy but barely threw the light of a firefly. Everything gleamed and Ella winced as the neon reflected off slick, shiny surfaces. The metallic booth table was cold beneath her elbows. An equally metallic song with a heavy bass beat and no discernible lyrics throbbed around the room.

"This is horrible," Ella bitched.

"Yes," Rosie agreed, handing Ella the glass of Sauv blanc she'd bought for her. "I think we're gonna have to find a new TGIF watering hole, babe. This is more Holy Shit, it's Friday."

"But I liked it here," Ella moaned. Today was going from bad to worse. "And it's five minutes from home."

Rosie looked at her. "What's up?"

Ella took a sip of her drink. "The letter came today."

"Bastards!"

"Hear, hear."

"Pen pushing, beaurocratic assholes."

Ella nodded, her friend's colorful insults music to her ears. Real music, not the techno-crap that was currently vibrating around them. "What you said."

"That lot couldn't organise a piss-up in a brewery. How dare they do this to you? Fuck them. Fuck them all."

Ella smiled despite the air of depression that had settled around her since opening the ominous yellow envelope at eight am. Rosie's profanities had long since failed to shock. Growing up around side-show alley was bound to have rubbed off and her best friend's unique way with words was just one of the things Ella loved about her, along with her don't-give-a-damn attitude, her dramatically dyed black hair and the chunky-heeled black army boots she favored. Not to mention the blood-red lips, eyebrow piercings and studded dog's collar that always graced her neck.

She raised her glass and clinked it with Rosie's. It was good to have such an ardent supporter in her corner. "Amen."

Ella's self-appointed champion since the age of seventeen, Gypsy-Rose Forsythe had been exactly what tightly wound Ella had needed. People who knew them often wondered what two women so completely opposite had in common. But Ella didn't—she knew she owed Rosie her life. That fateful day when the carnival had driven in to Huntley had been a major turning point in her life and she thanked her lucky stars for it, for Rosie, every day. Two misfits against the world.

"How long have they given you?"

"Till the end of the year," Ella said gloomily. "If my enrollments haven't picked up and my truancy record improved and if the school's image continues to be dragged through the muck in the media, they're going to shut us down."

"Don't those fuckwits know the demographic you're dealing with?"

Ella swirled the contents of her glass gloomily. "I never wanted this damn job. I never wanted to be principal."

"I know."

She threw a desperate look at Rosie. "I'm a math teacher."

Rosie reached across and squeezed Ella's hand. "And a damn good one."

Ella gave her friend a lop-sided smile. "How were any of us to know that Kelvin was going to crack under the pressure? This position was only meant to be temporary."

"It's not your fault no one wants to work there."

Ella sighed. "They're not bad kids. Not most of them. They're just living really tough lives."

"I know," Rosie murmured again. And she did know. They both knew how rough it was to grow up standing on the outside, looking in. To be one of the have-nots.

"But they need Hanniford High. The whole community does. Even if they don't realize it. I can't turn my back on that. Not like Kelvin."

"What are you going to do, babe?"

"I don't know. I just don't know. But I've got nine months to come up with something."

"You will." Rosie squeezed her friend's hand again. "We will."

Ella smiled. This was the Rosie she knew and loved. Behind the uncouth mouth, behind the dramatic clothes and don't-fuck-with-me attitude, Gypsy-Rose Forsythe was a bona fide pussy cat. She gave to buskers—even the crap ones—she helped in the local soup kitchen, bought street magazines from homeless people, wrote letters of protest for Amnesty International and collected strays.

Including Ella.

"Enough of me," Ella dismissed, removing her hand and feeling unaccountably emotional. "How's it going with preppy boy?"

"Ah, Simon. I had a breakthrough today."

Ella saw the gleam in Rosie's eye and the grin that split her face was infectious. She leaned in. "Oh, do tell."

"I dragged him into the stationery cupboard and pashed his lips off."

Ella laughed. Rosie, in complete contradiction to her appearance, worked at the city council as a systems analyst. "Oh my God. What did he do?"

"Well, at first he said it was highly inappropriate and broke the rules of workplace conduct from 11a through to 19b."

Ella gasped. "He did not!"

Rosie grinned and nodded. "I swear to God he did."

"He sounds arcane. How old did you say he was?"

"Thirty."

"God, Rosie. He's a baby."

"I know. I'm a bad, bad person." Rosie sighed dramatically. "I'm probably going to hell."

Ella rolled her eyes. Like the thought of a fiery afterlife wasn't a turn on for a crazy, semi-Goth chick. "So what did you say?"

"That I really didn't mind being sexually harassed by him and that he should take full advantage of my appalling lack of morals and just shut up and kiss me."

"And?"

"Let's just say that man follows directions to the letter."

Ella laughed. "I don't get what you see in him. He sounds too strait-laced for you. Not like your usual type at all."

In Rosie's quest for "the one", Ella had seen a procession of men through her life and none of them would ever be described as preppy. Her men were edgier. They rode Harleys and got into bar fights. Her men didn't give a damn about the rules of workplace conduct.

"Yeah, but there's something so—so *endearing* about him. He's so neat and prim. I just want to, I don't know … mess him up a bit."

Ella shook her head, wishing for the thousandth time she could have just an ounce of her friend's faith that Mr. Right was out there somewhere. Or her ability to get back up and get out there again. If Rosie's life was a song it'd be 'I Get Knocked Down (But I Get Up Again)'. What would her life song be? '(I Can't Get No) Satisfaction'?

"They're not toys, Gypsy-Rose," she tutted.

"Well, this one certainly ain't. His great-grandfather was governor of the state back before World War I. His grandfather was a federal minister. His father is the Lord Mayor's right-hand man and his mother is some hobnobbing charity queen. His family is about as blue ribbon as they come—very serious, conservative people."

Ella raised an eyebrow. Rosie getting involved with a political dynasty? Her friend was the antithesis of conservative. It'd be like Lindsay Lohan marrying a Kennedy. Did she know what she was getting herself into? "So, he's a challenge?"

Rosie winked. "You know how I do so love a challenge."

Yes, she did. But for the first time ever since she'd known Rosie, Ella saw a flicker of doubt, a brief hesitation before the confident wink. Something told her Rosie wasn't as sure of herself as usual.

"Hey, maybe Simon can use his connections to help with the school thing?"

Ella shook her head. "I doubt it. He might be able to help with getting that developer off Daisy's and Iris's backs though."

Rosie's wound a lock of her black hair around her finger and thumped the table with her other hand. "Yes, goddamn it! Yes. Kick that greedy bastard to the curb for once and all."

The measures being employed in the battle royale for their beloved home were becoming increasingly desperate. The rickety old house owned by Rosie's aunts was the center of their universe. It had been their sanctuary after fleeing Huntley for Brisbane all those years ago and was most definitely not for sale. At any price. Unfortunately, big-money developers weren't used to being denied and the pressure was on. Current tactics involved obscene amounts of money.

It had been quiet since Daisy and Iris had knocked back the last offer and, while the aunts took that as a sign of capitulation on behalf of the developer, Rosie and Ella weren't so optimistic. Their entire street had sold out and the sharks were definitely circling.

"I haven't seen Curtis at the house all week," Rosie said, changing the subject.

"We decided it was best to stop seeing each other."

"Oh, babe." Rosie reached across the table and squeezed Ella's hand. "I'm sorry."

Ella sighed. "Don't be. I think it was possibly the dreariest relationship I've had to date."

Rosie whistled. "That's saying something."

Ella didn't bother to protest her friend's statement. It was depressingly accurate. In the last two years, in her effort to exorcise the ghost of the best sex she'd ever had and the fact that it had been with the one man on earth she shouldn't have had it with, she'd decided to only date Jake's complete opposites: nice men who had proper jobs and didn't give a damn about sport. Arty men. Intellectuals. SNAGS.

"Don't get me wrong, he was very nice. Just a bit—"

"Blah?"

Ella shook her head. "Too—"

"Boring?"

Ella shot her friend an impatient glare. "SNAG-ish."

Rosie nodded. "Lousy lovers."

Ella cocked an eyebrow. "And Rosie, queen of SNAG lovers, would know this how?"

Rosie gave a sheepish grin. "So I've heard."

Ella rolled her eyes. Rosie had heard it from her, about a million times. "They want to talk. Get to know me."

Rosie suppressed a smile. "That's terrible. Just awful."

She shot Rosie a quelling look. "You know what I mean. Is there something wrong with wanting a man to take the lead for once? A little bit of masterfulness?"

Rosie smiled. "Ah. So you want to be dominated?"

"No!" she gasped. "I want ... I don't know what I want."

Rosie looked at her dearest friend. "I do. You want head-banging sex without the emotional vulnerability. SNAGs get too close and, thanks to Rachel, you've spent your entire life keeping men at a distance."

Sometimes Ella hated how well Rosie knew her. "No, Miss Smarty-Pants," she denied, placing her wine glass down. "Do you know what I found myself thinking about when Curtis and I were between the sheets last time? I was thinking about Pythagoras' theorem."

Rosie laughed. "Because A squared plus B squared equals C squared is some kind of twisted math geek aphrodisiac that gets you off? Are triangles some kind of new phallic symbol I haven't heard of? Are they the new black?"

Ella laughed and then groaned, laying her head on the table. "No. But he was being so gentle and kind and considerate. You know, touching all the places in the correct order, the correct number of times. Honestly, it was like sex-by-numbers—totally boring. And he kept talking. You know, asking if I was okay, did I like it? Was there anything I needed? Tell him to stop if I wasn't comfortable. I mean, whatever happened to talking dirty, Rosie? My mind just drifted."

"To Pythagoras?"

Ella sighed, even more depressed that instead of conjuring up some filthy fantasy like sex with a boat load of marauding pirates, her mind had drifted to a dead Greek scholar.

"Yes." She took a sip of the crisp white. "In my defense, I had been trying to explain it to Cam a couple of hours beforehand. And," she said, pointing a finger at her friend while still keeping a grip on her glass, "Pythagoras was supposed to have been a bit of a hottie."

Dubiousness quirked Rosie's eyebrow.

"It's true, I've seen busts."

Rosie pressed her lips together. "Uh huh."

"Oh God, what's the matter with me, Rosie? If I have to fake another orgasm, I think I'm going to join a convent." Ella stopped and frowned at her friend. "Are nuns allowed to masturbate?"

"I would have thought it a prerequisite," Rosie said "Of course," she continued, "there is the teensy tiny problem of you not believing in God. Although ... I guess you could fake it." Rosie burst out laughing at the dirty look that sailed her way. It took a minute for her to control the laughter. "Sorry. Couldn't resist."

"Yeah, yeah."

"Look, it sounds to me, babe, like you need dirty foot-baller sex again."

Ella opened her mouth to protest. Footballer sex was exactly what she *didn't* need. What she'd been trying to purge from her system. But hell, at least Jake Prince had made her come three times in forty minutes. That was three times more than any other man had made her come over the last two years. And he hadn't stopped to ask her what she did or didn't like, he'd just thrown her on the bed and taken charge. Told her what he was going to do to her in the most smutty, explicit terms possible. Even now her toes curled at the memory.

"Well, I certainly wasn't thinking about Pythagoras when I was with Jake."

"I like Jake."

Ella rolled her eyes. "You've never met him."

"He made you come right?"

"Three times."

Rosie grinned. "I triple like Jake." She raised her glass. "To multiple orgasms."

Ella clinked her glass against Rosie's. "Amen." At the moment though, she would have drunk to just one. She threw back the contents of her glass. "Well, I don't know about you, but if I have to listen to one more minute of this techno-crap garbage I'm gonna burst a blood vessel. I'll get us another round and put something decent on."

Ella groped her way carefully into the darkened environment, more than a little pleased to find the original jukebox where it had always been. It reminded her of the one in the Crown back in Huntley, and she felt curiously comforted by its presence. Maybe the new owner had a heart after all.

As another synthesized musical monstrosity assaulted her ears, she eagerly scanned the list of songs, quickly growing dismayed. All her favorites were gone. Talking about Jake, thinking about the Crown, had put her in the mood for 'Living Next Door to Alice'. But it was gone. All the country hits were gone. As was all the great seventies and eighties rock. All the good music was gone!

The antique shell held a cold neon heart.

Instead there was a who's who of gangster rap, dance music, hip-hop and electronica. The sort of stuff Cam and half the students at her school listened to incessantly, blaring from their MP3 players at eardrum-piercing volumes.

Ella shuddered. This had to be a joke! Talk about adding insult to serious injury. After the day she'd had, messing with her jukebox was unforgiveable. The absolute last straw.

Whoever this new owner was, he was about to get a piece of her mind. She could forgive him the neon and the big-screen televisions but Smokie? That was going too far.

\*

Jake Prince felt the rough bricks at his back as he leaned against the alley wall, sucking on his Corona. He was drinking too much. Perhaps buying a pub hadn't been such a swell idea, but what else did washed-up sportsmen do? If it was good enough for Sam Malone it was good enough for him. Of course this was Brisbane, not Boston. Or a television show. And none of his bar staff remotely resembled a Diane Chambers, but they were trifling details. He grimaced. Great. A new low. Half pissed and fantasizing about Shelley Long at barely six in the evening.

He raised the bottle to his mouth again and took a long pull. Damn, that tasted good. He'd learned the perils of alcohol as a young rookie the hard way and had been practically teetotal for the rest of his career. But with that in the toilet and his father's genes tightening their grip, his fondness for the amber liquid had returned with a vengeance.

A clatter further down the alley disturbed the peace. Jake turned to locate the cause and noticed a sad-looking excuse of a mutt backing guiltily away from some upended wooden crates. It was the most forlorn street mongrel he'd ever seen: painfully skinny, ribs well defined beneath mangy fur. It eyed Jake warily.

"Hey, boy." Jake slid down the wall, feeling the bite of brick snagging at his black T-shirt. He reached out a hand and waited patiently for the neglected animal to come closer. "You lost, boy?" he murmured as the dog approached tentatively, a slight limp making his countenance even more pathetic.

The poor animal looked like he'd been kicked when he was down one too many times and Jake could relate to that. The mutt's steps grew even more hesitant the closer he got and in the end it was Jake who gently bridged the distance between them. "I'm not going to hurt you," Jake crooned, scratching the soft spot under the dog's ear. "What's your name, buddy?"

Jake looked for a collar, not surprised there wasn't one. "Are you a runaway, boy? Are you homeless?" He cupped the dog's head and looked into those sad, mistrustful eyes. He wasn't a young dog; the fur around his nose was significantly grayed. Old and down on his luck. Jake could be looking in the mirror.

"Yeah, life's a bitch, ain't it."

The dog whined and Jake petted the length of his coat, feeling each dip of his ribcage. "You hungry, boy?"

The door beside him opened abruptly and the bass throbbed into the sultry ripeness of the alley as the dog pushed himself closer into Jake.

Pete Jones whistled. "That's one ugly dog."

The dog moved closer again and Jake grinned at him. "It's okay, boy, Petey won't hurt you. He's a friend."

Pete ambled over and crouched beside Jake then let the dog sniff his hand. "Some woman's at the bar bitching about the jukebox and demanding to see the heartless bastard who's ripped the soul out of her local."

Jake sighed and stood, still fondling the dog's head. Running a pub in the big smoke wasn't like back home. It wasn't like TV either. He drained the last mouthful of beer. "Guess that's me."

Pete stood too and clapped him on the shoulder. "Good luck. Man, is she pissed," he said gleefully as he headed back inside.

Jake looked down at the dog, who gazed back up at him with don't-leave-me eyes and gave the most pathetic tremble Jake had ever witnessed. "It's okay, boy. I'll send Pete out with some grub shortly."

The monotonous beat vibrated through Jake's chest as he entered and even he winced at the soullessness. Give him Jimmy Barnes screaming 'Khe Sanh' into the mike any day.

God, he was tired.

He walked past his office and through the area behind the bar, stopping to snag another Corona from the fridge. He cracked the top and took a long drag, not caring how long he made the dissatisfied customer wait. She could always go find somewhere else to drink.

He frowned as he approached—the complaining woman's voice was eerily familiar. This day had suddenly got a whole lot more interesting.

"... I mean, just how old are you? Obviously not old enough to appreciate a classic when you hear it. You ever heard of the Stones, the Eagles, Johnny goddamn Cash?"

Jake smiled at the imperious index finger pointing in Pete's face. Somehow, with her finger jabbing the air, Ella managed to make "goddamn" sound exactly the way it would coming from a high school teacher with a stick jammed up her ass. "The Dixie Chicks?" she asked in desperation. "You know, something with a lyric and more than one note?"

"Well, well, well. Looks like you can take the girl out of Huntley but you can't take Huntley out of the girl."

Ella dropped her hand and grabbed the edge of the bar as a familiar teasing baritone fluttered straight to muscles deep down and low in a wild kind of sexual recognition. She turned to see an unhurried sexy swagger as she squinted into the gloom behind the bar.

"Jake?" Had her flat-lined libido actually conjured him up?

Jake took another slug of Mexican nectar. "Ella."

They stared for a while. A long while. "You *own* this place?" she squeaked.

He raised his bottle to her. "Surprise."

Ella frowned. "I thought you played football?"

Pete looked at Ella then at Jake and raised an eyebrow at his boss. Jake smiled at the kid's incredulity. "I ... retired."

"Oh," Ella said completely forgetting her reason for being at the bar in the first place. Jake Prince owned a bar in her neighbourhood? She looked at him blankly for another moment trying desperately to not think about dirty footballer sex as he drank his beer.

Jake waited patiently for her to say something else. Two years since she'd thundered into Huntley and dragged him upstairs and yet the memory was as vivid for him as if it had happened yesterday. She was different though, dressed more conservatively, in a calf-length skirt and white cotton blouse. Her layered, shoulder-length hair was still the rich color of his on-tap stout but she wore it pulled back into a loose ponytail.

He'd always had a thing for ponytails.

Her eyes didn't have that sadness, that trapped look they'd been sporting last time. He remembered how they had briefly filled with tears after her first screaming orgasm, before she'd shut out his attempts at comfort and demanded more, her eyes lighting up with a startling fierceness. Now she looked as cool and detached as the Ella he had known as a kid and, for some reason—maybe it was the beer—it irritated the crap out of him.

"Was there something in particular you wanted? You know this establishment doesn't have rooms, right?"

For the first time since walking into the Black Hole of Spring Hill, Ella was grateful for the subdued light as heat flushed her cheeks. She glanced at Pete. "Oh, nice, Jake," she said icily. "Real nice."

"Don't worry," he said belligerently as Pete wisely moved away, "what happens in Huntley stays in Huntley." He leaned forward, his elbows on the bar. "Your secret is safe with me." He winked.

"Don't flatter yourself, Jake. It wasn't that good."

He grinned—he knew she was lying. She wanted to slap him almost as much as she wanted to drag him into the nearest dark corner.

Fortunately for her there were plenty to choose from.

"Sweetheart, I wouldn't mind betting that I'm the best you ever had."

Well considering his competition that wouldn't be hard. "You're mighty sure of yourself," she said.

"What can I say?" He took a swig of beer. "I'm gifted."

Yes, he was. Dear God, he was. In fact with her teaching experience, she'd classify him as being savant-like. But oh, the arrogance! "I faked it," she blurted, hurling the barb directly at his over-inflated ego.

Jake laughed. Ella had come so loudly she'd shattered glass all over Huntley. "All three times?" he enquired innocently.

She stood a little straighter and looked him directly in the eye. "All three."

"Well then, darling, you deserve an Oscar. Meg Ryan could learn a thing or two from you."

"What can I say," she said sweetly. "I'm gifted."

"Lots of practice, huh?"

She glared at him. *Bloody cheek*. Even if the man was right, didn't mean it wasn't the epitome of bad taste to point out her sexual inadequacies.

In a public bar.

He drained his beer and slapped it down on the wood.

Ella narrowed her gaze. "Are you drunk?"

He reached for another beer, cracked the lid and took a deep swallow. "Not yet."

"Drinking the profits, Jake?"

It was low but no lower than he'd already sunk. If he could imply she was good at faking it because she'd never had the real thing then a little historical reminder was fair game. She felt a moment's satisfaction at the slight clench of his jaw.

"My father gambled the profits, Ella. He didn't drink them." Which wasn't entirely true, it just so happened his father's gambling debts added up to more than his top-shelf habit.

"Hey babe, a girl could die of thirst waiting for you." Ella turned to find Rosie at her elbow and could have kissed her for her timing. "What's up?" Rosie asked. "This the owner?"

Ella nodded, unable to wrap her head around the events of the last few minutes as Rosie looked at her expectantly for an intro.

Jake smothered a grin. "Jake," he said, holding out his hand.

The woman shook it. "Rosie," she said distractedly and paused. She turned to Ella. "Jake? *The* Jake?"

"*The* Jake?" Jake repeated, looking at Ella, a smile playing with his mouth.

"The Jake who made you come—"

"Comes from Huntley, yes that's right," Ella interrupted. "The big meat-head footballer. Yes."

Jake chuckled. "Pleased to meet you, Rosie." Ella's friend was … different, unconventional. But even on such short acquaintance the closeness between them was evident.

Rosie grinned at him. "I've heard so much about you."

Jake glanced at Ella's mortified face. "Well now, I'll just bet you have. I was just explaining to Ella, I am gifted."

"She was referring to your career," Ella said acidly, even though all three of them knew Rosie wasn't. Rosie's interest in football was as dismal as hers.

"Ah, well, I'm gifted there as well."

Rosie turned to Ella. "His ego's healthy."

"That's one word for it," Ella agreed.

Rosie looked back at Jake. "So Jake, you're going to be in the neighbourhood. You should drop by one day. We're just a few streets away."

Jake watched the look of horror that Ella shot her friend. He took a swig of beer. "I may just do that, Miss Rosie."

Rosie turned to Ella, ignoring the daggers being hurled at her. "Have you asked him about this god-awful noise yet?"

Ella shook her head. "Haven't gotten around to it."

Rosie nodded and faced Jake. "I don't know if this had escaped your attention, Jake, but this music is utter crap."

He laughed. "Yes, it is."

"It's got no soul. We can't come to a place every Friday night to unwind from the week's stresses and listen to synthesized whales on crack, can we, babe?"

Ella shook her head. "God, no."

"You wouldn't make us find somewhere else to ponder the meaning of life, would you?"

"No, ma'am. I'll get a wider range of music put in first thing tomorrow. Will that be more to your liking, ladies?"

Rosie whooped and punched the air above her head. "Ace."

"Thank you, Jake," Ella said more sedately. "That would be much appreciated."

Those were the words Ella had used two years ago, before she'd sauntered out of room seven. *Thank you, Jake, much appreciated.* He felt his gut clench as he favored Ella with the most frankly sexual stare he could muster. "I aim to please."

Ella nearly came on the spot.

# CHAPTER THREE

Simon Charles Henry Lewis stood at a chain-mail gate barely supported on either side by a ramshackle white picket fence. At least, it had been white at some stage—the paint was peeling and completely worn in places. He adjusted his trendy wire-framed glasses.

Rosie lived here? He smiled to himself. Where else? He checked the skewiff number on the rusty letter box. Yep. This was the place. Set back on the massive block, the rambling old house was framed by two poinciana trees, their umbrella-like canopies almost touching. A long concrete path bisected the front yard, leading to a short flight of wide steps. The house's steeply pitched red corrugated-iron roof, spacious wrap-around verandahs and cladded exterior marked it as a classic.

Renovated, it would be a sight to behold. Rosie had told him about the regular complaints the council fielded from neighbours about its state of disrepair and he could instantly sympathise with the upwardly mobile residents. The area had undergone a dramatic facelift in the last decade and sadly, this old place just didn't fit the new image. All the large blocks with their sprawling, turn-of-the-century houses in the inner city area had been bought up by developers and turned into havens for DINKs. Looking around the street now, Simon was conscious of the discreet apartment blocks surrounding him. Nothing over three stories, they were all glass and concrete, tastefully decorated in muted earthy tones and gleaming chrome and finished off with the obligatory splendor of patio gardens.

He pushed opened the squeaky gate, careful not to catch his Ralph Lauren trousers. The grass was sparse either side of the path due to the large shade area thrown by the massive poincianas. As Simon made his way toward the house, a dog barked, followed by another and in a blur of fur he was surrounded by four canines, all in various stages of excitement. Simon stopped, holding the wine and the flowers out of the way as an eager Golden Retriever leaped up onto his chest.

"Genghis! *Genghis!* Down boy!"

Simon looked up to find Rosie running down the path, her pigtailed black hair flying behind her. She hushed the noise, pulled Genghis—Genghis?—away, planting a kiss on the dog's snowy head, and shooed them.

"I'm sorry, Simon." She laughed at his alarmed face. He looked like he'd never seen an animal in his life. He had dog hair on his very sexy black round-neck skivvy that clung to his killer pecs and she brushed at it with her hand. He looked so damn straight and cute she wanted to skip the blow-your-head-off curry she'd made him and get straight to the good bit.

"You have ... a lot of dogs," he said, kissing her on the cheek as he kept a wary eye on the nearby animals.

Rosie grinned. She pulled his head down for a hard, brief smack on the lips. "Yes, we do." She grinned and dragged him by the arm up the path.

"Do you ... do you have permits for all of them?" he asked, looking at the frolicking dogs.

Rose turned on the bottom step, causing Simon to careen into her. He was still a smidge taller than her and she put her hands on his shoulders to steady him and looked into his earnest eyes. "Nope."

Simon blinked at her honesty. What the hell did he see in her? Why the hell had he been letting this woman drag him into stationery cupboards for the last three weeks? She was entirely unsuitable for the life he had mapped out for himself in public office: she swore like a drunken sailor, dressed like a confused teenager despite her six years' seniority, lived in a rundown house with two maiden aunts and several large unregistered animals, and had her eyebrow pierced. He suspected there may also be tattoos.

His mother would hate her. The thought cheered him.

"Are you sure your aunts don't mind?" Simon asked.

Rosie shook her head. "They're dying to meet you."

"I bought flowers for them. And wine," he said, holding out the fuchsia gerberas and expensive bottle of red.

"Oh goody." She clapped. "They do so love men bearing gifts."

Simon swallowed as he watched Rosie mount the stairs, her lace-edged black miniskirt flaring with the movement, caressing the tops of her chunky-heeled, thigh-high, lace-up boots. He had the strangest feeling he was about to be devoured. He followed her up the steps and onto the verandah. The front door was wide open. "This is an interesting old house," he commented as he set foot on the bare boards and they shifted under his weight.

"Ooh, that it is. Come in," Rosie threw over her shoulder. "I'll show you around." She entered a short hallway with distinctive tongue-and-groove paneling and walked through an open doorway to the left. "This is the lounge room."

Simon didn't even notice the threadbare shabbiness of the carpet as he looked around the imposing room with soaring twelve-foot ceilings and decorative cornicing. The clutter assaulted his *House and Garden* sensibilities and he knew without a doubt his mother would have required smelling salts had she been here.

Two massive leather lounges—one a deep ochre color, the other fairy floss pink—were covered in an eclectic arrangement of scatter cushions ranging from tapestry to lurid faux fur. A massive wall-mounted television dominated one corner. A chrome and black cabinet beneath it boasted an array of electronic gadgetry from CD players to PlayStations to hard-drive recorders. For some reason, a bar fridge sat in another corner. A heavy wooden bookshelf stuffed with spines sat against one wall. Knick-knacks ranging from Doulton to plaster of Paris sat collecting dust on old-fashioned doilies on every available surface. The walls were laden with art with no discernible theme or order, although "art" was probably a little too generous. A Picasso print shared space with an amateurish oil depicting a bowl of fruit. A framed *Gone with the Wind* poster butted against a bright Ken Done harbour print. A boomerang and a Spanish fan were wall buddies.

"You like it?" Rosie said, grinning at the look of utter perplexity on Simon's face.

Like it? Rosie's house needed to come with a warning. Something like: Beware, this home could induce psychosis. Or enter at own risk if suffering from high blood pressure or epilepsy. The kaleidoscope of color was not for the faint-hearted.

"It's …" He searched for a word other than bizarre. "Eclectic."

Rosie nodded enthusiastically. "We call it shabby chic."

"Well, yes … that fits too."

"Through here is the dining room," she said, grabbing his hand and dragging him to the next room.

He followed her rather dazedly, his head still spinning. They walked under a fancy colonial arch to find more clutter. A massive silky oak table took pride of place in the middle of the room. A modern glass and chrome china cabinet boasting a profusion of glimmering crystal sat against one wall. Next to it, an old-fashioned cabinet with curved, stained-glass doors and ornately carved legs boasted older, daintier china.

But the room was dominated by the chatter of clocks. One wall was completely covered to the ceiling in ticking timepieces: big ones and small ones, classy ones with beautiful inlays and garish ones with tacky shapes and ostentatious decorations. Simon's eyes darted from one face to the other, realising that, miraculously, they all seemed to be keeping reasonably the same time. As he looked, a cuckoo ducked out of one and noisily pronounced the hour.

"Wow."

"Yeah. We don't really eat in here. Daisy always says she can't eat and listen to herself grow old at the same time."

"I can see why." There was something a little freaky about the ticking—kind of like dining in a bomb factory.

They walked through another arch into the kitchen. The lino was cracked and the floor seemed a little uneven but the appliances were A-grade, from the huge stainless steel twin-door fridge and freezer complete with ice-maker to the gleaming coffee center. The windows still boasted the original colored glass but the thick granite benchtops were ultra-modern.

Simon shook his head as he looked back through the arch into the dining room and beyond to the lounge room. He was beginning to wonder if the aunts weren't blind cat burglars.

"Where did you get all this stuff?"

Rosie kissed his bewildered cheek and removed the wine and flowers from his grasp. "My aunts are OCD."

Ah, that explained it. Surely only the mentally ill on a manic spending spree could think all this stuff crammed in together worked. He nodded sympathetically. "Obsessive compulsive?"

Rosie smiled. "Obsessive contest divas. Actually it's more than obsession. I think 'fetish' is a better word." Long before Ella and she had come to live with them, Daisy and Iris had made entering competitions an art form. "It's how they spend their days. Magazines and newspapers are their main source but they like radio and television comps too."

"They must be … very lucky," he said, trying to wrap his head around this latest bizarre twist.

"Nah. The law of averages is on your side when you enter as many as they do." She looked around at the unapologetically kitsch chaos. Having grown up in probably one of the most colorful environments on earth – a carnival – Rosie felt right at home. "Come on, there's more."

"Oh," he said to her disappearing back, wondering if it could get any worse.

Rosie waited for him to follow her into the hallway and put her arm through his when he did. She stopped at the next open doorway. "The bathroom."

She announced it with such a flourish he was almost afraid to look. He wasn't disappointed. There, hanging above the toilet, was a massive crystal chandelier. The afternoon sun was slanting in through the open louvers and caressing the tear-drop prisms that dripped from its frame, throwing rainbows around the room.

"Is that a Swarovski?"

Rosie shrugged. "Yes, I think it is."

"Let me guess. They won it?" Rosie nodded. "So you decided to hang it in the toilet?" He squinted, examining the craftsmanship with a practiced eye. It was a beautiful piece.

"Well, we thought it was a little too ostentatious for the rest of the house." She was standing beneath a mounted trout with a cheesy grin moulded to its cherry-lipped plastic mouth.

He raised an eyebrow at her. "You're kidding, right?"

Rosie laughed and shrugged. "We're not really into grand here. This way we get to enjoy it and stay grounded at the same time."

Simon reached above her head and pressed the button near the trout's head. It wriggled and flopped, miraculously staying attached to its backing board, and sang 'Splish Splash I was Taking a Bath'. He raised his eyebrow again. He didn't think there was much of a risk of anyone living in this house getting above themselves and he fell a little more for this unpretentious woman who was dragging him right out of his comfort zone.

"Cool, isn't it?" Rosie smiled.

Simon thought it was probably the most hideous thing he'd ever clapped eyes on, maybe an even bigger crime than hiding an expensive piece of crystal in the loo. But with Rosie grinning up at him so obviously at home in her little alternative universe he couldn't help but grin back. This place suited her. "Very."

Rosie sucked in a breath. He was humoring her, she could tell. But he was doing it so nicely and with such a sexy smile she took his comment on face value. Give him a while—this place was strangely addictive.

A bit like the Hotel California. You could check out but you could never leave. "Down the other side of the hallway are the bedrooms. This place was purpose built as a Christian boarding house."

"Like a YMCA?"

Rosie nodded. "Without the leather and feathers." She pointed to the rooms to her right. "The first three are empty, the one opposite the bathroom is Ella's. The next one's empty too. We were going to give it to Cam but—"

"Cam?"

"Ella's younger brother. He's fifteen."

"Oh. So why not put him next door?"

Rosie leaned back against the wall and grinned. "Because mine's the one after that."

Simon nodded, waiting for her to elaborate. "So?" he prompted eventually.

She smiled at him. "Ella didn't think it wise to give an impressionable teenager such an early sex education."

"I think I'm gonna like Ella."

"You should. She's much more your type."

Simon smiled and leaned in toward her. She was wearing an amazing perfume that smelled like passionfruit and sin. "I have a type?"

"Oh yeah, baby."

"And that would be?"

"A quiet, responsible woman who wears pastels and pearls."

Simon groaned. She'd just described his ex, Penelope. "Jeez, I sound boring."

"Someone who has elegant nails. Perfect hair. And never, ever, ever says fuck."

"Sounds dull," he murmured.

"Oh go on, you hate my potty mouth."

He pulled away. Her potty mouth excited him way more than it should. He'd never found vulgar women attractive but Rosie's quick-witted profanity and her unapologetic delivery had been a surprising turn on. "I do not."

"You get this little frown between your eyebrows," she said. "Like just now." Rosie smoothed the wrinkle gently with her finger.

Simon slid his hand around her waist. "I love your mouth. I just prefer to keep the dirty talk for the bedroom. Or the stationery cupboard."

Rosie smiled. "I'll remember that." She extricated herself from his arms. "Speaking of which." She pushed away from the wall and continued down the hallway to the next door. "This is my room."

As Simon walked in his feet sank into black shag-pile carpet. Blood red walls surrounded him. Several vases of tall white aruam lilies sat on low tables draped in red cloth along with candles of all shapes and sizes. Some were pristine, their line unspoiled. Others were crusted with use, rivulets of melted wax adding layers that reminded him of gothic castles and grizzled stalactites.

A bar fridge sat in one corner and Simon wondered if that was where she stashed the vials of blood.

His gaze was drawn to the enormous black four-poster bed in the center of the room. Black netting draped from the ceiling and cascaded down to sheath the bed in a gossamer embrace. Through the gauzy filter, the sheets, pillows and coverlet formed a richly embroidered tapestry of red. The bed beckoned like a fiery furnace. How about that—hell did have bedrooms.

He spotted a pair of silver handcuffs hanging from the iron bedhead behind the pillows. So, apparently, did heaven.

It was as far removed from Penelope's soothing pastel creation as was possible. There were no pretty bedside lamps, Monet prints or teddy bears vying for attention among a mountain of artfully arranged pillows. It had taken ten minutes just to find her bed beneath all the stuff. Rosie's bed looked … ready.

He turned to her. "You sleep here?"

"Among other things. Not quite what you expected?"

Simon nodded. "My ex favored pastels and stuffed animals."

Rosie laughed. "I hate to disappoint you. The only animal in this bedroom is me."

Simon thanked his lucky stars. "Oh, really?"

She nodded. "If you're good I may bring you back here to elaborate."

"If I promise to be bad will you use the handcuffs?"

Rosie laughed. "Oh, you can't handle the cuffs."

Simon grabbed his chest dramatically. "You wound me."

He spotted the small wooden crucifix complete with Jesus hanging on the wall above her bed; about as out of place as a hooker in convent. "Interesting," he murmured.

Rosie grinned. "The previous owner had one in every bedroom. Iris and Daisy took them all down but I kind of liked the irony. Lucky for me they never throw anything out."

He would *never* have guessed.

"Come on. The aunts are waiting."

Simon followed her out of hell and down the hallway a bit further. It was lined with all kinds of bizarre objects—the singing trout looked almost normal amid the contenders: a narrow cabinet displaying coffee beans of the world, some very odd-looking masks, some sad-clown prints and a line of ducks that appeared to be flying up the wall.

Rosie turned left into another hallway and Simon kept close.

"Three more bedrooms and a bathroom," Rosie explained. "Daisy, Iris and Cameron live in this section."

Simon noticed a series of framed black-and-white, portrait-style prints hanging on the walls between the doorways. They were of two women, very beautiful although quite young. He realised they were twins: they both had long dark hair and wide-set eyes. One was sitting at a table, her wrists laden with thin bangles, big hoops hanging from her earlobes. Her beringed fingers cradled what he could only describe as a crystal ball. She had a faraway look in her eyes, like she knew something no one else did. A secret.

The other woman stood behind her twin, hands resting on her shoulders. She wore a sleeveless dress with a modest neckline, leaving her thin arms bare. Except they weren't—they were covered in tattoos from wrist to shoulder. The shot was taken from too far away to see the detail but the skin art was highly visible. Her gaze was more frank, piercing even, as though she could sum you up in an instant.

"These are unusual," he commented.

Rosie nodded and sighed, fingering a frame lightly. "I love these."

Simon could see why. They had an allure and a mystery about them but an honesty as well. Each portrait had been taken from a slightly different angle, the background one of those innocuous backdrops from an old photographic studio, but each seemed to capture the essence of the sisters—the similarities as well as the differences.

Looking again at the women in the pictures, he saw a startling resemblance in Rosie's own wide-eyed gaze. "Relatives?" he asked.

"My aunts."

Simon blinked. He'd expected her to maybe admit to long-lost cousins several times removed. He looked at the picture again. "Your aunts are ... circus people?"

Rosie smiled at the photo with great affection. "They were. It's the family business."

He looked at her incredulously. The surprises just kept coming with Rosie. And yet somehow it all seemed right.

His mother was going to have a cow.

Rosie led Simon out onto the back verandah into a plume of cigarette smoke and a cacophony of bird noise. Two frumpy grey-haired women sat at a table, a tumbler half-filled with amber-colored liquid in front of each of them and an overflowing ash-tray between them. One shuffled a pack of tarot cards. The other thumbed through a magazine. A teenage boy sat at the other end of the table playing a game on his iPhone. The dogs lifted their heads and thumped their tails against the boards in their reclined positions.

"Here they are," the one with the cards said, looking up. "We thought you must have gotten lost."

Rosie smiled. "Just showing Simon around."

Two pair of eyes fell on him. Age had grayed and frizzed their formerly long dark locks and there were wrinkles around their eyes and mouths. There was meat on their bones, their bosoms ample, their laps generous, but they were unmistakably the same women from the pictures he'd just seen.

The one with the cards gave him a dreamy look while the other one, her tattoos still vibrantly colored and on full display, looked at him shrewdly.

"Simon, hey?" she said. "Well come over here so I can get a proper look at you."

Simon walked closer and Rosie introduced them.

"Bit young for you isn't he, Gypsy-Rose?" Daisy commented, looking him up and down.

Simon shot a glance at Rosie, who was grinning affectionately at her curmudgeonly aunt. "I believe age is irrelevant," he said politely.

"Hmph!" Daisy grunted. "Very gallant. Speak to me when you're sixty-two."

"You're a goat, aren't you?"

Simon looked at Iris, her dreamy eyes staring up at him. Did she mean a silly goat? A randy goat? A kid? He cleared his throat. "A goat?"

Rosie rescued him. "Capricorn. Your star sign."

"Oh, right." He gave a half laugh. "Yes actually, I am."

Iris nodded and presented the pack to him. "Pick a card."

He hesitated. He didn't believe in astrology or tarot or crystal balls—any alternative mumbo-jumbo. He believed in science and facts and hard work. Then he looked at Rosie and realized that alternative had its upside.

Rosie held her breath as Simon prevaricated. She'd not been sure how he would take the whole Forsythe extravaganza. And she was surprised to find that she actually cared that much.

Great, she was doing it again. Rushing in head first. How many times had Ella warned her about not losing her head?

"Pick one," Daisy insisted.

"Go on," Rosie said, injecting a teasing note into her voice to disguise how very, very much she wanted him to take a card. "Live dangerously."

Simon looked at the three women staring at him. Even the boy had given his thumbs a temporary reprieve from RSI and was watching with interest. "Okay." He pulled a card from the middle of the pack and stared at it blankly.

The Fool. Excellent.

He didn't have a clue what it meant in fruit-cake land but he had to figure it wasn't good.

He turned it around to show Iris. She looked at the card and then at him, sighing heavily as she relieved him of it.

"There's going to be trouble," she muttered.

Simon looked at Rosie and she gave him a lewd wink. God knew she was trouble with a capital T. With her hellfire bed and gothic dominatrix image, he should be running for the hills.

But trouble had never felt this good.

Daisy nodded slowly. "Don't mind a spot of trouble. Pull up a seat."

Simon sat feeling like he'd passed some kind of test. Rosie sat next to him. They were quickly enveloped in a heavy plume of smoke as Iris and Daisy stubbed out their cigarettes and each lit another one.

Hell also apparently had a waiting room. And he was sitting in it.

He coughed as he felt his bronchioles start to narrow and looked around for a distraction. Another massive wooden cabinet sat pushed against the outside wall of the house. Inside it was more state-of-the-art electronic equipment. Another wide-screen television and other associated machines. He couldn't believe they would have such expensive gear sitting unsecured on their verandah. Weren't they worried about it being stolen?

Rosie placed her hand on his thigh and under cover of the table she slowly moved it closer to his crotch. He clamped his hand down hard on hers, instantly forgetting all about local crime, his tendency to asthma and the hazards of passive smoking.

"You feed birds," he said, grasping the first topic that came to mind and saw Rosie's quick smile in his peripheral vision.

Their gazes were drawn to the hundreds of rainbow lorikeets huddled around tin plates lashed at intervals to the wires of the clothes line. They squawked and chatted and fought for position, their wings flapping indignantly, revealing the brilliant tangerine, crimsons and purples in the plumage of their breasts. The noise was incredible—like an avian rock concert.

It reminded him of the time his parents had taken him to Currumbin Bird Sanctuary as a kid. He'd held out his tin plate with everyone else and the birds had flown down and landed on the side. And on his head. And his shoulders. When one had pooped down his shirt, his mother had dragged him away in disgust. But for a few minutes he'd felt completely awed, like a normal kid for once, getting dirty and reveling in nature.

"Someone had to. They knocked down all the flowering trees that used to thrive around here to make room for these hideous apartments," Daisy griped.

Iris nodded. "Where were they supposed to go? We planted those wattles ten years ago," she said, pointing to the five trees lining the back fence, their silvery green foliage shimmering in the fading sun, "to help the situation, but it's not enough now."

"I guess that's the price you pay for progress," Simon mused.

"Fuck progress," Rosie said. Simon looked at her and got that little frown between his eyes again. "I mean ... scr ... er ... stuff progress," she ended lamely. But then Simon smiled at her with his gorgeous geek-boy smile and she practically melted.

Iris and Daisy exchanged a look. Even Cameron glanced up at Rosie's inarticulate stumbling. One thing Rosie had always been was articulately vulgar.

"They're kind of loud," Simon said. He wondered how many complaints had flooded into council about the noise from the pampered parrots.

Iris and Daisy grinned at him and said, "Yes," simultaneously.

He grinned back. He could tell they were fucking with progress in their own way.

# CHAPTER FOUR

Ella had arrived at Jake's bar too late this evening to grab the usual booth and with Rosie cooking dinner for Simon at home it didn't make sense to take up an entire table. She just wanted a couple of quiet drinks, some good music and a chance to think before meeting the new man in her friend's life. So she'd chosen a bar stool and was consequently balancing precariously on an inadequate piece of chrome and plastic while her butt cheeks fought and lost the battle with gravity, oozing over the edge. She felt like an elephant sitting on pogo stick. How the hell she was going to get off was a total mystery.

She'd fought with Cam today. Again. He'd wagged school. Again. How was she supposed to be the authority around Hanniford High when she couldn't even control her own brother? She was the principal, for Pete's sake. Damn it. Why wouldn't he let her in?

God, she was depressed.

A man sidled up to her and said, "Hi."

Ella looked up from her wine at a tall, nice-looking guy about her age. He was wearing a suit, his tie pulled loose, and she could see his mates nudging each other in her peripheral vision. Her depression intensified.

She was a regular tropical low.

"Haven't I seen you some place before?"

Ella groaned inwardly. She really didn't have the patience tonight; she was probably just a dare anyway. "Yes," she said unsmilingly. "That's why I don't go there anymore."

The guy's confident smile slipped and for a moment Ella felt a twinge of guilt but his friends' loud guffawing in the background hardened her heart.

He turned away and slunk back to his mates, who slapped him vigorously on the back. Ella returned to her wine and realized Jake had appeared behind the bar.

"That's the third one to crash and burn in the last twenty minutes," she heard Pete whisper to him.

"Ella," Jake murmured, topping up her glass of Chardonnay. "Are you torturing my customers?"

She looked at him, noticing the nearly empty beer he held in his other hand. Noticing his hands, period. Hands that knew their way around a woman's body. Magic hands. Her abdominal muscles contracted in primal recognition. Or was it yearning?

"I try not to feed the animals."

Jake gave a faux horrified gasp. "That's not a very nice thing to say."

The group of men broke into a chorus of loud cheers behind her as their footy team scored a goal in full Technicolor splendor on the four big-screen televisions. They punched the air and grunted like a pack of gorillas.

She raised an eyebrow at Jake. "I rest my case."

Jake grinned and downed the dregs of his Corona. "Now, now, Ella. They've been working hard all day. All they want is to sit around with their friends, watch a bit of footy and maybe get laid tonight."

Three giggling women came to the bar and called to Jake. They were blond and big-boobed and impossibly young. He grinned at them. "Don't go anywhere," he said to Ella before sauntering off.

His imperious command bothered her but not enough to shift her ass off the pogo stick—she preferred not to execute a move with such a degree of difficulty in front of the Barbie triplets. She rolled her eyes as one by one they held out their forearms and Jake signed them. They waggled their fingers at him and left, giggling. He sauntered back.

"Looks like you're the only one getting laid around here tonight," Ella said.

Jake shrugged as he inserted a slice of lime into the neck of his next Corona. "They just wanted my autograph."

"Oh please. I saw the way they were batting their eyelids at you. You could have had all three of them at once."

Jake laughed. "Ménages aren't as fun as they used to be."

Ella's mind went blank. Ménages? *Plural?* "Poor baby," she said derisively.

He leaned forward on his elbows. "I prefer to devote all my energy to one woman at a time."

His eyes were twinkling. Twinkling, damn it! She could barely see her hand in front of her face in here most of the time but she could see the bloody twinkle in his ridiculously sexy eyes.

"Well, I'm sure they'd all take a number, Jake."

Her deliberate insult missed it mark by a good mile as Jake hooted with laughter.

"Where's Miss Rosie tonight?"

"She's cooking her sure-thing curry for Simon."

He raised an eyebrow. "Because it works every time?"

She nodded, depressed further by her friend's very healthy libido. "*Every* time."

Jake narrowed his eyes. "We're not talking about curry now, are we?"

Ella shook her head.

"Ah. I see. Does she add some secret aphrodisiac potion to it?"

"Nah. She just makes it so bloody hot they have to go lie down."

Jake's laughter was drowned out by another round of loud hooting erupting around the bar. He looked at the nearest screen. The Brisbane Heroes were winning. It might have only been a pre-season game but they were coming out strong and he felt a surge of pride in his team mix with the familiar itchy-feet feeling.

The old resentment that he hadn't been quite ready to hang up his boots also reared its ugly head. Even at an ancient thirty-six his relatively injury-free career had put him in good stead to captain the Heroes for another couple of years.

But no, he had to go and open his big mouth.

Tony Winchester's face filled the screen. Speak of the devil. Jake's resentment intensified. His arch nemesis sat casually in his chair joking with the two other commentators, his blond good looks disguising his black, black heart.

They'd started and ended their careers together and had spent the intervening years butting heads on and off the field. Tony Winchester was an asshole. How he could even hold his head up in public, let alone score a commentator gig, was beyond Jake.

Jake took a long swallow of his beer observing Ella rolling her eyes and placing her forehead on the bar.

"Who do you barrack for?" he asked

Ella's head snapped up. "Oh please. I'd rather stick a red-hot poker into my eye."

Jake laughed. "Not a fan, huh?"

Not a fan? Boy, now that was an understatement. "I hate it with a passion that consumes my entire being."

He whistled. "What did football ever do to you?"

She felt the familiar sense of impotence and unfairness rise in her. How could she say, "It took you away"? How could he understand that although they'd barely ever spoken, Jake had been some kind of lodestone for her? Someone else in their shitty town who truly understood what it felt like to be standing on the outside.

"Nothing. I just ... hate the ... slavish devotion we have in this country for twelve sweaty men—"

"Thirteen," Jake interrupted.

"Who do nothing more than kick a dumb pointy ball around a stupid bit of grass."

"Actually it's not quite as easy as that."

"Jake," she said sharply and slapped her hand down on the bar. "It's not rocket science. They're not trying to split the atom or find a cure for cancer. I mean, those things are worthwhile at least. But no, you take a bunch of boys who aren't necessarily the sharpest tools in the shed, stuff their pockets full of money, ply them with gifts and alcohol, tell them their shit doesn't stink and let them loose in public."

Jake drank his beer in silence. Ella was in full flight and as much as he knew she was making sweeping generalisations, a lot of it couldn't be denied. He'd witnessed more than his fair share of disgraceful behaviour by ego-tripping teammates.

Tony Winchester being a good case in point.

"Then what do they do? They drink drive, conduct sordid text affairs—"

"Ah, I think you'll find that one's cricket."

"Oh, like there's a difference. Different balls, same grubby little boys with swollen egos," Ella snapped. She paused. "Where was I?"

"Text affairs."

She nodded. "Right. Then there's the party drugs. The trashing of bars and hotels, the violence both on and off the pitch—"

"The field."

"Field. Right. The way that they're so used to being surrounded by yes-men they don't seem able to take no for an answer, particularly if it comes from a woman. But for some strange reason our society hero worships these guys."

"Well, when you put it like that—"

"Jesus, Jake, there are children in Africa starving but we don't have the money for that. People live in abject poverty all round the world but we don't have the money for that. We have kids here in Australia who can't read or write or add up but we don't have the money for that. They're trying to close my school down, for crying out loud. But never mind, there's always money for football."

Jake watched Ella slump over her glass and stare morosely at the contents. Well, she wasn't kidding. It did consume her. "Finished now?" he asked quietly.

She sighed. She wished she felt better for getting it all off her chest but she didn't. They were still shutting her school down and her brother still hated her. "Finished."

"Jake, your damn dog's howling," Pete said, coming in from the back.

"You have a dog?" Ella asked, straightening.

"Kind of."

She blinked, wondering if she'd consumed more alcohol than she thought. "You *kind of* have a dog?"

"He's a stray who's been hanging around. I don't suppose you know anyone in the neighbourhood who could take him do you?"

As a matter of fact she did. She lived at stray central and Iris and Daisy were the queens. But she held back; she didn't want to be another of Jake's yes-women. In fact, she really didn't want to get involved with him at all. "Why don't you take him home?"

"No pets allowed in my building."

No. She supposed he lived in some riverside penthouse somewhere. A place where everything was marble and leather and designer pooches that fit in handbags were fine but dirty strays did not belong.

Jake could see her prevaricating. He shot her his best I'm-too-sexy-for-this-bar smile. "I think you owe me one," he said.

His look told her she owed him a hell of a lot more than that. In fact she owed him three. *Bastard!*

"He'd be a great watch dog. Protect two vulnerable women living by themselves. He's got a great bark and a menacing personality."

She held his gaze for a moment, knowing that the aunts would never forgive her if she said no. She drained her glass of wine. "Show me."

She prayed the Barbie triplets were busy drinking their fruity cocktails and no one was watching as she dismounted the pogo stick and followed Jake behind the bar and out to the alley.

"Cerberus?" Ella looked from the dog to Jake then back to the dog.

"Uh huh," Jake confirmed, squatting to give him a pat.

The dog looked up at her and gave his tail a wag as if in apology. As if even he knew that the name was rather ambitious. She may not have been expecting three heads but she'd certainly expected a more impressive specimen. This was the most miserable-looking hound of hell she'd ever seen. She couldn't have been more surprised had it been a Chihuahua called Satan.

"This is the watchdog with the menacing personality?"

Cerberus licked her hand and gave her one of his well-timed pathetic trembles.

Jake nodded again. "Underneath this flea-bitten exterior lurks the dark heart of a ninja dog."

Amy Andrews

She crouched down next to Jake. "Ninja dog, huh?" she murmured scratching behind the dog's soft, floppy ear. Cerberus angled his head to allow Ella more access and gave a shudder of ecstasy. "What do you say, boy? Want to come live at my house?"

Cerberus whined his agreement and Ella smiled. "Okay, then."

Jake watched her as she ran her hands down the length of Cerberus's body. "Thank you."

Ella glanced at him. A mistake. Out of the neon gloom his features were sharp and defined. He was breathtaking. As a teenager he'd been good-looking but as an adult his attraction had matured into a lethal weapon. Their heads were close and she watched as his gaze dropped to her mouth. How often had she dreamed about Jake's kiss? The thrill of it was still burned into her lips two years on. She could smell beer and lime on his breath and her eyes fluttered closed as the air in the alley became heavy with anticipation.

Oh God, this was bad.

She forced her trembling legs into action and stood. She cleared her throat. "Consider us even."

Jake laughed, pushing himself upright too, a raised eyebrow calling her to account. "Oh, I don't think so."

*Bastard.* "Come on, Cerberus. Let's go home."

Jake fell into step beside her and she stopped. "What are you doing?"

"I'm walking you home."

"I'll be fine."

"What kind of a gentleman would I be if I let a lady walk home by herself in the dark?"

"It's not dark yet, and anyway, I'm not alone, am I? I have the hound from hell, ninja dog with me."

They both looked down at Cerberus, who wagged his tail and trembled at the same time.

Jake rolled his eyes at the pathetic combination and started walking again. "I insist."

Ella refused to move. She didn't want him to accompany her. She didn't want to spend time with him. She'd relived those three orgasms obsessively over the last few weeks and frankly she was so horny she didn't trust that she wouldn't try to jump him before they even left the alley.

"I'm a big girl, Jake. I don't need a chaperone." If anyone needed a chaperone it was him.

Jake stopped, walked back to Ella, grabbed her arm and pulled her along. "Oh, come on, Ella."

"What about the pub?" she asked, resisting.

"Pete can handle it."

Ella dug her heels in. "He's kind of young to have that sort of responsibility, isn't he?"

Jake gave her a patient stare. "Don't worry about Pete. He can handle himself."

Ella reluctantly let herself be dragged along. She shook her arm free when they exited the alley and took some deep, steadying breaths of the warm March air. She congratulated herself on not slamming him against the bricks and having her way with him.

They ambled along the footpath, Cerberus between them, the techno beat from the pub gradually fading. "So what do you want to talk about?" Jake asked.

Ella, who was pretending she wasn't walking next to God's gift to the female anatomy, was grateful for the silence. "Talk is overrated."

Jake laughed. "Now you sound like my kind of woman."

Ella rolled her eyes. "More the wham, bam type, Jake?"

"Well, you'd know, sweetheart."

She gritted her teeth at his ungentlemanly reminder. But still those muscles deep inside her did another wild tango.

They walked in silence for a moment or two, Cerberus trotting between them as they appreciated the sultry twilight and the first sprinkling of stars.

"So what's the story with you and Rosie?"

Ella didn't answer for a while. Where did she start? How did she sum up their relationship in one or two sentences? How could she adequately convey just how much Gypsy-Rose Forsythe meant to her? How did you put almost two decades of friendship into words?

"It seems to me like you've known each other for a long time."

Ella nodded. "Nineteen years."

Jake did a quick calculation and frowned. "Do you know her from Huntley?"

She nodded again. "Rosie came halfway through twelfth grade."

"Has she always been … alternative?"

Ella grinned. "Always. Her family are carnies. She grew up in a circus. I think she was a little extreme though, even for them."

He laughed. "I bet Huntley wasn't ready for that."

His laugh was delicious. Rich and warm, oozing over her like warm treacle, and it gave her goose bumps despite the warmth in the air. Those muscles did their thing again. The way she was going, she'd have the tightest pelvic floor around. Which could be a plus. At least when they shut her school down she'd be able to get a job as an exotic dancer firing ping pong balls out of her twat.

"Huntley most definitely disapproved."

He looked at her speculatively. "So you befriended her?"

Ella caught the trace of skepticism. "Yes." Actually, Rosie, recognising a fellow misfit, had invaded her personal space and refused to leave. Thank God. "Is that so hard to believe?"

Jake shrugged. "You were always such a … loner."

Ella snorted. "Do you think that was through choice, Jake?" She stopped walking and Cerberus looked up at her and gave a low whine. "None of the good mothers of Huntley wanted their precious little girls playing with Rachel's daughter." Ella had learnt early that loneliness was preferable to rejection.

Jake nodded. He knew the feeling well. He hadn't been good enough for the daughters of Huntley either. Fortunately for him teenage girls and their mother's often didn't see eye to eye. "The mothers of Huntley were a mob of prissy, small-town, narrow-minded, bigoted bitches."

Ella held Jake's gaze. She knew he was right but, oh, how she had longed to go to Sarah Charlton's eighth birthday party along with all the other girls in her class. Or any of the other birthday parties.

Cerberus's cold nose nudged her palm. She looked down at him as she scratched his head—another misfit. "Yes, I know that—now. But as a kid, you just want to fit in. To be like the others."

Jake shook his head. "That's what I liked about you. You were different from the others."

He'd liked her? "Jake, we barely said boo to each other."

"Yeah, but you never judged me, Ella. You never condemned me because my father was a drunk or blew all our money on the horses."

"That would have been completely hypocritical of me, wouldn't it?"

"Huntley thrived on hypocrisy, sweetheart."

Ain't that the truth. Ella stared for a few more moments then started walking again. Jake and Cerberus joined her.

"For what it's worth, I really liked your mother."

"You knew Rachel?" Jake looked at her. Of course. Everyone knew Rachel.

Ella remembered the first time she realized what her mother did and why they were ostracized. She'd been in fifth grade and overheard some teachers talking. She remembered the shock as if it was yesterday, trying to comprehend how the woman who danced with her to 'Blue Moon' every morning and had home-made choc-chip muffins waiting for her after school was the same person these adults were talking about.

She'd always known her mother wasn't like the other mums but she'd actually kind of liked that. Rachel had been the prettiest mother by far and Ella had been secretly proud. She used to sit and watch her mother's make-up ritual every morning, totally entranced, longing for the day when she would be old enough for red lipstick and pink cheeks.

Of course the fact that Rachel was always in her silky dressing gown, day and night, should have been a clue. As a kid, Ella had just loved the cool slippery feel of it against her face and the way it smelled of perfume and powder. It had seemed so sophisticated. So adult. Later she'd grown to hate it and all it represented.

"Yeah, well," she said derisively shaking off the memories, "she tended to have that effect on anyone with a Y chromosome."

Jake shook his head. "She always had the time of day for my dad. A lot of people didn't. It meant something."

They stopped at a traffic light and Ella glanced at him. He was looking at her with sincerity blazing like a beacon in his eyes and she stopped herself from pointing out it was her mother's *job* to give people the time of day. It was startling to hear someone defending Rachel and she felt like a child again, desperately wanting her mother to be the person Jake knew her to be, not the one Huntley had painted her as.

The red man turned green and the moment passed. When they got to the other side, Ella turned right, away from the main road and into the back streets.

"So you two have been friends since twelfth grade," Jake prompted.

Ella nodded. "We hitched out of Huntley together, ended up in Brisbane at her aunts' place. Rosie always jokes she's probably the only kid in the world who ran away from the circus to join home."

Jake laughed. It filled the warm air around her and cocooned her in a comforting embrace. "So, you didn't flee with the principal that night?"

"No. Contrary to popular opinion, Mr. Edmonstone and I were not having an illicit affair."

"He liked you though."

"Yes. He did. He was the most inspirational person I had ever met. He told me about all the places he'd been and the people he'd met. He encouraged me to aim high. To get out of Huntley and make something of myself. Go to uni. Travel. Expand my horizons. He was a good teacher. The kind of teacher every student should have. I owe him a lot."

Jake nodded. "He was a pretty decent guy. I wasn't much of a scholar but he never gave up on me."

As Jake had spent more time outside Mr. Edmonstone's office than he'd spent inside a classroom, Ella figured he spoke from experience.

"He certainly didn't seem the kind to run off with a student."

Ella couldn't agree more, still pissed off at the rumour. "How were we to know he was high-tailing it out of Huntley that night too? He told us he was going to a curriculum meeting in Wombialla."

"Guess he must have just flipped," Jake mused.

She nodded. "It must have been hard for a worldly man to settle in such a bigoted backwater. I think he just couldn't take it another moment."

They drew level with her gate. The night was almost completely upon them now and the trees framing the house looked like stands of black coral against the velvet sky. Cerberus sniffed at the gatepost with great interest.

Jake blinked at the massive old Queenslander. "That's a big house for two chicks."

Ella smiled. "Two chicks, two crazy old aunts, several stray animals and a teenage boy."

"How is Cameron?"

Ella's hand tightened on the gate. "He's fine," she said, a little too quickly.

Jake saw the white of her knuckles. "He's what, fifteen?" He whistled. He remembered what a handful he was at that age. How full of hormones and rage he'd been. "That's a tough age."

"He's ... it's ... difficult at times." Now there was the world's greatest understatement. She felt like she'd been beating her head against a brick wall for the last two years. She was somewhere between concussed and rupturing a blood vessel. Even the thought of having to go in and confront him now over his latest misdemeanour was bringing on a headache.

Jake put his hand over hers. "Don't forget, he grew up in Huntley, too."

She looked down at his hand. She was trying hard, really hard, to remember. God knew she'd cut him enough poor-kid's-grown-up-in-whacko-central slack to last a lifetime. But she was nearly at the end of her rope. Her brother was so hostile and she didn't understand how blowing off his education, his one true chance at leaving his upbringing behind for good, was going to make anything better.

"Do you want to come in?" The husky invitation was out before she had a chance to recall it. She really didn't want to face Cam and was willing to use whatever delaying tactics she had at her disposal. She shrugged. "It's usually a three-ring circus but if you're game ..."

Jake could sense her desperation. Something inside was waving a giant red flag. This was cosy, family crap. Dangerous waters. But something else, something bigger, wrapped his resistance in a giant tentacle and yanked him forward at the same time Cerberus nuzzled his hand. He looked down at the dog and received an enthusiastic tail wag/ whole body wiggle.

Surely seeing Cerberus settled was the responsible thing to do? He smiled at Ella. "I'm always up for a challenge."

Ella smiled back, bolstered by his presence, and pushed open the gate. "Virgin sacrifices first," she said and gestured for him to precede her.

Jake grinned as he moved past her. "Should I be afraid?"

"Very. Daisy loves fresh blood."

A sensor light shone through the tree canopy and lit the path almost immediately as a rumble of barking and a flash of fur tumbled down the stairs to greet them.

"Whoa," Jake laughed as Genghis leaped up at him. He ruffled the dog's head affectionately and razzed him up for a few seconds before crouching to pat the other dogs too. They spent a bit of time watching while the dogs all sniffed Cerberus's bottom and generally got to know the skinny intruder.

Ella decided not to take him through the house. It was a bit like entering an alternative reality and as much as she was grateful he was beside her tonight, this house was the only place she'd ever felt at home and she didn't want to share it with him. How could someone who lived in a sleek riverside address understand her total devotion to this sagging old beauty?

She led him around the verandah, the dogs charging ahead. The cigarette smoke greeted them long before they reached Iris and Daisy's table. She was nervous and wasn't at all sure it was totally to do with Cameron and his truancy.

"And who do we have here?" Daisy held Cerberus's head in her hands and stared into his eyes. He wagged his tail.

"That's Cerberus," Jake said.

Daisy looked at the pathetic mutt and raised an eyebrow, then she looked up and appraised the other newcomer through a waft of blue smoke. "And who are you?"

Ella performed the introduction and Jake felt an instant rapport with Daisy. She reminded him of his own aunt, Thelma. Well actually, she'd been his great aunt, his mother's aunt. But she'd raised him for many years after his mother's desertion with the same shrewdness he saw in Daisy's gaze. She'd died of a heart attack when he'd been twelve and he'd missed her every day since.

"Jake!" Rosie leaped from the table and gave Jake an enthusiastic hug. "Sit down. I have some curry left."

Jake looked at Ella, who gave him an almost imperceptible shake of her head. He glanced at who he assumed was Simon, his nose shiny red, gulping greedily from a large cup of water. "Er, thanks but I can't stay for long. I have to get back to the pub." He took the seat opposite Simon with views over the backyard. He noticed Cerberus was making himself at home by methodically lifting his leg on every tree and bush. Genghis followed after him peeing over the top of the newcomer's wet spots.

"You're a Sag, aren't you?" Iris asked.

Jake smiled at the older woman with the dreamy voice as Ella introduced him. "Yes, I am."

Iris nodded, picked up her tarot cards, shuffled them and presented them to him. "Pick one.'

Jake grinned as he looked from one Technicolor twin to the other. He chose one from the middle of the pack and flipped it over.

It was Death.

The whole table stared at it in silence. "Guess that's bad, huh?" Jake grinned, unperturbed.

Iris glanced at Daisy. "Trouble, I tell you," she muttered, picking it up.

Simon blinked at the laidback guy who'd joined them. The heat of Rosie's curry had finally eased its strangle hold on his vision and he realised his fellow newcomer looked familiar. "Good God," he said. "You're Jake Prince." He rose from his seat and extended his hand across the table. "I'm a big fan. It was a tragedy to see you go."

Jake shook Simon's hand as Rosie introduced him. "It's a pleasure to meet you."

"Do you miss it?" Simon asked, sitting back down.

"Sure," Jake said also taking a seat. *Every moment, of every day.* Football had been the only thing he'd ever been any good at.

"What do you think the Heroes' chances are this season?"

Ella rolled her eyes at Rosie. "Where's Cam?" she interrupted before the conversation descended into a cave man-like dialect that required either a degree in anthropology or a Y chromosome to decipher.

"Watching the footy. Where else?" Daisy said, eyeing Jake with interest. "That kid watches too much TV."

Ella nodded, Daisy's bluntness washing over her. She knew Daisy had her own thoughts on the way Cam was being raised, which she generally kept to herself. She doubted any of them involved the softly, softly approach that Ella had thus far favored. Certainly Cam wouldn't be game to give Daisy the amount of crap he heaped onto her. But she had a lot of years to make up for and she was trying to get by as best she could. At least when Cam was glued to the box, she knew where he was. And watching football made him less sullen. No doubt it was his way of trying to piss her off further.

"Some girl rang him earlier," Rosie chimed in. "Miranda. Or something like that."

Ella blinked. A girl? Her brother had the communication skills to converse with a girl? "Really?" She sat down next to Jake. "How'd that go?"

Rosie grinned. "Kind of silent this end. He did a lot of nodding."

No surprise there. Cam usually only stretched to more than grunts and one-syllable words when absolutely essential. Ella had a glimpse at what it must have been like for Neanderthal woman and wasn't surprised they all died young. Probably from sheer boredom.

"Any more thoughts on a plan of attack, dear?" Iris asked.

Ella came out of her thoughts and smiled sweetly at lovely Iris for changing the subject. "Not really, Iris. What do the cards say? Anything hopeful?"

"I'm sorry, dear." Iris shook her frizzy head. "It's all very unclear."

"Problem?" Jake asked.

"They're trying to shut Ella's school down," Rosie said. "Mob of moronic beaurocratic fuckwits."

Simon raised an eyebrow at her and Rosie chewed on her lip contritely. "Sorry. Some situations require the F word."

"I can't believe they're actually going to do it." Ella grimaced. "These kids don't have much but at least they're getting an education." She turned to Jake. "At least at school they get to escape from their home life for a while to a place where they know that people care about them. Who's going to feed the Breakfast Club kids if we close our doors? Their parents certainly won't. And what about the school-based apprenticeship scheme that I busted my ass to get up and running? It was giving them a real alternative. Something better than shelf-stacker or the dole queue."

He watched Ella worrying a linen napkin between her fingers. Had it been paper it would have been torn to shreds. He liked that she'd become a teacher—it was fitting. And it was apparent that it was more than just a job. The school and its students obviously meant the world to her. They were clearly more than just numbers.

He listened as the women threw ideas around in the smoke-filled bubble that ranged from the whacky to the dubious. Simon, who had been silently assessing the situation too, squinted through the haze of smoke and locked eyes with Jake.

"I've got it," he announced with a snap of his fingers.

Everyone turned to face him. Even Cerberus, who had plonked himself down next to Simon and was gratefully accepting the odd smuggled spoonful of curry. The other dogs, lounging far away from the table, knew better.

"Does the school have a football team?" Simon asked Ella, absently patting Cerberus's head.

She frowned. "A group of kids who play touch on the oval at lunchtime." It was about the only time she could guarantee that Cam would be at school. She shrugged. "There's no money for extracurricular things like that. We don't even have enough PE hours in the budget for all the kids to have their mandatory one lesson a week."

"What if you formed a football team and entered the BSFC? No way would they shut down a school that took away that prestigious sucker."

Ella blinked. Enter the Brisbane Schools Football Competition? A competition schools trained for years to win? She stared at Simon and wondered if he'd been dropped on the head as a baby.

Jake, whose shoulders had tensed, relaxed. Ella looked like she was about to have a stroke. Or at the very least a seizure. And he thanked God for her pathological dislike of football.

"Cameron would love it," Daisy commented.

"Just like that. Just win a comp like that?" Ella asked incredulously.

"Well, I'm not saying it'll be easy. But you do have a secret weapon. You have a first-rate retired rugby league player under your nose. Probably the best fullback this country has ever seen."

Ella turned and looked at Jake. "He means you, right?"

Jake glared at Simon. "No." Jesus. The last thing he needed was this kind of hassle. He was retired. He was running a pub and drinking beer. Life was one long happy hour.

"You could coach them," Simon pressed.

"Ohmigod, yes." Rosie clapped, bouncing in her seat. "It's perfect."

"No," Ella and Jake said in unison. They looked at each other.

"I'm retired," Jake said, looking back at Simon.

"He's retired," Ella repeated.

"The winner gets to take on the private school boys for the Schools Cup," Simon continued, looking straight at Ella. "Win that and you'd be untouchable. Maybe forever."

Ella hated to admit it, but Simon was right. Slavish devotion to football started early and the inter-school football comp was extremely high profile. The temptation was massive but even so, she couldn't believe she was considering it. The irony cut too deep. Could the one thing she'd despised more than anything—football—be the one thing to dig her out of the hole she was in?

"But we'd have to win," she said to Simon. "That's ... impossible. We'd need a miracle. We'd need more than Jake. We'd need God's gift to football."

Simon looked at her. "He *is* God's gift to football."

She looked at Jake and he shrugged and grinned. Well, now, how unfair was that? God had favored Jake Prince with one too many gifts. She glanced at Simon. Then back to Jake. She didn't want to want this. She didn't want to need this. She didn't want anything to do with football. And certainly not anything to do with someone from Huntley, and least of all someone who was such an integral part of a past she'd spent nearly two decades trying to forget. But unfortunately she also knew what Simon was saying was right. The Schools Cup was extremely prestigious and highly sought after.

Iris, who had been setting out a spread of cards, pursed her lips. "The cards are favorable."

Ella sighed. Well that was that, then. If the cards said so then both Daisy and Iris were already committed.

"The cards are telling me it could be very good for Cameron," Iris added.

Ella looked at Iris, shying from the force of her mental arm twisting. She'd never questioned Iris's gift. Rosie had had her convinced of her aunt's ability even before they'd arrived in Brisbane and she'd been privy to its accuracy on more than one occasion.

"Do they say we'll win?"

Iris gave one of her mystical smiles. "You know they don't deal in absolutes."

Ella looked at Jake speculatively. Maybe she could use Australia's criminal devotion to sport in her favor? Make the bloody game work for her? Work for good. And besides, what else did she have? Apart from sleeping through the upper echelons of the education department?

Jake shook his head. "No."

She gave him a reproving look.

"I'm retired," he said, exasperation in his voice as everyone stared at him.

"So you have plenty of time on your hands," Ella reasoned.

"I run a pub."

She almost faltered at his vehement rejection. She glanced at Iris again, who nodded at her. It sounded crazy. A stupid, hare-brained whim, but it beat the hell out of a dozen or so sexual favors with a bunch of men who looked like Menzies had been PM the last time any of them had seen any action. She was pretty sure they hadn't even discovered the g-spot back then.

"Challenge too big for you, Jake? Not up to it? Prefer to fritter away life drinking beer and signing women's body parts?"

He snorted. "Hell, yeah."

Ella rolled her eyes. "This is important, Jake. More important than beer and women."

"Nothing's more important than beer and women."

"Margarita land every day for you, huh?"

"Yes, ma'am."

Ella swallowed. "Please, Jake."

Jake shook his head. "A public school has never won the Schools Cup in its ninety-year history."

Ella started. She looked at Simon. "Is that true?"

Simon nodded. "Doesn't mean yours won't be the first."

If there was one thing Ella hated more than football it was the whole elitist sport bullshit that went on at private schools. The temptation to be the ones to change that—poor, under threat Hanniford High—was amazingly enticing. Oh God. Was she that desperate?

She turned to Jake. "We could be the ones."

"You told me not even an hour ago you despise football."

Ella nodded. She did. But. "I'm prepared to tolerate it."

Jake looked at her, exasperated. "Don't you have a plan B?"

Ella shrugged. "Sleep with the entire education review panel."

Jake smiled. "There you go, then. Problem solved."

Cameron chose that moment to enter the fray. Ella's heart contracted as it always did when she saw him. He looked so much like Rachel. Sure, he was a big kid, solidly built from his thick neck to his broad shoulders down to his tree-trunk legs. He obviously took after his father—whoever the hell that was. But his face; some of his expressions were so like Rachel it was uncanny.

He ignored everybody, reaching for the iPhone he'd left on the table.

"Hi, Cam," Ella said trying to sound casual and friendly. Cameron grunted at her. "Can you let me know when the footy's finished? I need to talk to you."

Cameron rolled his eyes. "Shit, Ella. Nag, nag, nag. That's all you do," he said glaring at her as he grabbed his phone.

"Cam," she called after him as he turned to go back inside.

"Fuck off," he threw over his shoulder.

Jake blinked at Cameron's profanity, shocked by his utter rudeness. He looked at Ella and saw her complexion pale as her knuckles grew white against the back of the chair. Then her cheeks turned pink as everyone at the table sat in uncomfortable silence.

He felt a white hot welling of anger bubble up inside him. No wonder Ella had looked so strained earlier. Her brother needed a serious attitude adjustment. But amid the heat simmering inside him was a kind of primal recognition.

Cameron Lucas was a product of Huntley.

As he had been.

Cameron Lucas was him—before football.

"Okay," Jake said.

He stood to leave. If he stayed he may be tempted to give Cameron the whopping he deserved right now instead of making him pay for it on the field.

"I'll be there Monday at three o'clock. You got yourself a coach."

# CHAPTER FIVE

Iris wrestled the official-looking envelope from Genghis's mouth on Monday morning. She didn't need her psychic powers to know that anything with Brisbane City Council on it was not going to be good news and she almost gave it back to Genghis for annihilation by slobber. One of them might as well get pleasure out of the damned thing. Unfortunately she didn't think the council would accept "the dog ate the notice" from a grown woman.

She hurried up the stairs with the dogs at her heels. Her metal bangles, thinner every year, jingled with the rhythm. She could feel an edge of anxiety, never far away, kick up a notch—her psychic ability came hand in hand with a fretfulness she'd never quite mastered and to say she felt uneasy right now was an understatement.

Her recurrent dream didn't help. She woke most mornings desperately trying to hold on to the wisps of a vanishing dream that her intuition told her was important. But it always slipped from her grasp and she was left with just two words—yellow gold. Important words.

If only she knew what they meant.

Fortunately, her sensitivities had not been replicated in her twin and Iris couldn't wait to offload the offending envelope to Daisy. "It's from the council," Iris said, rounding the corner of the verandah, dropping the letter on the table the second she drew near enough to hit her target.

Daisy grunted and didn't bother looking up from rolling the day's supply of cigarettes; some things were more important than envelopes with windows. She ignored the multiple packets of filters, lying among the debris of newspapers and magazines on the Formica table top, that Ella and Rosie regularly bought for them. The girls' hearts were in the right place and the sisters made a point of using them in the evening when the girls were home, but they'd been smoking rollies since they'd been eleven and were too old to start looking after their health now.

Iris picked up her pack of tarot cards and shuffled them, eyeing the letter, then put them down again. She looked out over the yard, watching Cerberus scratching at the hard earth beneath the middle wattle. He seemed to have adopted that tree since arriving and had chosen well. Of the five wattles, it was the one that produced the most stunning display of yellow each season. The others always seemed to struggle in comparison. She called him away, not wanting him to kill their best flowerer with his digging, and turned back to Daisy. Her lips were pursed in concentration as she loaded tobacco onto the paper and Iris felt her anxiety raise another notch. She picked the deck up again and rubbed her thumbs over the top card, taking a measure of calm from their familiar texture.

"Daisy."

Daisy looked up from licking the edge of the cigarette paper and momentarily resisted the reproach in Iris's gaze. Being one minute older had it advantages. But even after sixty-two years on earth together she was still a sucker for her twin's emotional vulnerabilities.

She passed Iris a rollie and picked up the envelope.

"What does it say?' Iris demanded the minute she'd taken her first fortifying, unfiltered drag.

Daisy scanned the letter and then scrunched it up and threw it to Genghis. "Asbestos."

Iris felt her heart stop momentarily in her chest and she coughed several times as the acrid smoke swirling in her lungs irritated her airways. She stared at her calm sister. "We have asbestos?" she gasped.

"Nah," Daisy said in her gravelly voice, lighting a cigarette. "They're just fishing."

Iris shuffled the cards. "They're sending someone, aren't they?"

Daisy shrugged. "They have to get past the dogs first."

Iris flicked ash off the end of her cigarette into the over-flowing ashtray. "When?"

"They didn't specify. Sometime in the next few weeks."

Iris pressed her lips together, squinting through the smoke at her sister, still shuffling her cards. "What if we do have it?"

"If we do have it then we're probably all doomed anyway."

"It'll cost a fortune to get rid of."

"It'll be fine."

"It's not just the asbestos, Dais. Look at this place. We can fill it up with as much modern stuff as we can win but it's still a ninety-year-old house falling down around our ears."

"So?" Daisy took a deep drag of her cigarette, looking for calm amid her twin's rising panic. "We'll remortgage it."

Iris snorted. She felt a flow of energy in her hands and pressed the deck between her palms for a moment before laying out a three-card spread.

"That developer has his finger in everyone's pie. He's obviously decided upping his offer isn't good enough and is stepping up his plan. He has to have friends in local govern-ment to be able to pull this trick," she said, indicating the letter being patiently masticated by an ecstatic Genghis. "Our bank manager is probably on his payroll."

Daisy shrugged again. "We'll find another bank."

"Daisy, have you forgotten this house has already been mortgaged twice? We don't exactly have a good track record. We're in debt to our eyeballs."

Daisy eyed her twin, cursing her tendency to get a little strung out over trivialities. "Forget? No. But I don't regret any of it either. Gypsy-Rose and Ella got the best education at one of the country's finest universities and little Stevie's coming up to his five-year anniversary since the experimental treatment in California."

Iris nodded, feeling churlish. She'd never for a minute regretted their choices either. The girls' education had been a no-brainer, as was second cousin Larry's plea for his baby grandson's life. Family was sacred. But she'd had a real itch up her spine for weeks now. Something big was going to happen. Something cataclysmic for them all. And nothing would be the same again.

Daisy took a long drag of her smoke and reached for her sister's hand. "What do the cards say, Iris?"

Iris blinked and looked down, surprised to see the three-card spread before her. The Tower card stared back at her in the future position. The very foundations of their lives were about to be shaken. A rude awakening lay around the corner for them all. She looked up at Daisy. "Is it too early for a drink?"

Daisy looked at her watch. It was barely nine. She stubbed out her cigarette. "It's five o'clock somewhere." She smiled and poured a slug of the ever-present sherry into their empty coffee mugs.

*

Jake's mobile jangled in the dark, quiet room like hell's door-bell. He woke with a start, groping around blindly for the offensive item, the noise like a hot needle in his temple.

"This has better be good," he growled as he punched the answer button.

"Good, you're awake." Pete's chipper voice grated along cerebral nerve endings that already felt like they'd spent the entire night on the rack.

"What the hell time is it?"

"Two."

Jake turned his head toward the sliver of light he could see through a gap in the heavy black-out curtains covering the window. "Two pm?"

Where the hell was he? An air-raid shelter? A dungeon? A coffin? As much as it hurt to think, he searched back into the abyss that was last night. There was poker. And drinking. And a girl. He reached out a hand and came in to contact with a warm naked thigh. The woman attached murmured something and rolled toward him, draping herself across his chest, her hand sliding down to the flat of his belly.

*Crap!*

"Uh huh. You have to be at the school in an hour."

Jake groaned. He wanted to crawl into a dark corner somewhere and die. He did not want to run around a football field with a bunch of rag-tag high school amateurs. At the moment, getting out of bed seemed way too big an effort. But then a picture of Ella's strained face at Cameron's insult the other night floated through the ninety-proof quagmire of his brain. He sighed.

"Okay. I'll be there."

"Cool."

Jake squinted into the darkness. "Er, Pete? I don't suppose you happen to know where I am?"

Pete laughed. "Well, sure. I dropped you and fan-girl back at her place last night. Would you like me to come pick you up?"

Fan-girl's hand moved lower and he grabbed it before it reached ground zero. "Hurry."

＊

Jake winced as he climbed into the passenger seat of his car and was greeted by an unbearable blare of noise that was the musical equivalent of fingernails down a blackboard. He reached for the dial and turned it down. "Jesus, Pete."

Pete grinned. "Did we practice safe sex?"

Jake glared at him. "What are you, my pimp?"

"Actually, Jake." Pete laughed. "I think I am."

Jake contemplated murder as Pete's laughter ricocheted like jackhammers inside his head. "I should have left you on the streets," he muttered.

Pete laughed even harder. "We're late. Ella's going to be ticked."

Well, Ella could get in line. He was pretty annoyed at himself. He couldn't remember the last time he'd written himself off enough to cause amnesia. Maybe two years ago when the club had given him his marching orders? Had he practiced safe sex? Hell, had he even *had* sex? He'd woken up with his clothes on and somehow he seriously doubted he'd have been capable ... Christ, he'd never not been capable.

Jake shut his eyes, his head throbbing double-time the harder he tried to remember. Unfortunately not even the combination of closed lids, an ultra-dark window tint and his aviator sunglasses was able to block the stab of harsh afternoon sunlight filtering through the smoky glass directly into eyeballs. They felt as if they'd been ripped out, stood on, rolled in shell grit and then stuffed in back to front.

"Just drive."

His head sank back gratefully into the spongy luxury of the leather interior as the powerful engine of his Saab surged forward. Thankfully, Pete didn't try to communicate any further and the construction crew in his head downed tools for a while.

He wasn't sure how much time had elapsed when the Saab glided to a halt but he knew he was going to need a hell of a lot more to even begin feeling human again. He peered out the window at a poorly maintained oval. The grass was patchy and mostly weeds. Large areas were totally bare. The goal posts had rust stains. A large crowd milled around run-down wooden bleachers. Bloody hell—he only needed seventeen for the team.

"How do I look?" he asked, taking his glasses off and turning to Pete.

Pete shook his head. "Like crap. And you stink of booze and cigarettes. Here." He rifled around in a backpack and passed over a can of deodorant.

Jake lifted his shirt, the action turning the bolts in his temples a little tighter, and sprayed. The car filled with a truly sickly smell, like Old Spice and Brut had a fight to the death and they'd bottled the festering remains. "Jesus! What the hell do you call this?" Jake asked.

Pete dropped his voice an octave or two. "It's Metrosexual Mojo."

Jake half-laughed, half-snorted both at the name and the delivery and then instantly regretted it.

"Laugh away, boss, but the ladies go crazy for it."

"This? This gets you laid?"

Pete winked. "Never fails."

Jake pushed his sunglasses back on, wondering what the hell was wrong with women these days. "Were the women of your generation born with malfunctioning olfactory centers?"

Pete laughed and sprayed some more deodorant in Jake's general direction, ignoring his boss's protest. "It sure as hell beats the Eau du Alcohol Poisoning you're sporting at the moment."

Jake wasn't entirely sure about that as the sickly aroma intensified in the closed confines of the car. "Let's just get this thing done."

*

Ella was torn between kissing Jake for showing and throwing the stupid football at his head when he finally arrived. This morning at assembly the student body had greeted her BSFC announcement with the kind of skepticism only those who had been continually let down by life could perfect. She'd spent all day assuring her students that yes, they were fielding a team in the comp and yes, *the* Jake Prince was going to coach it.

Most of the two hundred and eighty students had headed to the oval at three daring to hope for once that maybe something good was about to happen. The weight of utter depression as each minute slipped by without Jake's presence had been hard to bear. Some of them had already left, their opinion that adults lied and life sucked resoundingly confirmed.

Ella heard the car door slam and strode towards Jake. He was looking better than any man had a right to in his standard tight blue jeans, tight black T-shirt and a growth of overnight stubble that'd leave one hell of a beard burn.

"You're late," she hissed as he approached, nodding at Pete.

Jake winced. While her tone wasn't loud it was just the right frequency to twang his already fragile neurons. And frankly, it irritated the crap out of him. He was here, feeling like death warmed up, doing her a favour, saving her ass.

A little gratitude wouldn't go astray.

He squinted at his watch through the dark tint of his glasses, blinking his bleary eyes. "Ten minutes."

Ella shook her head. "These kids don't give you ten minutes."

Jake looked over her shoulder at the motley collection of students. They were watching him curiously but there was a wariness to their gazes he wasn't used to seeing. Usually, crowds surged forward, smiling and talking all at once. They slapped him on the back, shook his hand, shoved autograph books at him. These kids hung back and looked at him with a guardedness that was beyond their years. Jake rubbed his temple. "Tough crowd."

"You have no idea," Ella muttered.

Even through the pound at his temples, Jake couldn't mistake the dejection and disappointment in Ella's voice and his self-loathing raised another notch. "Hey," he said, lifting a hand to cup her face. "I'm sorry. It won't happen again."

Ella was curiously touched by the gesture and was suddenly pleased to have her back to her students. She almost succumbed to the urge to cover his hand with hers and maybe if Pete wasn't right there witnessing the scene she would have. But he was. Along with a sudden truly terrible stench.

"Oh my God, Jake. You stink!" she said, stepping back, his hand falling away. She'd thought a decade of teaching smelly, teenage boys double-maths after they'd run around all lunch hour had practically immunized her against odour. She'd been wrong.

The two octaves her voice had risen screeched through his brain and Jake reached for his temples. "Ella. Do you think you could keep it down?"

Ella blinked. "Oh my God!" she said again and reached up to whip his glasses off. His eyes were bloodshot. He looked like hell. "You're hung over!"

"Ella," he winced, grappling his glasses back and pushing them into place.

"How could you?" She stepped closer and lowered her voice. "What kind of example are you setting for these kids?"

"They won't know."

Ella snorted. "You smell like a collision between a brewery, a cigar shop and a cheap perfume factory."

"Hey," Pete protested.

Ella ignored him. "Half these kids have grown up in households destroyed by alcohol. Trust me—they'll know. Shit, Jake." She shook her head. "I didn't think I'd have to give you a code of conduct. I mean really—"

"Shh," Jake interrupted, placing two fingers against her mouth. His head felt like it was going to explode and her low, angry whisper was throwing petrol at the fuse.

Ella's diatribe stuttered to a halt. He was late and hung over and stank. God knew what he'd been up to or who he'd been with to get in such a state. She was mad as hell. But he was here and her heart did a funny triple beat at the press of his fingers into her lips.

Even hung over as he was, Jake felt the transient pulse of awareness as the softness of her mouth and the sigh of her breath against his fingertips streaked straight to his groin. He wanted to press harder, use his finger to smear the gloss from her mouth. It just wasn't the time or the place.

He rubbed his temple again. "Just go and introduce me, Ella."

It took a good few seconds for Ella to snap out of the haze. She turned and walked away from him.

"Okay, everyone." She raised her voice to hush the few murmurs that hadn't stopped as she'd approached them. "I'm sure to many of you, he will need no introduction, but I'd like you all to meet Jake Prince."

She turned slightly, and Jake took the cue, smiling and waving beside her.

"Jake apologises for being late, he's ... been unwell and dragged himself out of his sick bed to make this first session."

Jake grimaced at the paltry claps and cheers, realizing that his star-footballer rep alone would not be enough to win these kids over. They were obviously doing it tough and his tardiness had ruined any idolizing he'd come to expect as his due. Today he definitely had feet of clay.

Ella stepped aside and Jake was up. Unfortunately he just didn't have the patience for niceties today. So he was late. So they were pissed at him. He had a whole season to win their respect. Today was not the time for pleasantries. Today just had to be endured.

"Can I have—" Jake stopped as the effort to raise his voice caused a stabbing pain at the back of his head. He continued, his voice quieter, "Only the students interested in joining the team over at the goalpost."

There were a few moments of shuffling and low murmurs before a couple of boys peeled hesitantly off followed by more and then more. Jake nodded. "The rest of you want to watch on the sidelines, you're most welcome. We'll be here every afternoon at three."

Jake headed toward the boys who were waiting for him at the goalpost, Pete trailing behind. Every step reverberated through his head, kicking his headache up another notch. If he stood very still for the next hour maybe his head would still be on his shoulders by the end of it.

Ella blinked, staring after his departing back with its very interesting landmarks—broad shoulders, tapered waist, buns of steel. That was it? No team building, no rah-rah speech? No talk of honor and glory and mateship or whatever else dumbass excuses footballers used to forgive their appalling behavior.

She hurried to catch up to him, arriving in time to hear his first words. Maybe they'd be slightly more inspirational.

"We need seventeen guys," Jake announced to the assembled boys. He turned to Pete. "How many here?" The realm of counting was beyond him.

"Forty."

Jake nodded, the action jarring through his temples and he wondered again how the hell he got roped into this. He spotted Cameron among the hopefuls and glanced at Ella standing nearby. Hell.

"Right. This week is the selection process. Pete here," Jake slapped Pete's back, "is going to put you through your paces and next Monday I'll announce the team."

Pete looked at Jake with startled eyes and turned his back to the assembled students. "Er, Jake?" he asked quietly.

"You know what to do," Jake assured calmly. "You've been to every Heroes' training session since you were twelve years old."

Pete took a moment to absorb his boss's comments. He did know the grueling training schedule backward. He nodded. "Okay."

"Run them into the ground," Jake murmured.

Pete smiled. "Yes, sir."

"So that's it?" Ella demanded, falling in beside him as Pete rallied the troops.

Jake grimaced. "Yup."

"What? No pep talk? No encouraging words from a rugby league great?"

"Nope."

Ella glared at him. "As much as I enjoy monosyllabic conversations, would you care to elaborate on your game plan here?"

Jake folded his arms. "I've got to cut forty to seventeen."

She waited for him to elaborate a bit more. "And? Is there some sort of criteria for that?"

"Run their asses off for an hour and keep the ones still standing at the end of each day."

Ella blinked. "That doesn't seem very technical. Is this strategy from the hung-over school of coaching? The half-assed, I've-got-a-shocking-headache-don't-bother-me school of thought? I mean, don't you need kids with specific skills?"

Jake shook his head and almost groaned out loud at the pain behind his eyes and in his temples. Her sarcastic commentary was magnifying it tenfold. "Skills can be taught, practiced. Stamina is paramount."

"But aren't—"

Jake cursed under his breath as he massaged his temples. "Ella. Please shut up."

Ella glared at him. "Hey, it's not my fault you're hung over. I'm just trying to help—"

"Ella," he interrupted again. "If you want to help you'll go find me something, anything, to ease the sledgehammer pounding in my brain."

"I thought footballers could hold their booze?"

"It's been a lot of years since I mainlined Tequila." He grimaced.

Ella shook her head. "What on earth possessed you, Jake? Did coming here today scare you that much?"

Jake gritted his teeth at her insight. He'd deliberately gone out last night with the express purpose of getting trashed enough to forget about this hare-brained scheme he'd agreed to. Sure, it had been under the guise of a poker game but deep down he hadn't wanted to be alone in his apartment with nothing but thoughts of today.

"Yes." He didn't know why it did, it just did. Whether it was Ella or returning to football or the ghosts of two years ago or even further back to Huntley—he didn't know.

Ella blinked, surprised by his admission.

He must be hung over.

Being around Jake scared the hell out of her too. He was everything she'd turned her back on when she'd run from Huntley. Everything she'd been determined to never have anything to do with again, determined to forget. He was the only one who really knew her. Knew all about her. Her mother, the smears, the humiliations, her loneliness, her isolation.

Not even Rosie knew her as well as Jake. And here she was arm to arm with him. The one person from Huntley, from her past, who knew all her dirty little secrets.

She looked at him for a long moment hating that she couldn't see his eyes behind the tint of his glasses, itching to remove them from his face. The fact he could see her but she couldn't see him made her feel vulnerable. And she'd left vulnerable behind in Huntley.

"I'll go get some Panadol."

Jake watched her walk away, her hips swaying in her long brown skirt, her ponytail swinging. She'd worn her hair in a ponytail back in high school too and he felt a familiar urge to pull the band out and let it fall free like it had been at the Crown when she'd hauled him upstairs to room seven and bonked his brains out.

She was wearing a cream shirt of thin cotton that sat wide on her shoulders and through which he suddenly realized he could see her bra strap. God damn! He *must* be hung over to the point of near death to have missed that when she was closer and facing him! He made a mental note to check out the front view when she returned.

He turned his attention to the field in time to see a couple of boys run into each other, too busy checking out their hottie principal than watching where they were going, and he smiled for the first time since waking up with a splitting headache in a strange woman's bed. He wished there'd been a teacher of Ella's caliber when he'd been in high school—he may have enjoyed it more. He may have made a bit more of an effort to attend.

*

Ella returned ten minutes later and watched Jake as he tracked her progress across the field.

"Nice blouse," he commented as she passed him two tablets and a bottle of water.

Ella looked down at one of her favorite shirts. It was peasant style and fairly modest by today's standards but she found herself blushing anyway. She looked at him and watched as he gave a half grin that died an ugly death as a wince.

She quirked an eyebrow. "Thought you were hung over?"

"Hung over, Ella. Not dead."

Ella felt that funny pull down low again and couldn't drag her eyes away from him. She didn't need to remove his glasses to know he was staring at her—she could feel it.

"Jake! Jake!"

Ella turned around at the excited squeal, pleased for the distraction. The relief soon changed to surprise as fifteen-year-old Miranda Jones hurled herself at Jake, clinging to his neck and jumping up and down, chattering excitedly about the team and the comp. Funny, she'd never pictured Miranda Jones as the hero worship type. She'd taught Miranda math in eighth grade. She was a nice kid, well bought up, smart and motivated. Ella frowned as the hug continued. It was hardly appropriate behaviour for a school girl with an adult male and she was annoyed that Jake didn't get that there were some things you just didn't do in a school yard.

Although to give him his due, he did seem to be trying to settle the girl, if only to stop the incessant squealing that must be playing havoc with his headache. Ella allowed herself an evil grin, hoping the noise was a particularly virulent form of torture.

"That's enough, Miranda."

Ella turned to see a woman about her age approaching. She was blond and redefined petite. Ella felt like an Amazon next to the diminutive proportions of the newcomer. Ella searched her memory banks. This was Trish Jones, Miranda's mother.

The similarities between the two were amazing. Miranda was a tiny blond, like her mother, and cute as a button with a perky smile and a personality to match.

"Hello, Jake."

Jake set aside Miranda. "Trish." He smiled and kissed her on the cheek before wrapping her up in a hug.

"Oh God, Jake," Trish said pulling away. "You stink. Are you hung over?"

"Mum!"

Ella laughed at the look of horror on the teenager's face. Even Jake managed to crack a smile.

"Trish Jones," the woman said, turning to Ella and holding out her hand. "I think we've met once before."

Ella shook the proffered hand. Miranda's mother had an easy smile and an open, friendly face. "Yes, we have. At a parent–teacher night. Ella Lucas."

"Don't mind Miranda. Jake and I go way back—she's known him since she was born. She was so excited when she rang me at lunch time to tell me she had to come back to school straight after her dentist's appointment to watch Cameron try out and that Jake was going to be here."

Ella blinked. Cameron? *Her* Cameron? Could this be the Miranda from the phone the other night? Mature, articulate, Miranda Jones? The straight-A student?

Ella didn't get a chance to process the information before Jake butted in. "This is Hanniford High?" He looked at Ella, frowning. "You never said you were principal of Hanniford."

Ella shrugged. "You never asked. I assumed you knew. You got here, didn't you?"

Yeah. Thanks to Pete. Great. Jake's headache, already at screaming point due to Miranda's excited chatter, wound a little tighter. Now there was no way to back out of this dumb plan. God, why oh why did Trish have to send Miranda here? He'd offered to pay for her to go to the best girl's school in Brisbane. But no, Trish had wanted her daughter to stay grounded. Now he not only had to do this for Ella but there was no way he could sit back and let anyone shut down Miranda's school.

"This is a great thing you're doing, Jake. Really amazing," Trish said. "Haven't I been saying you should coach?"

Ella returned her attention to the field, curious as hell but not wanting to intrude on a private conversation. Just what was Jake's relationship with Trish Jones?

She forced herself to concentrate on Pete putting the students through their paces, searching for Cam, praying he wasn't among the boys who had already fallen by the wayside. He was beefy, all muscle, built like a tank—not for speed but endurance. And, thankfully, he hadn't faltered.

Trish laughed and Ella found her attention drawn back to them as she watched surreptitiously. The woman was standing quite close to Jake still and his hand at her waist confirmed their casual intimacy.

Had they been lovers? Were they still? Miranda leaned in then and said something Ella couldn't quite catch but all three of them laughed like they'd been doing it for years. Even Jake. They looked like a family.

And suddenly Ella felt like she was back in Huntley. Standing on the outside looking in.

# CHAPTER SIX

The following Monday there was a knock on Ella's door after lunch. "Come in," she said. She held up her hand as she quickly finished the paragraph she was reading. She looked up, her smile faltering as she saw her brother standing in her doorway.

Ella sighed and shut her eyes. "Oh, Cam, what have you done now?" she asked. Normally she received a phone call as a bit of a heads up before one of Cam's teachers sent him down to see her.

"Bloody hell, Ella. Nothing. Just forget it."

Cam turned away and Ella wished a sharp knife had been handy to cut her tongue out. She stood and called out to him, "No, wait," and was pleased to see his hand still and the door not bang shut with the full force of teenage outrage. He was seeking her out? Voluntarily? Her pulse picked up at the thought.

"I'm sorry, Cam. Please come and sit down."

Cameron glared at her and the chair and then back at her before sullenly acquiescing, slumping himself down with as much surliness as was possible.

"You wanted to see me about something?"

Cameron nodded and she waited patiently for him to start. He sat staring morosely at the ground, his mop of overgrown hair obscuring his eyes from her gaze. Ella detested the latest shaggy-hair fashion the male students were sporting. Her mind wandered to Jake's uber-short spiky do and she wished she had the power to line all the boys up and shear their bushy noggins in one sitting.

"Cam?"

"Do you know who Jake's chosen yet?" The question was fired at her with his usual hostile edge, as though everything bad in the world was her fault.

"No."

Cameron snorted. "What, he hasn't even given you a peek at the list?"

Ella ignored his belligerent tone. "No."

"But you're the principal. Surely he has to check with you about it?"

She'd not spoken to Jake all week. She'd seen him a couple of times when she'd gone to the oval to check on progress but had deliberately kept away from him, including avoiding the pub on Friday night. He was here in her school performing a necessary evil and she was grateful, but she was acutely aware of her attraction to him and she was damned if she was going to put herself in the path of that truck.

"No, he doesn't. He's the expert. It's his team. We'll all know in a couple of hours," she said.

"Has he hinted at all, maybe, that I'm in?"

Ella heard the desperation in his voice. She'd never seen Cameron so gung-ho about something. So motivated. He seemed to live life with a permanent scowl and this interest was heartening. "I haven't spoken to him all week."

She regarded the boy/man who just wouldn't let her in. He was so big, already a foot taller than her and growing out of his shoes at a rate of knots. "You really want this, don't you, Cam?"

Cameron looked up from the floor. "Yes, I do."

Ella swallowed as emotion welled in her throat. This was only the second time in two years he'd looked her straight in the eye. The other time had been after their mother's funeral, when he had told her he hated Rachel, despite the tears streaming down his face. She'd tried to reach out, to gloss over what their mother was but he'd just turned away.

"Well, you've trained hard. You've stayed standing. I think you're in for a good chance."

Cameron shook his head. "But what if I don't? Can't you … can't you use your influence with him?"

Ella felt a prickle at the base of her spine. "My influence?"

Cameron looked at the ground again. "You know him from Huntley. And … I see the way he looks at you. Maybe a … favor might help convince him."

Ella felt time whir to a halt around her. A pain built in her chest, making it impossible to breathe, like he'd picked up a knife and rammed it straight through her heart.

"You want me to use sex to get you in the team?"

Ella felt as if she was watching the scene from a great height. She couldn't believe how calm she sounded, how composed she looked, when her heart was breaking.

He shrugged. "It worked for Rachel."

His words fell like stones into the silence and Ella drew in a shaky breath. It was like he truly didn't know that he'd insulted her more deeply than she'd ever been before. "I hope you're not comparing, Cam."

"Oh no, what, me?" He snorted. "Compare the saintly Ella to Rachel? No, no, no, I wouldn't dare."

Ella dragged in a swift breath at the pure scorn in his voice. There was a whole minefield of emotions behind his words, stuff from Huntley that he never talked about no matter what she tried to get him to open up. "I'm not the enemy, Cam."

"Then prove it." He was looking her in the eye again. Talking about stuff he had no idea about. Speaking with the confidence of youth—fifteen going on fifty.

"You know," she said quietly, disappointment and hurt warring for top billing inside her, "it's been a lot of years since a boy made me feel so cheap. I guess you Huntley guys know how to do that really well."

Ella took no pleasure from the stain that spread across her brother's cheeks as her rebuke hit its mark and he looked to the ground again. She hoped he was ashamed, that he felt as dirty about making his comment as she did being on the receiving end.

"I know you think that I owe you, Cam. That I left you behind in Huntley and didn't care about you. Even though you know I wasn't aware of your existence."

Cameron snorted. "All you had to do was pick up the phone and call her, Ella."

Ella swallowed, the deep-seated guilt she'd always felt about cutting herself off from Rachel, from Huntley, returning. The underlying ache she heard in his sneered reprimand stuck like barbs in her flesh. He was right. If only she'd made the effort, maybe there wouldn't be this great gulf yawning between them now.

"I think you know that I'm sorry about that."

She looked at the set of Cameron's jaw, the bitterness glittering in his gaze. He'd never given her an inch and it looked like he wasn't about to start.

Cameron shrugged. "Forget it. Just forget it," he said. "I did alright without you for thirteen years and I don't need your help now."

Ella watched as his chest puffed out, looking like the boy of two years ago who'd told her he didn't need a sister—he didn't need anyone. To go back to Brisbane and leave him alone. It hurt that after all this time he still felt the need to hide behind that façade. To pretend he didn't need her. But for once she wasn't going to be guilted in to backing down. What he'd said was unacceptable.

"I think you're wrong. I think you do need me. But just for the record, I'm not going to assuage my guilt by getting you something you haven't earned. And you can hate me for that if you want, that's fine, but it's just not the way I operate. You need to achieve things on your own merit."

She reached across the desk to touch his hand and felt his rejection as a body blow when he snatched it away before she made contact.

"Have a little faith in your abilities, Cam."

Cameron rolled his eyes. "Well, I'm sure that works out real well in Ella land but in the real world, things aren't always so dandy. Thanks," he said, pushing up out of his chair. "Thanks for nothing, sis," he threw over his shoulder as he yanked the door open.

Ella braced herself for the bang as Cameron made his disgruntled exit. He didn't disappoint, the window rattling at the force.

She sat for a moment, her elbows on the table, her head in her hands, her whole body shaking at the confrontation. She felt ill and for a moment wondered if she was going to lose her lunch as his suggestion that she do a Rachel to secure a spot on the team for him appalled and sickened her all over again.

"Can I come in?"

Ella looked up, startled, to see Jake standing in the doorway. "Oh," she said, her brain momentarily freezing, "I'm sorry, I didn't hear you."

Jake frowned. "I noticed Cam leaving here pretty steamed," he said, shutting the door and sauntering toward her. "Are you okay?"

Ella gave a half laugh and rubbed the back of her neck. "Not really, no."

Jake perched on her desk. "Did you argue?"

Ella looked at him, the muscles in his denim-encased thigh moving interestingly in her peripheral vision as his leg swung at the knee. He was wearing another T-shirt that fit snugly over his nicely tanned and rounded biceps. His jaw was clean shaven and somehow just as tempting to touch as when it was covered in stubble. His green eyes were looking down at her with a frankness and intensity that was compelling.

They knew her, those eyes.

"We didn't yell at each other, if that's what you mean."

"But he upset you," Jake persisted "What did he say?"

Ella felt absurdly like bursting into tears and wished Rosie was here. She blinked hard, not wanting to cry in front of him. She focused on the swing of his knee, finding it hard to even look at him as Cam's words made her feel dirty all over again.

"He suggested that I sleep with you to secure a place for him on the team."

She looked at him then, Cam's implication hurting so much that not even the potential embarrassment could stop her from seeking solace in his gaze. "After all, that's what Rachel would have done. Like mother, like daughter, right?"

Jake felt his fists curl around the clipboard he held in his hands as a thin slither of rage wound its way around his gut. Cameron Lucas needed a damn good kick up the backside. And he was just the man to do it.

Cam was going to be sorry he ever wanted *on* the team.

"You're nothing like her, Ella."

His soft rebuttal was more powerful than an outraged rejection and Ella swallowed hard. She was ashamed to admit there'd been a time when she'd wanted to be exactly like Rachel. When she'd been little and her mother had just been this beautiful creature with yellow-blond hair and a laugh that could light up a room.

"I know that, Jake. You know it. But does he? I mean, half of the boys back home thought I was tarred with the same brush, didn't they?"

"They were jerks. And Cam's just yanking your chain."

Ella nodded, pleased to hear Jake's quick dismissal of the boys who had contributed to her Huntley hell. "But why wouldn't he think that, growing up in Huntley under Rachel's roof? Why wouldn't he think that all women use their bodies for favors?"

"He knows right from wrong, Ella. You shouldn't cut him so much slack."

Where had she heard that before? "You sound like Daisy."

She knew he was right, they were both right, but a large part of her sympathized with the kid. Cam was exactly what she'd wanted to be all those years in Huntley: tough and not afraid to take anyone's crap. Just like Jake. Instead, she'd been meek and mild and let Huntley treat her with disdain. Maybe part of her just didn't want to break through the shell around Cameron because she recognized it for what it was—a way to protect himself from the disappointments of the world.

Jake grinned. "I like Daisy."

Ella knew full well that the feeling had been one hundred percent mutual. The phone on her desk rang and she was pleased for the reprieve from his laughing green eyes.

"Yes, Bernie?"

"I have Gwen for you."

Ella nodded, asking her administrative assistant to put Cameron's biology teacher through. "Hi, Gwen."

"Hi, Ella. Have you finished with Cameron?"

"Yes. About ten minutes ago. Hasn't he returned to class?"

"No."

Ella appreciated the gentleness of the reply. Unfortunately it didn't make the situation any better. "Okay, thanks Gwen. Write him up."

Jake watched as Ella replaced the receiver. She looked utterly defeated. He'd seen that look before, a long time ago, and couldn't bear to see it again. "Cam taking some time out?"

Ella snorted. "That's one way of putting it."

She stood, her impotence with the situation making her suddenly restless. She went to the window and watched a city train waiting at the station over the road. She'd like nothing more than to walk out the gates, get on the train and never come back.

"Does he wag very much?"

Ella placed her forehead against the glass. "Cam's truancy record puts yours to shame."

Jake whistled. "Impressive."

"Oh, he's really talented."

Her quiet sarcasm cut through his attempt to lighten the mood. She had her back to him, her shoulders slumped. He took a moment to admire the way the floaty hem of her black skirt fluttered around her calves. His gaze dropped to her sensible black pumps and he found himself picturing how much sexier she'd look in a pair of killer high heels.

She turned to face him. "Is he on the list?"

He eased himself off her desk and walked toward her, extending the clipboard. "Rest easy, you don't have to sleep with me."

She took it from him and he leaned his hip against the window sill while she ran a finger down the names. Her grip tightened on the clipboard and her finger stilled when she spotted "Cameron Lucas" neatly printed among the seventeen names.

"Oh God," she said, looking up at him. "This list is a veritable who's who of the truancy brigade."

But that didn't matter right now. Cameron was on it and that was all that mattered. She shut her eyes as relief flooded her system. She hadn't realised how tense she'd been about this damn list until this moment. She took a deep breath and looked at him, a question hovering on her lips despite the rapturous bubble of overwhelming gratitude she was floating in. She hated to ask, but knew she had to. "Are you doing this as a favor to me?"

Jake didn't hesitate for a second. "Every kid on that list deserves their spot."

Ella's teeth dug in to her bottom lip as tears stung her eyes and she looked down quickly, the names blurring before her. She nodded. "Thank you."

"Ella?" When she didn't answer he gently lifted her chin with his thumb and forefinger.

She shook her head. "I'm sorry. It's been—he just doesn't have any confidence in himself ... but he's smart, you know?" She swiped at a tear that managed to avoid her rapid blinking and spill over. "All his teachers say so, he just doesn't apply himself ... he's too angry—with me and Rachel, and I know how much he wanted this ..."

"Hey," Jake said, his thumb drying another tear. "Don't cry."

She gave a gurgle of embarrassment as she shook her head, trying to evade his touch and his gaze. "I'm sorry. I don't know what's the matter with me. I'm not usually this emotional."

Jake nodded. He would never have described her as a weepy woman and God knew he'd known a few of them. In high school, despite often extreme provocation, she'd been Little-Miss-Aloof. She'd perfected a shrivel-up-and-die stare that had put even the most moronic teenage boy into a hasty retreat. Hell, even at her mother's funeral she'd been dry-eyed and stoic.

"It's just—it's been a tough couple of years and ... I never thought I'd suck this badly at being a big sister."

He was nodding and his eyes were full of compassion, full of knowing, and that was the clincher: Jake *did* know. And

Ella hated it. Hated that this guy ... this *footballer* guy knew stuff about her past. Knew about her ostracism, her isolation, her loneliness. Knew that behind the woman she was today and the aloof teenager she'd been, there lurked a little girl who'd just wanted to be accepted. His eyes were telling her he understood and despite how much she hated it, on the back of Cam's insult, it was surprisingly comforting.

"I swear to God, Jake, if you don't stop looking at me like that then I'm going to be bawling like a baby."

Jake smiled. "Like what?"

His thumb swept across the ridge of her cheekbone and it was so gentle Ella felt her eyelids flutter closed. They opened again and the look in his eyes had changed. His pupils had dilated, the green intensified. He was staring at her mouth. Was he closer? Her body swayed a little.

"Like what, Ella?"

*Like you want to kiss me.* "Jake."

He heard the warning note in her voice. Except it was husky with more than a hint of hunger and when he took a step closer she didn't back up and when her gaze dropped to his mouth kissing her became a force that would not be denied.

Ella sighed against his mouth as his lips settled on hers. They felt good, soft and gentle and she welcomed his slow, lazy exploration. But when his tongue stroked along the seam of her lips, a heat down low took hold and she wanted more than gentle. She wanted to feel the full force of his kiss. She wanted open mouths and questing tongues and warm, bare skin. She parted her lips, inviting him in and when he obliged, she moaned and gripped the front of his shirt, pulling him closer.

The trilling of the school bell echoing around the building was like the proverbial bucket of ice water. They both pulled away, their pulses leaping at the unexpected intrusion, panting from pure, unadulterated lust.

It took a second for Ella to grapple her thoughts back from the abyss of pleasure still swirling around her feet and sucking at her belly. She looked around. She could hear students rushing by in the corridor, laughing and joking on their way to their final lesson for the day.

They were standing in her office, in front of the window. For the entire world to see. Anyone could have caught them. A student. A parent. Donald Wiseman from the education review board with the creepy smile and a habit of touching himself an awful lot during his many unannounced visits. God knew the train full of passengers sitting at the station opposite seemed to be inordinately interested in the goings on. Just as well the bell had rung or they may have been treated to a much more interesting show. A moment ago he could have stripped her naked, pushed her against the glass and taken her from behind and she would have given them a performance worthy of Paris Hilton.

"Of course, if you want to sleep with me then I could always make Cameron team captain."

Ella blinked, surprised to find she was still in the cradle of his arms. He cocked an eyebrow and she found herself responding to his teasing suggestion with a smile of her own.

She pushed out of the circle of his arms and walked to her desk on legs that weren't quite steady. "Forget it. I'm not going to sleep with you, Jake."

"What? Ever?"

She smiled again at his mocking tone. "Ever."

He chuckled. "Well that's a long time."

She shrugged. "It's called self-control. Maybe you should try it some time."

He walked toward her desk, stood on the opposite side and planted his fists on the edge. "You weren't big on self-control a couple of years back."

Ella swallowed at the mention of that day. She should be mad but with today's kiss still fresh on her lips, she was just plain turned on. Goddamn it! This was her office, her dominion. He might have invaded it but it was still her turf. And this was an entirely inappropriate conversation.

"The sex with you was just anger and frustration and to prove a point, Jake, and you know it. I'm not going backward."

He cocked an eyebrow. "I'm backward?"

"You're Huntley, Jake—I left there a long time ago and I'm not going back."

"It felt like you wanted to go back when you stuck your tongue in my mouth just now."

Ella felt a rush of heat and beat it back, deciding to change tack. "You do know that abstinence doesn't kill people, right?" God knew she'd have been dead a long time ago.

Jake nodded. "It sure makes them mighty pissed off though." He pushed off the desk and picked up his clipboard.

"And this you would know how?"

He grinned. "See you at the oval."

\*

Ella watched Cameron's face as Pete read out the names. A lump rose in her throat as she watched the play of emotions. First stunned disbelief, then a slow dawning as a tentative smile grew into a grin as big as the Great Australian Bight. The lump swelled to life-threatening proportions as his eyes sought hers and she saw tears shining in his tough-kid gaze.

She gave him the thumbs up and he actually returned them. In fact every kid whose name was called out stood an extra inch higher and Ella couldn't remember ever feeling such a charge of optimism in all her years at Hanniford. A transformation was happening before her eyes. Kids who never had any expectations from life suddenly looked bullet-proof and she dared to hope for the first time that they might just pull this off.

But her heart went out to the guys who weren't picked. She knew what it was like to be the last one standing when it came to being chosen for teams and then being reluctantly included. She knew they'd put their all into the process and she could see their shoulders slump as the one bright light on their horizon was snuffed out.

She made a mental note to talk to Eddie Springer, the P.E. teacher. Maybe he could get a couple of touch teams together and organize an in-house comp. Girls could join too. They could really build on the momentum that had begun. Engage some more students, keep them interested in school, let them know that she and Hanniford High cared.

Jake turned to the shaggy-haired, inexperienced crew before him and wondered how the hell he was ever going to pull this off. Sure, there was some good raw talent, but he had to create in one season what professionals, what the other teams in the comp, would have built up over years and years of playing and competing: unity, synergy, trust.

He looked at Ella and then at Miranda, so like Trish, who was waving at him from the sidelines and knew he had to try.

"Okay now, listen up," he called above the back slapping and high-fiving that was going on among the successful students. "There are a few ground rules before we begin. You want to be on the team, there are three non-negotiables." He watched the boys. Their smiles faded a little. "Pete?"

Pete dug around in his backpack and came out with a pair of hair clippers. He held them up and switched them on.

"Number twos. All of you. Here, now, this afternoon."

There was a collective groan and Jake plodded on. "Training is every day. Every day. Three o'clock sharp. Even the holidays. We have a month till the first game and a lot of ground to cover."

None of the boys were smiling now. Good, he finally had their complete attention. "Lastly, one day off school, just one," Jake held up a finger, "without a doctor's certificate—wag it just once and you're off the team. No exceptions."

Silence greeted him and he glanced at Ella. Even she looked slightly aghast. But Jake knew boys like this, like Cameron—he'd been one himself. Angry, disenfranchised. If it hadn't been for Huntley's police sergeant getting him in to football and setting impossibly high standards, God knew where he'd be today. It was time to pay it forward.

"Those of you still keen, come join me."

Ella held her breath as the boys looked at each other. Then they looked from Jake to Pete, still holding the clippers, and back to Jake. Cameron was the first to move and the rest followed.

Jake nodded. "Alright then. Go with Pete." The scruffy rabble shuffled off. "Cameron, not you," Jake called.

Cam frowned as he fell back. Ella approached, looking at them uncertainly. "Everything alright?" she asked.

"All good," Jake dismissed.

Ella glanced at a nervous Cam and opened her mouth to say more but was interrupted by an out-of-breath Trish Jones lugging a large shoulder bag. "I just got your text," Trish said. "You want me to do what?"

Jake nodded behind him. "Shear some heads."

Trish looked at the boys in the distance and then glanced at Ella. Ella shrugged and Trish smiled. "It'd be my pleasure."

Ella laughed as the diminutive Trish practically levitated her away across the oval. She looked back at Jake and Cam standing tense and awkward obviously not requiring her company. "I'll join her," Ella said. Jake nodded.

Cameron eyed Jake nervously as Ella retreated. "Did you want something, sir?"

Jake looked at the kid who could almost meet him eye to eye. He was big, stocky, and probably one of the few guys on the team with real talent.

"I'm not your father, Cameron, nor am I a teacher. You can call me Jake or coach."

Cameron swallowed. "Yes, coach."

Jake regarded him seriously. "I understand you. Probably better than you understand yourself. I know Huntley gave you a tough time. I know you probably spent your life with your fists up defending someone you didn't like very much in a shithole you didn't give a damn about."

Cameron remained silent but Jake could see the hostility in his gaze and the set to his jaw.

"But for the next six or so months, your ass belongs to me and if you want in this team, then you got to prove it to me—more than the other boys. Do you understand?"

Cameron nodded. "Yes, coach."

"I don't know if you know this or not but I was at your place one night a few weeks ago when you told your sister to fuck off. If you ever talk to Ella like that again—ever—you're out. Got it?"

Cameron ground his teeth together so hard Jake thought he was going to break some. "But—"

"No buts, Cam. Men just don't talk to women like that. That's the number one rule, mate. Are you a man or a boy? This is where you decide."

"But—"

Jake held up his hand. "Ella's not the enemy, Cameron. Maybe you should cut her some slack? Don't forget, she grew up in Huntley too."

He shrugged. "She's my sister. She was supposed to look out for me."

Jake shook his head. "No, Cameron," he said, clapping him on the shoulder. "That was Rachel's job."

Cameron looked at Jake's hand on his shoulder and then looked back at Jake.

"Got it?" Jake repeated.

Cameron looked at his feet. "Got it."

*

Ella suppressed the urge to ask what had transpired between Cam and Jake when Jake joined her ten minutes later. Cameron looked pretty sullen but as that was his modus operandi these days, she let it slide. And besides, she didn't want anything to ruin the unadulterated delight she was experiencing at Trish's and Pete's handiwork. God knew she'd been tempted to creep into Cam's bedroom in the dead of night and execute a dawn raid on his head too.

"Not that I don't appreciate it," she said, "but what's the purpose of the number twos?"

Jake smiled. "Ahh, grasshopper, you have much to learn. The reasons are threefold."

Ella rolled her eyes. "Oh, this ought to be good."

He laughed. "Firstly, it's a test. I needed to know their level of commitment."

"Good test." Ella whistled. "Trust me, no one's more committed to awful bushy hair than a teenage boy."

"Secondly, they can see the ball better when they haven't got hair in their eyes."

"Ah. Excellent point."

"Lastly, it makes them look mean. And bluff is just as important in football as it is in any sport."

Ella looked into Jake's face, his number two delineating his nicely shaped skull and emphasizing the leanness and perfection of the planes and angles. It looked sexy. Hot. Wild. Far, far from mean.

But as she watched Pete and Trish going to work on a bunch of indignant-looking teenagers with an efficiency that would have put the best shearer in the country to shame, she had to admit he was right. On these surly, burly boys, caught halfway between adolescence and manhood, it looked mean as hell. They looked like Satan's helpers. Even their floral capes didn't detract from the don't-mess-with-us vibe.

"Whaddyareckon?" Trish asked, bounding down to join them, inspecting her handiwork.

"Amazing." Ella nodded. "Are you free to knock over the rest of the school tomorrow?"

Trish laughed as she eyed off the other boys who didn't make the cut. Literally. "Tempting, isn't it?"

Ella felt an insane urge to laugh. This whole thing was mad, but it was really happening. Cameron was on the team, the bleachers had been turned into an impromptu hair salon and Jake, Jake Prince from Huntley, was standing by her side. The idea seemed less and less crazy each day. If she hadn't seen it with her own eyes she wouldn't have believed it. She wanted a photo to remember this moment. Hell, she wanted a photo to prove to everyone it had happened—to the other students, to the parents and the community.

"We need the press in on this," Ella said suddenly. Maybe a bit of a media profile and some community support would help them in their endeavour. And maybe a bit of publicity would keep the wolf, aka Donald Wiseman, from her door.

She turned to Jake. "Can I invite some local media to a training session? Maybe we could re-create this scene?" Ella could see the photo now. The kids might hate it but the publicity could be fantastic. "Trish would you come back one day and pose for us?"

Jake felt Trish tense beside him and felt for her hand giving it a squeeze. He looked down at Ella. "No press."

Ella smiled. "Oh come on, big famous footy star, not afraid of the *Western Suburbs Post* photographer are you?"

Jake knew that the news of him back on the scene, coaching, would break soon enough, especially if they managed to pull off a miracle and become real contenders. And he'd deal with that then. But he wouldn't court them before they came knocking. "No. Press." Jake's voice had gotten softer and Ella frowned.

"It would be good for the school."

"Any press and I'm out of here, Ella." He held her gaze for a few moments. "That's number four. No. Press. That's not negotiable."

Ella blinked as he walked away. She looked at Trish. Trish shrugged and bounded away again approaching the next unwilling participant, caping him up and turning on her clippers.

# CHAPTER SEVEN

Rosie woke to the cool serenity of an off-white ceiling and was momentarily disorientated. Where was her blood red paint and black netting? Then Simon murmured and stretched along the length of her and she became aware of his naked ass filling her palm. And suddenly all was right. She squeezed it just to reassure herself he was actually here.

"You're killing me."

Rosie smiled at his sleepy voice. Last night she hadn't been able to wait an extra ten minutes to get home and they'd ended up back at his place instead—for the first time. It had seemed only sensible, being mere minutes away from the restaurant and given her total disregard for the road rules as she'd considered his zipped fly fair game.

"I don't know," Rosie murmured, her hand moving from his ass to other interesting regions. "You younger men, no stamina." She hit pay dirt and smiled, her hand encasing the evidence of his state of readiness.

"You were saying?" Simon murmured before flipping her over and pinning her to the bed in one swift, well-executed move, forcing a surprised little squeal from her mouth.

Rosie laughed. "I may have been wrong about the stamina."

"Damn straight you were," he muttered as his mouth lowered onto hers.

The door opened and both of them froze as a voice floated toward them. "Simon, darling, I just noticed your car here."

Simon cursed under his breath, placing his forehead against hers briefly before rolling off to stare at the ceiling.

"Mother. Have you ever heard of knocking?" He sat up, the duvet bunching around his waist.

Mother? Rosie lifted her head off the bed to sneak a peek at the woman advancing into the room. She looked like a cross between Camilla Parker Bowles and Barbara Walters.

"I'm sorry, darling. You're so rarely home these days I—"

Rosie heard the reproach in her voice as a pair of cold, slate gray eyes settled on her. She gave a small smile and waved.

"Oh, sorry, I didn't realize you had—"

Rosie, completely starkers under the covers, felt like even they'd been stripped away by Simon's mother's scrutiny. It didn't take Iris's gift to know that she didn't exactly measure up. She felt the shrewd gaze on her bed hair, her heavily kholed eyes—no doubt panda-esque by now—her eyebrow piercing, the studded collar encircling her throat. Rosie waited for the floundering matriarch to finish her sentence, half expecting her to say, *a prostitute in your bed.*

"—a guest."

Rosie smiled as good manners won out over motherly disdain. She flicked a glance at Simon. "You live with your mother?" she murmured.

Simon looked down at her. "You think I live in a mansion by myself?"

*Mansion?* Rosie blinked and looked around at the room. It was rather *spacious*. She squinted—was that the river she could see through the French doors? She suddenly wished she'd paid her surroundings more heed last night. But the truth was, the only surroundings she'd been interested in were the fabric ones preventing access to his body and how to get them off him in the shortest space of time.

Simon looked at his mother and sighed. "Mother, this is Rosie. Rosie, my mother."

Rosie wasn't sure of the etiquette after being sprung in bed with your thirty-year-old boyfriend by his mother. She was thirty-six years old, for fuck's sake!

"Pleased to meet you Mrs. Lewis."

"Geraldine, please."

Rosie nodded at the tight smile, fairly sure that Simon's mother was merely being polite. There were a few moments when nobody said anything and Geraldine looked at Rosie like she was Monica Lewinsky and her son like he'd just been caught picking up a blue dress from the drycleaners.

"Er ... was there something you wanted, Mother?"

"Yes, of course." Geraldine smiled another tight smile. "I was going to ring you a little later. Henry Lichfield is coming for lunch today. He wants to meet you."

Simon whistled. That was quite a coup. He was wealthy and connected and didn't do pity lunches and could be a useful ally for his future political aspirations.

But.

"Can't, sorry, Mother. I have another engagement. You'll have to reschedule."

Geraldine became very still. "Reschedule? Do you have any idea how difficult it was to arrange this today."

"Yes, Mother, and I really am sorry but I just can't make it."

Geraldine pressed her lips together. "And what, pray tell, is more important than your future?"

Simon knew that note in his mother's voice. He'd grown up with that steely resolve to have her own way and he had to admit it grew more impressive in its execution every year.

Rosie squeeze his thigh under the covers and he thanked God she didn't scare easily as he said, "A football game."

"You're going to blow off a man with enormous political influence to watch *football?*"

Rosie marveled at the way Geraldine Lewis made football sound like the dirtiest word ever invented. Ella was going to love her.

"Rosie's friend, Ella, is principal of Hanniford High. Their team is playing in the BSFC today. It's their first match." He shrugged. "It was sort of my idea."

Rosie felt the brief sideways slide of Geraldine's gaze that blatantly said, *Hmph, your friend—figures.*

"Hanniford High?" Rosie almost laughed at the way Geraldine's eyebrows had practically hit her hairline. There was no doubt the older woman knew exactly of Hanniford's rep.

"I promised, Mother."

"Darling, if you want to get involved in local school sport I'm sure the Brisbane Grammar would welcome your involvement. They won the Schools Cup your last year, didn't they?" She looked at Rosie. "Simon went to the Grammar. He gave the valedictory address his senior year. He was dux." *And you're corrupting him.*

Rosie was getting the message loud and clear. Well—her hand slid higher on his thigh—she'd do her damnedest.

Simon had had enough. He wasn't going to have a career discussion with his mother on a Saturday morning while his girlfriend—if that's what he could call Rosie—watched on like an engrossed Wimbledon spectator above the covers and a sex maniac, her hand finding its way into his lap, beneath.

"Please give my apologies to Henry," Simon said sharply as Rosie gave him a very intimate squeeze and he fought to keep his eyes from closing on a surge of pleasure. "I'll talk to you later."

Geraldine looked from one to the other and then sniffed. "Very well." She nodded at Rosie and exited with practiced regal grace.

Simon fell back against the bed. "Sorry 'bout that."

Rosie waited for the door slam and was surprised to hear only a dignified click. Man, she was repressed! There was some serious passive-aggressive stuff going on with good old Geri.

He rolled up onto his side as her silence stretched, his hand resting against her belly. He frowned. "You're speechless, aren't you?"

Rosie shook her head. "No, just waiting for Jeeves to enter with the morning paper."

Simon chuckled. "It's his day off."

Rosie gave a half-hearted laugh before the opulence of the room sobered her. It was the ultimate in *Vogue* chic. "Seriously though. You're kind of ... rich, right?"

Simon winced at the description. If his mother was here she'd have corrected Rosie instantly. *Wealthy*, Geraldine had always insisted. *Rich* was so common.

He dropped a kiss on her shoulder. "I'm afraid so."

A small smile was playing on his delicious mouth and her heart swelled in her chest. Oh God, what was he doing with her? "How rich?"

"Disgustingly. Is it turning you on?"

"Fuck, no."

"Would you prefer it if I was poor?"

Rosie gave a rueful smile. "Yes, actually." Poor she could do. Poor she was used to. She was the daughter of a carnie, after all. Poor boys turned her on. God knew, she'd dated enough of them. Sure, she'd known he wasn't like the others. She'd known he was from blue ribbon stock, but this level of wealth was surprising. To say she felt a little out of her depth was an understatement.

Simon stroked a hand down her flat stomach and felt her muscles react. She was looking so serious suddenly and he wanted Rosie from last night back. Rosie who'd laughed as he'd sworn and nearly swerved the car off the road when her hand had found its way past his zipper and her head had followed.

"Do you want me white-collar poor or *Oliver* poor? Because you know I know how to beg, right?"

Rosie smiled despite the weird depression settling around her and the certainty that this could never last. "I know you can in handcuffs."

He nuzzled her neck. "Please, Rosie, I want some more."

She shut her eyes as the touch of his mouth on her skin made her want things she didn't want to get too used to. "Your mother doesn't like me."

He smiled against her neck. "My mother doesn't like anyone. I'm pretty sure she doesn't even like me most of the time." He kissed up her neck. "She barely tolerates my father."

"I bet she liked Penelope."

Simon stilled, then he flopped onto his back and sighed. "She adored Penelope. In fact I'm not sure she's forgiven me for breaking it off."

It was Rosie's turn to roll up on to her elbow. "How long were you together?"

"Five years."

"Five years!" Rosie's statute of limitations was more like five weeks.

Simon chuckled. "That's bad right?"

"No." She shook her head. "Not at all. It's ... sweet. It just seems so ... mature. You're obviously the adult in this relationship."

He groaned. "I'm guessing that's not a compliment."

Rosie smiled. "It's not that. It's just ... settling down with one woman and having all this expectation on you about your future ... Don't you want to just, I don't know, live a little first? Leave the heavy stuff for middle age?"

"This country needs young, energetic politicians with a vision for the future. Politicians that stand an outside chance of actually being alive to see their policies come to fruition rather than making pie-in-the-sky promises that they know they're not going to be around to see through."

Rosie's heart tripped a little. He was right. She smiled at him. "I like it when you talk clean. I think I just came."

Simon laughed and kissed her neck. "Orgasms are no extra cost."

He nuzzled her neck for a bit and she shut her eyes, enjoying the sensations that fizzed in her blood and pricked at her skin, ignoring the dull nag inside her. If a life of civic duty was truly what Simon wanted then she'd be nothing but a liability. He needed someone like Penelope. She pushed away from him.

"Why *did* you break it off with Penelope? It seems to me she's probably the type you need by your side."

"You're right. She was. But I suddenly realized that while she was everything I could ever ask for in a political wife—serene, demure, unopinionated, unflappable, organized, with this great ability to blend into the background—she was, in actual fact, mind-numbingly boring."

Rosie didn't have to look in the mirror to know that blending wasn't her forté. "Not the kind of girl who'd give you a blowjob while you were driving?"

Simon laughed. "Oh, no. Penelope never went down."

Rosie blanched not quite believing what she'd just heard. "You were with her for five years and she never sucked your dick?"

Simon looked up into her horrified face and smiled. "Never. In fact, I'm not even sure she touched it at all."

God! No wonder he was with her. She looked into his handsome face, his dimples like a siren's call to her bleeding heart hormones. "Oh no, poor Simon," she crooned, her hand sliding down to fondle his neglected penis. "And it's such a nice specimen too."

Simon grinned. "I like to think so."

He grew hard in her hand. "And look at that." Rosie gave him a scandalised look that would have been well at home on a Victorian virgin except for the Goth-cum-dominatrix dog collar. "It's in full working order."

After a marathon session last night Simon was amazed it worked at all. "Gee. I wonder where I can put that?"

Rosie gave him wicked grin. "I have the perfect place for someone with as much catching up to do as you."

As she disappeared beneath the covers, Rosie pushed aside thoughts that maybe this was only about the sex for Simon. Maybe she was just a stopgap until he found Penelope mark II: demure on the outside but slutty in bed; a politically correct, oral-sex junkie.

Because two things were for certain. She could never be a Penelope. And whatever version of Penelope he ended up with, she hated her already. Suddenly she knew this was about more than the chase. More than taking Mr. Neat and Prim and messing him up.

Simon Charles Henry Lewis was well and truly under her skin.

*

Geraldine bade them a stiff goodbye a couple of hours later. "Why do you still live here?" Rosie asked as she watched Geraldine's stony face slowly get smaller in her side-view mirror.

"Aside from the river views being a great way to impress chicks?"

Rosie rolled her eyes. "But of course."

He shrugged. "Convenient. Close to work. Great venue for entertaining." He flashed her a smile. "Rent free." He frowned at her unimpressed look. "It's expected, I guess, and I can come and go as I please. I have my own wing, my own privacy."

"Oh, like this morning?"

"It freaks you out that she caught us, doesn't it?"

"No," Rosie blustered. "I just ... can't believe you still live at home. With your *mother*."

He lifted an eyebrow. "This from someone who lives with two crazy old aunts."

She looked out the window and muttered, "That's different."

"How?" he asked trying to keep the amusement out of his voice. "How is you living with Selma and Patty any different to me living with Rose Kennedy?"

Rosie smothered a smile at his apt character portraits and turned to face him. "I live there because I want to. Not because it's convenient or expected. Because I love those crazy old ladies and that crazy old house."

Simon nodded. He could see that. He tried to imagine feeling such attachment to the Lewis family house and just couldn't. Growing up the only child in a cold, stone mansion had been a lonely life. No siblings to climb the trees with or play hide-seek in the many, many rooms. Not that such frivolous childish antics would ever have been tolerated. "You're lucky."

"Yes. I am." She looked out the window and watched the scenery whiz by.

"Hey," she said a few minutes later as Simon drove in the opposite direction to the football field the Hanniford Demons were scheduled to play at today. "Wrong way."

"Thought I'd swing by your place and pick up the mascot."

"Mascot?"

Simon nodded. "A footy team needs a mascot. A symbol of their potency. A representation of their strength. Something to strike fear into the hearts of their opponents."

Rosie shook her head—private school boys! "And that's at my place?"

Simon nodded again. "Cerberus."

"Cerberus?" Rosie paused for a second. "I hate to break this to you, but he's hardly a spritely specimen of canine virility. He's old and suffers from an abandonment complex."

Simon smiled at her. "He's Cerberus, the hound from hell. They're the Hanniford Demons." He shrugged. "It's symbolic. Besides, won't Daisy and Iris want to come?"

Rosie blinked at the tears that sprang like a flash flood to her eyes. God, this man was so sweet and, suddenly, as she looked at him she could hear the "Wedding March" in her head. But he didn't get the whole home and hearth thing and as much as they were having fun, she *so* wasn't his type. She wasn't a Penelope. She tried to channel Ella and lectured herself about the perils of falling too hard, too early, but it was no use. It was already too late. Maybe she could learn to be a Penelope?

*

Ella was so nervous she couldn't decide whether she was going to throw up or have a full-blown panic attack. From her vantage point in the opposition stands, she watched Jake and Pete talking, or rather strategizing, if their hand gestures were remotely indicative.

Jake wore a baseball cap tugged low on his forehead and a pair of dark sunglasses but still she could see people nudging each other and pointing at him. Although that may not have anything to do with who he was and everything to do with how he looked and the fact that eighty-five percent of the spectators were women. And not just any women, but mothers. Ella had seen enough of them over the years to re-cognize that if any one group of women could use a bit of gratuitous eye candy from time to time, it was mothers.

And Jake certainly didn't disappoint. The man was simply mouthwatering in his jeans and snug-fitting tee. He was like the Lindt chocolate of eye candy. The Ferrero Rocher. The Tim Tam. Ella could practically feel the fat cells on her ass multiplying as her mouth watered. She dragged her gaze away, focusing instead on the boys warming up on the sidelines, searching for Cameron. He was standing on one leg, stretching the other up behind, staring at the ground in fierce concentration.

The panic returned. Yes, they needed this win for the school but Cameron needed it more.

"Don't the boys look amazing?" Rosie said, nudging Ella's arm.

Ella nodded. They did. They really did. In fact she and Rosie were really going to have to stop thinking of them as boys. Today they looked exactly as Jake had hoped, in the red-and-black strip he'd bought for them with Hanniford Demons emblazoned on the front. They looked mature. A force to be reckoned with.

Ella had protested his generous gesture. Not only were the jerseys new but he'd also splashed out and bought each of his players top-of-the-range boots. In fact, he'd totally kitted them out. She had no idea how much it had all cost but it didn't look like the equipment came from the 7-11. She didn't want to be that indebted to him—she was in deep enough. But Jake had insisted that becoming a team involved claiming and projecting an identity. Ella had been dubious but damn if those boys—young men—weren't all standing a foot higher. They certainly looked the part next to the opposing team, who oozed confidence.

The Bribie Bullets had been in the comp for twenty years and were looking at the Demons like they were mere bugs on the footpath. Their football field was immaculate, decked out in yellow and blue flags, making Hanniford's oval looked like a mosh pit the morning after a rock concert by comparison.

Jake called the Demons together and Ella watched as they formed an eager huddle. Jake had well and truly made up for his tardy start. He only had to say jump and the boys wanted to know how high.

"This is your cue," Rosie urged. "Go down and give your team a pep talk."

"They're not my team," Ella murmured as she watched Jake geeing them up. What could she possibly offer?

Rosie placed a firm hand against Ella's fidgeting ones and looked her straight in the eye. "You're their principal. They're going to shut this school down. They're the only team you've got, babe."

Ella looked at her friend and then at Simon. He nodded and gave her an encouraging smile. "What do I say?" She didn't have a clue what all this secret men's business stuff was about. What did seventeen boys revved up on nerves and testosterone expect their headmistress to say to them? She'd spent the last two years trying to figure out teenage boy speak to no avail. She hated to admit it, but she just didn't get them.

Simon shrugged. "Tell them they'll get detention for a week if they don't win."

Rosie dug him in the ribs. "Not helping, Simon."

Simon half laughed as he rubbed at Rosie's point of contact. "Tell them to listen to Jake."

Ella nodded. That sounded like very good advice to her. She stood and made her way down through the almost empty stand, ignoring the stab of disappointment she felt at the lack of Hanniford supporters. She knew the school wasn't known for its community spirit and this away game was quite a distance from home, but she had hoped. So much was riding on today. Maybe a big show of support would make a difference?

Ella caught the odd word of Jake's speech as she approached. She didn't understand any of it but Jake seemed to know what he was doing and Pete and the team were nodding. She stood quietly, waiting for him to finish, feeling every inch the uptight school marm intruding on a male bonding ritual. Would they start picking nits off each other soon?

Jake finished his pep talk and looked up. Ella was nearby shifting from foot to foot, looking great in jeans and a T-shirt, her hair loose and had she been smiling, she would have been totally bootylicious. But instead she was looking at him like she was about to face a root canal.

He noticed Miranda leaving Trish's side and coming down the stands toward them too. The irony wasn't lost on him. These were the stakes.

Two unrelated females who had his nuts in a vice.

"Ella?"

She cleared her throat. "I was wondering if I could just talk to the team for a moment?"

Jake frowned at her and for a second she thought he might refuse her. What the hell? What did he think she was going to say? "Have you washed behind your ears and put some sunscreen on?" He gestured her forward and she fell in beside him.

Jake turned away from the team slightly and dropped his head so his mouth was close to her ear. "They're nervous," he murmured. "Keep it light."

Ella shivered as the low timbre of his voice slid into all her susceptible places. She gave a small nod and he pulled away. She cleared her throat. "Well, guys, this is not something I know a lot about but I just wanted to say that I'm proud of you." She caught Cameron's gaze and held it. "Very proud." He looked nervous and she wanted to reach out and give him a reassuring squeeze. For a second she cursed Rachel for keeping them apart for thirteen years. She'd wished she'd known him as a baby, bonded with him. Surely things would be easier now?

"So, um … I don't know." She turned to Jake. "Do you say break a leg or something?"

Pete slapped his forehead in the background and Jake shut his eyes and shook his head. "No, Ella, not under any circumstances."

The whistle blew and Ella was grateful for the interruption to her completely botched debut pep talk as thirteen boys stormed past her in a cloud of testosterone.

She noticed Cerberus watching attentively from the side-lines and called his name. He wandered closer and she sat on the low wooden bench behind her, reaching out to stroke the dog's soft ears. Cerberus, hound of hell, whimpered in ecstasy.

Play started and after a few minutes, Jake joined her on the bench. "I'm sorry," she said. "About the breaking a leg thing."

Jake, his gaze intent on the game, answered with a terse, "It's fine."

Except he seemed really pissed at her. "I just wanted to be … succinct and you know I don't know one end of the football from the other. I mean I know you guys like to pat each other on the bum—"

Jake snorted trying to watch the game and pretend he was listening to her at the same time. "That's cricket."

"Well, you hug then, a lot—"

He frowned as one of the Demons fumbled a pass. "Only when we score a try."

"Right." Ella nodded, faintly amused amid her consternation that Jake felt the need to clarify the physical contact. "But it's hardly appropriate for me to do that, is it? I'm their principal. There are boundaries. I want them to know I support them and God knows Cameron probably need this more than most and I'm going to really try hard but—"

"Ella," Jake interrupted, dragging his gaze off the field. "Must you talk?"

Ella glared at him, already bamboozled and bored by the game and so nervous she was contemplating hitting the toilets and going for the forced vomit to get it over with.

"What? Can't do two things at once?" she cooed.

Jake shot her a lazy smile. "I think we both know that's not true." He'd multi-tasked his ass off two years ago.

Ella blushed. She'd so picked the wrong man for that quip. "Sex doesn't count."

"Sex always counts."

They stared at each other for a moment. "Don't you have a game to be watching?"

"Are you going to let me?"

She held his intense gaze for as long as she could, wondering if he was thinking the same X-rated things as her, then she focused on the field. "I won't say another word."

Jake nodded and turned his attention back to the field. The Demons were going to get hammered and he felt like he was watching a bunch of lambs going to the slaughter. His competitive streak was burning a fiery path through his veins and he realised suddenly he wanted to win. Not just for Hanniford High or for Ella or Miranda but for him, Jake Prince, washed up ex-footy star.

He could feel the nervous energy radiating off Ella and it was distracting as hell. "Are you okay?" he asked impatiently.

Ella shook her head. "I'm so edgy I could puke."

"Don't be. This is in the bag," he said and smiled at her.

Ella believed him. She looked down at the four reserves sitting at the end of the bench and noticed that Cam was among them. Miranda was sitting beside him and they seemed to be involved in the same sort of conversation she and Jake had just had: Miranda was talking, Cam was watching the field intently, nodding occasionally.

For the next forty minutes, Ella sat on the edge of her seat. Rosie and Simon had joined her and she clung to Rosie's hand like the lifeline it had always been. Occasionally Jake would sit beside her and explain things but more often than not he was wearing a path in the sideline, yelling encouragement and direction.

Pete also trekked endlessly up and down the sidelines, video camera in hand. Jake explained that he'd use it to review the team's performance during the week. Cerberus shadowed Pete's every move, barking when things got exciting, whining when Jake's cursing got particularly animated, and taking shameless advantage of spectators, who threw the mangy-looking hellhound their hot dog leftovers.

Every successful kick or pass from the Bullets earned a massive roar from their supporters and triggered a peppy routine from their cheer squad. The squad was irritatingly perfect, with big plastic smiles, short blue skirts and tight yellow tees encasing their perky chests. Blond and bouncy, all twenty of them.

"Jeez, I didn't realize public high school science budgets ran into the millions," she murmured to Jake at one stage.

Jake frowned. "Huh?"

Ella nodded in the direction of the cheer squad. "Some genius at Bribie has managed to clone Barbie."

Jake laughed. "You don't approve of cheerleaders?"

Ella shot him a disgusted look. "Emmeline Pankhurst would be rolling in her grave."

Jake laughed again. Then the Bullets made a break for their try line and he was running up the sideline, calling to his team strategizing on his feet.

At the half-time hooter, Bribie had them by eighteen points. Ella watched with trepidation as the Demons walked off the field, all red-faced and sweaty, their shoulders slumped. Cameron didn't even look at her and Ella felt his dismay arrow straight through her soul. She sat on the bench, powerless, wanting to build the team up but not having a clue how to go about it. Luckily Jake seemed to know. He talked non-stop in the ten-minute break. Pete saw the team fed and watered while Jake talked: reviving their spirit, praising them, encouraging them. Reiterating their goals, focusing them on the next forty minutes. By the time the Demons ran back onto the field they were standing tall again.

And Ella was officially turned on. Jake had been magnificent. He'd been articulate and passionate, his belief in his team and his passion for the game blazing from his eyes. He'd been eloquent and animated and in those jeans, it was a potent combination.

The whistle blew and she dragged her attention away from Jake and forced herself to concentrate on the game. What an amazing forty minutes it was as the rejuvenated Demons clawed back control. She could barely watch as two minutes out, the Demons leveled the score. And then ten seconds before the final hooter, Cameron kicked a field goal.

The Hanniford supporters may have been paltry in comparison to the home team but when they rose to their feet in wild jubilation, they made just as much noise. Ella, who'd sat with her hands over her eyes for the last minute, stood too. Had they won? It certainly looked like they had from all the clapping, cheering and stomping that was filling her ears.

"How much is a field goal worth?" Ella grabbed an ecstatic Pete as he charged by, arms waving in the air.

Pete laughed. "One point."

He pulled out of her grasp as realization sunk in. They'd won. She watched Cam being enthusiastically picked up by his teammates and she thought her heart was going to burst right out of her chest. She'd never seen him so happy and tears came to her eyes.

"We won?" she shouted to an approaching Jake, still amazed and unsure. Still waiting for someone to tell her the score was wrong. Nothing much had gone right in the last two years—it'd be par for the course.

He grinned. "We won."

Ella felt the tears gain momentum as a heavy weight lifted from her chest. Maybe they could pull it off. "Thank you," she mouthed to Jake as he was dragged into the maelstrom of seventeen jubilant, hyped-up teenagers. She saw him touch two fingers to his forehead in a small salute to her before he was swallowed in a mass of sweaty bodies, high on their achievement. Her earlier state of arousal roared to life as she watched him laughing and joking, basking in the celebration.

Rosie came up behind her and gave her a huge hug. "Cam was great." She grinned. "Jake was great."

"Yes." Ella nodded, still watching Jake with the team.

Rosie nudged her friend's shoulder. "You're thinking about dirty footballer sex again, aren't you?"

Ella blushed. "Absolutely not." She waited a beat and then added, "How can you tell?"

"Are you kidding? After that brilliant performance? After watching him prowl up and down the line for eighty minutes? Hell, every woman here wants to jump his bones."

Ella sucked in a breath. *Over my dead body.*

# CHAPTER EIGHT

Several hours later Rosie, Simon and Ella sat at one of Jake's booths drinking, laughing and reliving the game. Something metallic and dreadful was playing on the jukebox but they didn't care. The man of the moment was caught up at the bar, helping Pete out with the early rush, but he kept on sending over cocktails for the women and beer to Simon and the three of them kept downing them.

Ella was feeling a gentle buzz when Jake finally joined them carrying more cocktails. It anesthetized her to the surge in her pulse and the hum in her veins as he squashed in beside her, his thigh pressed against hers.

"Jake, we've been talking about the game and I was wondering—"

His chuckle cut her off and she blinked at him.

"Who'd have thought," he said, grinning down at her, "Ella Lucas talking football for two whole hours."

Ella shrugged. "I'm pretty tipsy."

Jake laughed this time. She was looking up at him with bright eyes and pink cheeks, like the worries of the world had been lifted from her shoulders. He tried to remember if he'd ever seen her so ... carefree. "Wondering what?"

"The origin of the term 'dummy'."

"Ah." He nodded sagely, gathering the information from the recesses of his brain as he sucked on some Mexican nectar.

And then Ella picked the bright red cherry off the rim of her glass, held it between her thumb and forefinger and licked the creamy froth from its glazed skin and he completely lost his train of thought. Satisfied it was all gone, she sucked the cherry into her mouth with a moist, wet-sounding *phht* and her lips glistened with sticky glaze. Every ounce of blood he possessed rushed to his dick. Even when she looked at him, blinking cluelessly, waiting for him to respond and then frowning up at him in that impatient school teacher way she'd perfected, the blood refused to shift.

"Jake?"

He nodded, willing himself to speak. Nup. Blood still in pants. Not in brain.

"Jake!" She had this way of speaking that was like a bamboo cane cracking down hard on soft sensitive skin—a school principal dominatrix. That did it. That snapped him out of it. "Right."

He flicked a look at Rosie, who raised an eyebrow and winked at him. He looked back to Ella. "Don't know its historical origins I'm afraid, but I assume it came from the fact that you're a bit of a dummy if you fall for the fake pass."

"Or it could be referring to the fakeness, like store mannequins, also known as dummies," Simon added.

"Hmm." Ella frowned. "What's the use of having a rugby league legend in your camp if they don't know important stuff like this?"

Jake shook his head as the use of the word "legend" contributed to the major swelling action in his jeans. Even though he knew it hadn't been her intention to stroke his ego, his dick had no pride. "That's not important."

Ella frowned again. "Says who?"

"Says the rugby league legend."

"So what's important?"

"Winning."

Ella used the straw to swish the creamy content of her drink around the glass. "What about trying hard and doing your best?"

"All bullshit."

Ella rolled her eyes. "You're such a jock."

Jake grinned at her, a smile that she felt all the way down to her toes and she tried to remember why she hated jocks so much.

"Lucky for you I'm a jock who knows how to win."

Ella turned to look at Rosie. "There's that ego again."

Rosie smiled. "It's kind of cute."

Ella shook her head. "Puppies are cute. Fluffy yellow ducklings are cute. Little naked babies in pot plants with flowers on their head are cute. Men with egos the size of Tasmania are not cute."

*They were just damn irresistible.*

"Sure we are." Jake chuckled. "Maybe you just need another drink." He turned and gestured to Pete, holding up four fingers.

"Let me just—" she waved in the general direction of the ladies, "go and relieve my bladder of the first few."

Jake scooted out of the booth, holding his breath as she brushed past him, thanking God he had the good sense to keep the lighting subdued. Hopefully with the temptation of her body out of reach he'd be able to coax some blood flow back to his brain.

He sat back and tracked her progress. She was wearing one of those flowing skirts that moved with her body and almost brushed her ankles, elongating her shape. She disappeared through the ladies' door and he turned back to find both Rosie and Simon watching him.

"What?" he asked warily.

"Nothing," Rosie dismissed, waving her fingers in the air.

Jake wasn't falling for that. "What?" he demanded again.

Rosie glanced at Simon, who gave her a barely perceptible shake of his head. "Are you two going to step this up?" she asked, ignoring Simon's heavy sigh. "Or are we going to have to keep watching it in slow motion?"

Jake grinned. His groin was hoping for the fast forward version but there wasn't enough beer in Mexico to make him think, even for a second, that Ella wouldn't take her own damn sweet time. He looked at Rosie, so different from Ella and yet somehow so right for her too.

"What's the story with you and Ella? She said you met in twelfth grade."

Rosie nodded. She took a moment to respond. "I didn't get it, you know. She looked perfectly ... normal and yet she just didn't fit into any of the cliques. I mean I was a carnie kid, I was used to being a loner misfit but she took the cake. She was pretty enough to hang with the cool girls but she didn't. She was geeky enough to hang with the nerds, but she didn't. She was poor enough to hang with the welfare kids but they didn't want her either."

Jake nodded. She'd always been a loner. He'd seen enough of her around Huntley to glean that. All the other girls had hung around in groups or at least pairs but wherever Ella had gone, she'd gone alone.

"I asked her about it at the end of my first week and she just shrugged and said something about the sins of the mother."

"And yet you stuck?"

"Hell, yeah! If there's a bigger misfit around than me, I'm in. And besides, she didn't judge me, you know?"

Jake nodded. "Yeah." He knew.

"Jake? Jake Prince? Is that you?"

Jake looked up to find a vaguely familiar guy about his age looking at him like a long lost brother. But then he was as used to male adoration as he was female. He plastered on his best public smile and stuck out his hand. "Hi."

"Roger Hillman." He shook hands vigorously with Jake. "From Huntley High. We were in the same grade."

Jake smiled as he searched back through his memory banks.

"My sister Deidre had a major crush on you."

Ah. Bingo! Roger Hillman, or Rog as he'd been called, had been a prize wanker, always keen to rub Jake's lack of social standing in his face. But his sister, Deidre, on the other hand, hadn't been so fussy. In fact he'd go as far to say she'd been downright accommodating that day she'd stripped her top off and let him touch her breasts. It had been the first time he'd ever been allowed that far by a girl and he could still remember the total awe. He'd been a boob man ever since. "Oh right, yes, great to see you again," Jake lied.

"I've followed your career. Man, you were dynamite. Pity that piece of skirt ruined it there for you at the end though, hey?" Roger gave him a playful punch on the shoulder. "You had another couple of seasons in you, I reckon."

Jake's fake smile slipped as the ugliness of that time revisited and he pulled his hand out of the other man's grasp. Rog was too stupid to notice the cool change. "Why don't you go up to the bar and tell Pete your next one's on me?"

"Yeah? Cool man. I heard you'd bought a pub. Like father, like son, hey?" Rog gave a belly laugh, clutching his chest with one hand and patting Jake on the shoulder with the other and then ambled off toward the bar.

Twenty years later and a kickass international football career behind him, he was still Mick Prince's son. Jake turned bleak eyes back to his booth companions.

"What was that about?" Rosie asked.

"Ignore him, Jake," Simon said. "The guy's a loser."

Rosie frowned, and asked again, "What was that about?"

Ella arrived back at the booth. "What was what about?"

Simon looked at Rosie as Ella slid in next to Jake. "I'll tell you later," he murmured.

"I think I have room for that drink now," Ella said, her buzz making her oblivious to the awkward undercurrent.

"Of course." Jake smiled at her, pleased to be banishing Roger Hillman and his small-town attitude to the wayside.

Pete appeared miraculously with their tray of drinks and Ella kissed his cheek as he set hers down. "You're a bloody marvel, Pete."

"I know." He grinned.

"Where on earth did Jake find you? Did he free you from a lamp or something?"

Pete laughed. "Something like that."

Ella squinted, trying to picture Pete in nothing but harem pants and exotic turban, but found herself substituting Jake instead. His bare chest bronzed and oiled. His biceps bulging as he crossed his arms and declared her wish was his command. Her wondering if asking for a repeat of his triple-treat counted as one wish or three.

She took a large swallow of her cocktail and pushed it aside. *Time to stop drinking.* "Weren't our boys dynamite today?" she asked changing the subject.

Pete glanced at Jake. "Er ... sure, yep. It was great to see them get up."

Ella was not quite drunk enough to miss the hesitation or the sideways glance at Jake. She looked at the pair of them. "What? Am I missing something?"

Jake glanced at Pete. "No."

Ella looked at Rosie. "They just did a thing, didn't they?"

Rosie nodded. "Yep. There was a definite thing happening."

"A thing?" Jake asked.

"You did a look thing. He," Ella pointed at Pete, "hesitated. What's going on?"

Pete held up his hands, feigning ignorance. Ella narrowed her eyes. "Pete, aren't genies supposed to tell the truth?"

"Er ... I think that was the mirror on the wall."

Ella turned her gaze on Jake. "Out with it. Don't bullshit me."

Jake sighed. "We had a good result today but that's because we were lucky and the other team thought we'd be a walk over. They didn't try in the last half. They thought they had it in the bag. They were sloppy. We won on the back of their mistakes."

Ella turned to Pete, who nodded. Even Simon seemed to agree. She pulled her drink closer and took another hit. Rosie looked at her and shrugged.

"Does it matter?" Rosie asked.

Jake rolled his eyes. "Yes. It matters. It's alright for now, for the first game, but it's going to get tougher and if we want to win the comp we're only going to win it if we're the best. Don't forget this is just the first step in a long road. If, by some miracle, we win the public school comp we still have the Schools Cup. Counting on the other team being lazy or choking is not a strategy. We didn't win today. The other team lost."

Rosie and Ella looked at each other. "But you were so good with them after," Ella said. "So full of praise."

Jake shrugged. "They deserved their moment in the sun, to feel ten feet tall and bulletproof for a couple of days. But Monday afternoon they'll be coming right back down to earth."

She reached her hand out and covered Jake's. "Don't be too hard on them," she said. "They were so euphoric."

Jake nodded. "It's not going to win them the cup though." He watched her as she chewed on her bottom lip and looked anxious all over again. He sighed. "Don't worry, I'll tread carefully, I promise. We'll mainly be reviewing the tape with them so they can see their mistakes. It's often easier to show than tell, isn't it, Pete?"

"Absolutely. It's an invaluable tool."

Ella looked up at the skinny kid who didn't even look old enough to drink let alone work in a pub. He sounded so old sometimes. "Or maybe we can just rub our genie and make a wish?" She gave Pete's arm a rub.

Pete gave her a wicked grin. "Lower."

Ella laughed at Pete's non-threatening banter. "Pete," Jake growled. "I think you're needed at the bar."

Pete winked at Ella. "Can't blame a guy for trying."

They watched him go. "I should sack him," Jake mused. Pete had been giving him cheek and telling him how it was for the last seven years.

Rosie nodded. "We can take him home with us."

"Just what your place needs," Simon mused. "Another stray."

"Plenty of room," Rosie said.

"True," Ella agreed. "And Cameron would probably appreciate another male around."

"What's Pete's story?" Simon asked Jake.

Jake took a long pull of his beer. "Pete used to come and watch the Hero training sessions and home games religiously. He was a skinny thirteen-year-old with a quick wit and smart mouth. I was out late one night jogging along the river bank and I discovered he was sleeping under one of the bridges, doing it really tough. I kind of gave him a bit of a hand up. Haven't been able to get rid of him since."

Rosie beamed at him. "So, you collect strays too, huh?"

"Nah. Just Pete."

"And Cerberus," Ella chimed in.

"And the footy team," Simon added for good measure.

"Of course." Ella nodded. "A team full of strays."

"No wonder Daisy and Iris like him so much," Rosie added.

Jake watched them looking at him with a new appreciation. It seemed, suddenly, he was a regular caped crusader. It was a tag he really didn't want. Mother Theresa he wasn't. Roger Hillman's crack earlier had brought his thoughts around to Trish. She knew better than anyone that his feet were most definitely made of clay. The night was turning into a real downer—first Rog and now this. All he needed was Tony Winchester to walk through the door. Not that the son of a bitch would dare.

"You're actually a pretty decent guy, Jake, do you know that?" Ella said. Considering he'd been raised in a town that never let him forget he was the son of a drunk, it was amazing he had any humanity at all.

"No. I'm not."

Had she not been several cocktails down, Ella may have recognized the warning blazing in his eyes. "Sure you are," she insisted. "I think you're very gallant."

He wondered if she'd think that if she knew the truth. "I'm no knight in shining armor, Ella. Don't go putting me on a pedestal. I'm here to help Hanniford High win the Schools Cup. I'm not looking to be canonized."

"You shouldn't downplay this," Ella chided. "You've really gone to bat for us. For Pete. For Cerberus. It's a good thing you're doing."

Jake gave her a tight smile and drained his beer. She was looking at him like he was a god and he suddenly couldn't stand the weight of his sins. Okay, yes, she'd had a cocktail or two but she was far from drunk. Ella had always been good—a good girl, a decent woman, a compassionate teacher—and he felt totally unworthy of her praise. He had to get away. His past sucked at him as a surge of anger and regret filled his chest.

He stood. "I think I better get back to the bar. Pete's looking snowed under again. I'll send over another round of drinks."

Rosie raised her eyebrows as Jake hightailed it back to the bar. "Faster than a speeding bullet," she murmured.

Ella watched him go, his Levi's hugging his hips and his gorgeous ass, the broad planes of his back moulded to perfection in his snug black T-shirt. She frowned. What the hell was wrong with him? They were supposed to be celebrating.

And how was it possible to be annoyed and turned on all at the same time?

*

Jake worked the bar like a machine, grateful to be pulling beers and pouring shots and away from Ella's big, blue, trustful eyes. He could smell hops and the floor was sticky from spilled liquor. People laughed, girls batted their eyelashes, men shook his hand, a metallic beat played in the background and the till opened regularly with a satisfying *bing*!

It was just the type of good, honest work he needed to keep his mind off the black mood that had settled on his shoulders. He was fighting a rather overwhelming desire to smash things. The feeling was familiar, a blast from his past, and he struggled to push it back. Roger Hillman and his mates getting steadily trashed in front of him didn't help. But it had been a long time since he'd used his fists and he was damned if was going to regress on tonight of all nights.

He glanced up to see Ella and Simon laughing at something Rosie had said and he felt his gut twist tighter. What had she said to him a few weeks ago in her office? He was backward. He was Huntley and she'd come too far to go back. Maybe she was right. A few weeks in her company, a couple of hours with Rog buzzing around and he was spoiling for a fight.

Just like the bad old days.

*

An hour later, the group sitting at the booth were all feeling the hum from one too many cocktails.

"Jesus! This music is giving me a facial tic," Rosie complained. "I'm gonna put something decent on, then we should dance." She walked her fingers up Simon's chest and smiled at him.

"Dance?"

Rosie rolled her eyes. "Yes, you know—moving your arms and legs to music."

"Decent music," Ella added.

"Hmm. Not something I excel at," Simon said.

Rosie stared at him and shook her head. "What do I see in you again?"

"I don't know exactly."

She grinned. "Well, lucky you excel at other things."

Simon smiled back and Ella felt like the proverbial third wheel. Simon may not be Rosie's usual type but there was no denying they had chemistry. "Think I'll get the music," she said and climbed out of the booth.

Ella loaded the jukebox up with a selection of her favorites, effectively clearing the dance floor of all the bass junkies—which was pretty much everyone. Unperturbed, she and Rosie boogied until midnight, pulling out all the dance moves they'd perfected through their uni years and TGIF drinking sessions at this very establishment in its previous incarnation.

Simon couldn't be coaxed out and watched them from the booth, laughing and shaking his head at their moves. Ella noticed Jake and Pete watching from the bar. While she was having a ball, she knew her moves were a little two-dimensional, and Rosie was the real mover, her body undulating to the beat as if it came from within her. Ella felt like she was in some kind of a corny chick flick. Very *Coyote Ugly*. She half expected Rosie to force her to climb up on the bar. Which, in this skirt, could be interesting.

The oh-so-familiar opening chords of "Sweet Home Alabama" oozed from the jukebox and the dance floor filled—apparently even metal-heads had taste.

"This one always gets them up," Rosie said and grinned, undulating her hips and stomach.

"It's a classic," Ella agreed, doing a less successful version of Rosie's effortless Beyoncé hip shimmy. "Metal may come and go but classics will live forever."

"I'm getting Simon." Rosie strode to the booth, tugging on Simon's very reluctant hand. Ella laughed as she dragged him onto the floor. For someone who claimed he couldn't dance, Simon got into the groove quite quickly. But then dancing with Rosie plastered to him didn't actually require a lot of movement.

"Thought you said you couldn't do this," Rosie shouted.

Simon grinned as he pulled her hips in tighter. "This isn't dancing. This is fornication to music."

Rosie laughed. "I love how proper you make fornication sound."

"Fornication." Simon rolled the word off his tongue in a way that would have had old Mrs. Arbuthnot, his elocution teacher, calling for the smelling salts.

Rosie stood on her tippy toes. "See. You do know an F word." And then she kissed him.

Simon indulged briefly before pulling away. "Let's get out of here and I'll show you how improper I can be."

Ella rolled her eyes at the pair of them. The song came to an end and people started to depart. A hard male elbow jabbed Ella in the back and as she swung around, the man connected to the elbow stumbled against her, upending his beer all down her front.

"Hey mate, watch where you're going," Rosie snapped.

Ella stood looking down at herself as cold beer soaked into her shirt and bra.

"Simon, go and see if Jake's got a towel or something."

The man reached out to Ella. "Oh shit, sorry, lady, terribly sorry."

Ella dodged the slightly inebriated man's hands as they travelled toward her. What did he think he was going to be able to do? Rub her dry?

"Hey? Don't I know you?"

Ella looked up from her drenched clothes and raised her head to look at the man properly. Oh crap! Roger bloody Hillman.

"I don't think so," she said giving Rosie a get-me-out-of-here glare.

"No, no. I do," he said, grabbing her arm. "You're Ella Lucas. Little Ella Lucas. From Huntley."

She tried to pull out of his grasp. "I think you've mistaken me for someone else." Her lips were so stiff they might as well have been pumped full of collagen.

Roger leered at her as he shook his head. "Some things I never forget. What do you say? Are you doing anything for the rest of the night?" He ran the back of his forefinger down her arm.

Ella's skin crawled as the color drained from her face and her stomach plummeted to her toes. She felt cold all over; Roger Hillman may as well have thrown the icy beer in her face. She couldn't breathe. She couldn't move. She'd seen that leer before. Occasionally she had come face to face with one of Rachel's men and they'd get that look. Their gazes frank, knowing. Like it wouldn't be long before she was on the menu too. But she'd left that all behind in Huntley. Or so she thought.

Rosie watched Ella's color change and her entire demeanor deflate before her eyes. It took her back twenty years and she felt all the old protective instincts roar to life. She prodded the upstart in the chest. "Hey pin-dick, fuck off," she growled.

Pete was passing Simon a towel at the bar when all three men noticed the tense standoff happening on the dance floor. When Jake saw Roger Hillman with his smarmy paw on Ella's arm, he practically vaulted over the bar.

"Whoa," said Pete, who rapidly followed.

Simon quickly brought up the rear.

Ella looked down at Roger's hand on her arm, not really seeing it for the hundreds of memories that clawed at her gut. His touch was making her skin crawl and his voice was slurred and creepy but she was afflicted with a strange sense of paralysis. She could smell the beer, warm and yeasty against her skin, and she could feel the stares of curious onlookers. She just couldn't move.

"If you want to leave here with both your balls intact I suggest you let her go."

Ella looked up as Jake's voice sliced through her paralysis. He looked grim, his green eyes cold, reptilian almost. She'd seen that look before. Once. On the Huntley High School oval just before he'd taken a swing at some kid three years older than him who'd called Jake's father a stupid drunk. She took advantage of Roger's distraction and wrenched her arm free.

"Jake." Roger smiled and clapped him on the back, not noticing Jake's grim countenance. "Look who it is. Ella. Little Ella Lucas. You know, *Rachel's* daughter."

"Right," Jake said and grabbed Roger by his lapels, hauling him closer. "Get out of my pub."

"Hey," Roger said, his feet barely touching the ground. "C'mon, Jake, you know what Rachel was like."

Jake tightened his fists in Roger's shirt. "Shut your face."

"Alright, alright, you want her, you can have her." He gave Jake a nudge in the ribs. "I bet she's a goer though."

Jake had been looking for a place to put his pent-up anger and Roger Hillman's face was looking like the perfect spot. He could see a bright stain of color looking completely unnatural in Ella's bloodless cheeks. Rosie had her arm wrapped tightly around Ella's shoulders and a look on her face that would have put Mike Tyson to shame.

'Help me," Pete said to Simon before stepping forward between the two men. He grabbed Roger by one arm and Simon grabbed the other. "Out!" he demanded.

"I'm fine, Pete," Jake growled.

"Sure, boss. But Ella's not.' He indicated with his head. "Leave this miserable piece of dog excrement to us and go take care of her."

Ella looked at him with bewildered eyes. He hadn't seen her this vulnerable, this confused since the day she'd ridden into Huntley and dragged him up to room seven. She looked pale and shaken and as much as he wanted to wipe Roger Hillman's face all over the bar, pound on him, make him pay, make him hurt, he wanted to take her hurt away more.

He shoved Roger at Pete. "Don't ever show your face in here again. Red-necks aren't welcome in my bar."

Pete and Simon hustled a loudly complaining Roger out the door and Jake unclenched his fists. He looked at Ella still being hugged fiercely by her warrior princess. "Go home, Rosie," he said. "I'll take care of her."

Rosie nodded at the steely purpose in his gaze. "Make sure you do or you'll have to answer to me."

"Yes, ma'am." Jake held out his hand to Ella. "Come on, I have some dry clothes in my office."

She took his hand automatically and followed him like a docile lamb. He opened his office door, gesturing for her to go in first. She did and sat on his lounge chair, only vaguely aware of Jake moving around the office. Everything seemed to have shut down. Roger Hillman's poisoned words still dripped their venom into her system, infecting every cell. They wounded her with their malice. They reverberated around her brain and she recoiled from them. From the ugliness of them.

"Put these on."

Ella looked up to find Jake holding something out to her and it took a couple of moments for her to compute that it was clothes. The air con in Jake's office turned her beer-impregnated T-shirt into a froze wet-wrap. She felt cold all over—not only from the air-con's effect on her wet clothes—her nipples pebbled, her brain function was sluggish and she realised suddenly she was rubbing at the raised goose-flesh on her arms.

She reached out for the items, kicking off her shoes as she stood. She crossed her arms over her front, grabbed the hem of her T-shirt and hauled it over her head. She registered the surprise on Jake's face on a purely subliminal level. Turning away from him hadn't even entered her mind. It wasn't like he'd never seen her in her bra before. She pulled his old training jersey over her head then stripped off her skirt and replaced it with grey sweat pants. She rolled them up several times at the ankle and sat again on his chair, huddling into the layers of the jersey.

"Roger Hillman is a dickhead. Always was, always will be."

Ella nodded slowly, the pain not letting up but echoing around inside her. "I know. I just wasn't expecting—it'd been such a great day."

Jake gripped his glass. "Yes. It was a fantastic day."

Ella stared at her fingernails, tuning into the muffled bass of the jukebox—even playing god-awful metal crap, it was oddly comforting. It was certainly preferable to the maelstrom throbbing inside her.

"Do you know how many years it's been since a guy spoke to me like that?" she said finally. "Looked at me like that. Like I was a *commodity*?"

Jake cringed. "Ella."

The impotency she'd been feeling started to ebb as pure mortification took over. How many people had heard his ugly inferences? Had Simon? Had Pete? What about the people on the dance floor around her who'd also been caught up in the whole sick incident?

"Nineteen. Nineteen blissful years. And that ... that—" Ella searched around for an expletive worthy of Gypsy-Rose Forsythe's best friend and failed. "*Moron* has the hide to throw my past in my face tonight? Of all nights?" She hugged her knees to her chest, rocking slightly.

"Forget about him," he growled.

Ella shook her head. If only she could. But if living in Huntley had taught her one thing, it was that there was always another Roger Hillman. She'd just allowed distance to lull her into a false sense of security. She stood.

"How long, Jake? How many years does it take to shake her legacy? Until I get to be me. Plain old Ella Lucas, school teacher, and not Ella Lucas, *Rachel's* daughter?"

Jake felt his heart break at her desolate question, at the bleakness in her eyes. He shook his head. Underneath it all, the fame and the accolades, wasn't he still just Mick Prince's son? The publican's kid? Son of the town drunk, the loser gambler?

Ella pushed her hair behind her ear. "I thought I'd left all that behind me in Huntley. Why is it following me? First Cam and then you and now Roger bloody Hillman. I left there nearly two decades ago and still it keeps sucking me back."

She was looking at him like it was his fault. She wanted someone to blame and he was it. He let her go, she was upset and growing up in and around pubs Jake had learnt early that sometimes you just had to let someone run out of steam.

"I vowed when I left there I'd never look back. And here I am a thousand miles away but everywhere I look lately there are reminders of Huntley."

"Hey." Jake gave her a wounded look. "It wasn't all bad, was it?"

Ella felt a rush of emotion. After he'd left—the one person who, without knowing her much at all, had known her pain better than anyone—it had been unbearable.

"Yes, it was."

"Ella, I copped a fair bit of crap but even I had some good times."

Ella snorted. "Well, goody for you. I guess being the son of the town drunk gave you a little bit more latitude to let your hair down. But the town tramp?" Her voice wavered. It hurt even now to think of Rachel in that way. Even though she knew it to be true. "I never had that kind of freedom."

"Ella." Jake took a step toward her.

"Jake, Roger Hillman and his cronies, they used to … offer me money, ask me my … price." Ella's voice cracked and she stopped. She couldn't go on. All the old feelings of revulsion and fear swamped her. The gossips of Huntley had called her haughty but it'd all been an act to disguise her anxiety. She'd never been sure when one of the boys would try something on with her. They may not yet have been men but they'd been expert at playing grown-up games. Some days she'd felt so dirty, she'd stand under their rickety old shower for hours.

"Ella," Jake whispered as her first tears fell and he pulled her into his arms, holding her against his chest as a strangled sob tore from her chest. He held her firmly, anchoring himself, knowing that if he didn't hold on tight he'd walk straight out of his office, hunt Roger Hillman down and beat the crap out of him.

He ushered her to the lounge, pulling her into his lap, cradling her close as she sobbed great heaving sobs, loud and wet and snotty, right onto his shirt. And he didn't care. Until this moment he hadn't been aware of quite how bad things must have been for her. His jaw clenched thinking about what she had endured.

He may have been the son of the town drunk but his aunt would have boxed his ears if he'd disrespected a woman like that. In fact, Thelma had raised him with a healthy respect for the opposite sex.

Ella buried her face in his shirt and cried like she hadn't cried in a long time. She'd cried in his arms two years ago, the day after she'd buried her mother, as the orgasm he'd given her released unexpected emotions, but even then she'd refused to give into soul-deep grief. Now she was crying for Australia; for Rachel and Cam and her lost childhood and even Hanniford High.

His chest was warm and he smelled of soap and deodorant, not expensive cologne as she might have expected. And there were other aromas. Beer and coconut rum and bar nuts. She felt warm and safe and even though he was the last person she should be baring her soul to, she did it anyway. He rocked her and held her and she couldn't remember a time when she'd felt so right. Befriending Rosie and coming to live with Daisy and Iris had been godsends but she felt inexplicably at home within the circle of his arms. Two kindred spirits united in a shared memory.

So it wasn't such a stretch that she should fall asleep. She'd had insomnia for a week worrying about their first game—worrying about Cam doing well and Jake winning and how much Hanniford's future depended on the success of this venture. Frankly she was exhausted. And after crying a decades' worth of tears while Jake held her tight against his big, warm, delicious body, it was so easy to sigh, shut her eyes, push her nose into his neck and drift off.

So easy.

# CHAPTER NINE

Jake drew the cue back and jabbed the white ball into the cluster of colored balls, picturing Roger Hillman's face on the front of it. The satisfying smack was like music to his ears and his gaze tracked the blur of color as balls flew around the table. He wasn't sure how long he'd been playing for but it was his third game and he wasn't done with torturing snooker balls just yet.

Pete had stayed to help him clean up after closing and had hovered like a mother hen, challenging him to a game or two. But Jake had ordered him home and he'd gone, reluctantly. Pete was a good kid and while his self-appointed role as Jake's guardian was amusing and Jake indulged him, tonight he wasn't in the mood for Pete's wisecracking.

Jake inspected the table now the balls had settled into place and chose the longest shot, sending the white ball flying across the felt, smashing the yellow into the distant pocket. The clink of balls as he set about annihilating the table was also a good distraction from the echo of Ella's tears that needled at his subconscious. It was the second time she'd cried in his arms but it was different this time. Two years ago she hadn't allowed herself to wallow. She'd bitten down hard on her grief and channeled it into their sex, screwing like it'd been her last day on earth.

This time she hadn't held back any of it and he hadn't had to dig too deep to feel the echos of his own lost childhood. Her grief had been gut wrenching, hard to witness and frankly, he'd been relieved when the sobbing had settled and she'd grown heavy against him as she'd slipped into slumber. He'd never been good with weeping women but her sorrow had been particularly poignant and had reached deep inside him and squeezed great big handfuls of his gut. He smacked the black ball and it thunked heavily into the pocket. He wondered if Roger Hillman's face connecting with his fist would make the same sound.

Jake reached under the table and pulled the lever that released the balls and they thundered into the return slot. He set up another game. He had no idea how long Ella would sleep but he had no intention of waking her up. He drew back his stick and sent the white flying into the colors again and watched the chaotic scramble until all the balls were still.

"Is this a private game or can anyone play?"

Jake looked up from the table and squinted into the gloom. He'd turned all the lights in the bar out except for the one directly above the pool table. "You're up."

Ella moved carefully toward the light. "What's the time?" she asked, squinting as she stepped into the pool of light spilling over the table.

Jake checked his watch, ignoring the appeal of her messy hair and the just-rolled-out-of-bed rumpledness of her clothes. "Three-thirty."

They looked at each other for a moment. Ella pushed a stray lock of hair behind her ear. The silence stretched between them and it seemed out of place in a bar where only an hour and a half earlier music had throbbed into every corner.

"Have you—" Ella stopped and cleared her throat. "Have you got any change for the jukebox?"

Jake laid his stick against the wooden surround of the table and fished into the change pocket at the front of his jeans. He pulled out some coins and deposited them into her outstretched palm.

She smiled at him then walked away. He picked up his stick and returned his attention to the table. Even so, out of the corner of his eye he could see her hunched over the jukebox, the jersey she wore slipping off her shoulder, leaving it bare except for a purple bra strap. He forced himself to focus on lining up a shot, jabbing the white toward the target. It missed, for the first time tonight. He shook his head. Harry Ryan, his first coach as a rookie, had always said that women ruin men's focus.

Harry had been one wise old bastard.

Ella waited for the opening beats of "Breakfast at Sweethearts" to filter out before returning to Jake. He was bent over the table, his powerful legs spaced evenly apart, his knees bent. She could see the thick slab of his thigh muscle bunch beneath the denim as he rocked forward a little on his front foot and remembered how strong they'd felt against the backs of her thighs as he'd held her in his lap.

She drew close to the table and leaned her hip against the wood grain as she watched Jake shoot. His arms were strong as they braced for the shot. The snug sleeve of his black T-shirt barely contained his bicep as it tensed in preparation. Jimmy's rough baritone sang about hot coffee and brown toast and Jake slammed his cue into the white ball.

And missed. He cursed under his breath.

"Bummer," she said.

Jake took a moment to pull in a steadying breath then straightened up. There was a hum between them tonight, a connection evident even before the Roger Hillman incident and it scared the hell out of him. "Your turn." He reached to the nearby cue rack and pulled one down, passing it to her.

"Oh. No." Ella shook her head. "I'm hopeless at pool."

"We're not playing for sheep stations." Damned if he was going to play while she stood and watched, half falling out of his football jersey.

Ella resisted. "Rosie's the one that you need. Rosie can beat a bar room full of bikers."

Jake made a mental note to never challenge Ella's friend to a game. He lifted the stick and pushed the rounded end gently into her chest. "I don't want to play with Rosie."

Ella looked at him with big eyes. He was watching her all dark and brooding, his green eyes blazing. She took the cue, suddenly desperate for something to do with her hands other than putting them all over Jake.

"Which ones am I supposed to hit?"

He dragged his gaze away from her naked shoulder. If he kept looking at her like that there would be no question that she would end up on the table. "Don't worry about that. Just go for the easiest."

Ella had no doubt that if he kept looking at her like that she'd be the easiest thing at this table. She focused on the felt, her mathematician's mind admiring the patterns on a subliminal level while the chant of *shit, shit, shit* reverberated through her more conscious levels.

She drew the cue back to hit the nearest ball, missing by a mile.

Jake blinked. "Wow. You really are hopeless."

Her stance was awful, her cue positioning terrible and her aim shocking. His grip tightened around his own cue. Ordinarily he'd give someone this bad some pointers, especially if they were an attractive woman. He'd be up there behind her, draping himself along the length of her back, invading her space under the pretense of showing her how to hold the cue. But he didn't think he should lay himself bare to that kind of temptation tonight. Once again he found himself in a position where he wanted Ella but her emotional fragility put her off limits.

Ella glared at him. "You want me to point out the mathematical patterns on this table or work out the probabilities of each shot, I'm your girl. You want me to sink the ball? Not so much."

Jake chuckled. "Okay. So I'll play really badly and let you win."

She shook her head. "I know this may be a revelation to a jock like you, but I actually don't care about winning."

That's what she thought. "Yes, you do," he said, leaning over the table, setting up a shot for her that even Cerberus could make. "You just need the right incentive."

Ella's gaze flicked to his and she didn't have to ask to know what he was talking about. Hanniford High. She'd fight to the death for her school, her kids.

"Red into the center pocket," he said.

Ella dragged her gaze from his and looked at the indicated shot. She leaned over and hit the white with her cue. The red bounced off the edge and ricocheted to the far side of the table.

Jake winced. "Too hard." He concentrated on lining up another ball and dropped his voice an octave or two. "Sometimes you have to go softly," he said, demonstrating as he gently nudged the white to cozy up to a yellow that was sitting square with the pocket. He looked at her. "Sometimes you need a slow hand. A gentle kiss."

Ella felt hot suddenly. Very hot. James Reyne cautioning not to be too reckless floated towards them from the jukebox.

*Good thinking, James.*

Except the heat intensified As she leaned across the table and the too-big jersey slipped from her shoulder, she could feel his eyes on her, on the exposed skin, and glanced up to see his gaze drifting lower to where the V-neck fell forward, revealing her cleavage, her bra.

Her insides felt as if someone had jabbed them with an electronic cattle prod and she didn't even look at the table as she made the shot, pushing the cue toward the white ball, missing it completely. Not even James Reyne's melodic mournful warning could break through the sudden electric charge and it was on the tip of Ella's tongue to suggest strip pool. But she'd been the sexual aggressor with him once, she didn't have the nerve to do it again.

*And,* she reminded herself, *Jake was backwards.*

Jake drew in a shaky breath. His palms itched remembering how good the creamy rise of her cleavage had felt in his hands; soft and full. His mouth watered at the memory of how it had tasted, sweet like she'd been brushed with honey dust. His dick, predictable as ever, joined in the walk down memory lane and he knew there was no way it was going away while Ella's bra kept playing peek-a-boo.

She straightened and he breathed again, counting to three before he spoke. "You should keep your eye on the ball when you're shooting." He forced himself to peruse the table. "Here, try this one." He maneuvered the white into another good position.

They played on, the longest game of Jake's life. Between her hopeless aim and her damn cleavage, he was fighting a losing battle with his temper and his libido. He talked her through the moves, giving her pointers as they went, demonstrating with his own stance, his own cue, but Ella was stubbornly uncoordinated.

That should have made a difference to his dick, but it didn't. He really preferred sporty women, ones who enjoyed this type of recreation and could hold their own. He especially loved the ones who could whip his ass. But his erection didn't seem to care how bad she was as long as she kept bending

Amy Andrews

over, her bra on display, her ass in the air, snuggled nicely into his tatty old sweats.

The game finally came to an end when he potted the black with a resounding thud. It was four am. He was tired. And horny. He needed to get the hell away from her. Maybe he could dig out his little black book and ring one of a dozen women who would welcome a booty call even at this hour.

"Another?"

Jake opened his mouth to say no. No way. No how. No siree. There was Alicia and Candice and Jennifer—three willing women he could name off the top of his head.

"A proper one this time. I think I'm getting the hang of this."

His jersey slipped off her shoulder again and his "Honey, you have so not gotten this" was snatched away as the brain in his pants took over. "Sure." He cursed himself as he retrieved the balls and racked them up in the triangle.

*Stupid. Stupid. Stupid.*

"Can I shoot first?" Ella asked.

"Sure," he said again, stepping back a pace as she stood at the head of the table with him.

Ella bent over, balancing the tip of her cue between her second and third knuckles as Jake had taught her, acutely aware of his muscled presence a mere arms length away. She stopped and straightened, turning to look at him.

"Thank you," she said. "For before. For rescuing me from Roger. And being so … nice, in your office. I seem to make a habit of saving my meltdowns for you."

Jake knew all he had to do was take one step and he'd be pressed against all her soft feminine curves. He knew instinctively she'd have a different kind of meltdown if he dared to kiss her. There'd been a simmering passion raging between them since she'd first leaned over the pool table. But it had been an emotional evening, for both of them. Best to heed the wise words of James Reyne and Australian Crawl.

*Don't be so reckless.*

"I'm sorry you had to be exposed to his crap. I should have kicked his sorry ass out the second I saw him."

Ella smiled. "On what grounds?"

"Being a class-A dickhead."

She laughed. "Jake, you'd have to kick out half your clientele."

He shook his head. "That's the beauty in being the owner. I get to say who the dickheads are."

The silence stretched between them again and Ella found her gaze drawn to the strong line of his jaw and the incredible sensual curve of his mouth. "Well, thanks anyway. Much appreciated," she murmured.

She bent over the table, lining up her shot to hit the center of the pyramid while trying not to think about where that mouth had traveled. And how long it had been since a mouth had created anywhere near the havoc that Jake's had.

Naturally she ruined the break. The wonderful spider-webbing of balls she'd expected fizzled as the cue hit the white off-center and it barely made the colors move.

Jake hauled his gaze away from her ass, so beautifully rounded and so very, very near. "Why don't we try that again?"

He used the triangle to muster the couple of balls that had managed to escape during the most pathetic break he'd ever witnessed. And then, because a part of him couldn't bear to watch her cock it up again, but mostly because he was weak, he did lean over her as she bent again to take the shot.

"Here, let me show you." he said, fitting his body snuggly against hers, his stomach and chest pressed along the length of her back, his crotch fitting around her ass like it was made especially for him.

Ella forgot to breathe. His lips were at her temple, his breath warm against the sensitive skin. He fitted around her perfectly. Like a glove. Like a coat.

Like a lover.

"Like this," Jake said, determined to stay business-like even though the silky caress of her hair and its fruity aroma were digging seductive fingernails into his resistance.

Ella was aware of him like never before. His left hand curled around hers, steadying it as it balanced the cue. His right hand gripped the stick just above hers, pulling it in close to both their bodies. She could feel his lungs expanding, his pulse thumping against her back, the hard ridge beneath his zipper, brushing occasionally against her rear.

"You don't have enough control of your stick," he murmured, feeling like a total hypocrite. At the moment he was damned sure she had better control of hers than he had of his. He was trying to keep his distance down there and hoped she couldn't tell he was hard as a rock.

"You have to slide it like this." Jake demonstrated the motion, gliding the cue between her knuckles in smooth, easy movements. Back and forth. Back and forth. He thought he heard something remarkably like a whimper reverberate in the back of her throat. He swallowed, his hand tightening on the cue. Her smell was intoxicating and it took all his willpower not to drop his head and bury his face in her neck.

"Do you see?"

Ella was still none the wiser. She'd taken nothing in since he'd pressed himself against her. His voice, thick and rough went straight to her nipples and the sliding motion of the stick was utterly entrancing. It took a second or two to find her voice and then it was totally unintelligible. "Hmm."

Jake wasn't sure what she said but she didn't sound very confident. "Let's do it together," he suggested. "Draw back," he murmured into her ear, pulling the cue back a few inches, "and strike the center of the ball."

He punched the cue's tip into the white and it sailed down the table, hitting the cluster with a resounding smack and sending the balls flying around the table in a satisfying spider's web of color.

Neither of them moved. Balls careened crazily around their joined hands, narrowly missing them. Still they didn't move. Ella watched the spectacle without taking any of it in. Not the wonderful randomness or the mathematical possibilities or the sheer prettiness as the balls bounced and collided, spiraling off each other like fireworks squirming into the night.

They still hadn't moved when the balls eventually settled. The silence grew thick around them. Jake, stretched to the limit of his resistance, turned his face slightly and rubbed his nose against the tiny flutter at her temple. It was soft there, the fruity perfume from her hair infusing his senses. He barely hung on.

Every millimeter of Ella's skin felt alive, vibrant, waiting for Jake. When his lips touched where his nose had been an involuntary moan escaped her throat and even more involuntarily she pushed back into him, her butt cheeks grinding against the full force of his arousal.

Jake's pulse skyrocketed.

"Ella," he groaned and buried his face in her neck, her soft hair caressing his face. She pressed into him again and he shifted his hand from the cue to her hip and held her firmly to him.

Ella dragged in a breath that sounded like sandpaper rasping over wood. This was all kinds of crazy. She grasped for some sense. If they didn't stop this now it would be unstoppable. She moved, turned in his arms and he straightened up, allowing her to do so but keeping her against the pool table, his hand firmly attached to her hip.

She drew in another husky breath. "Jake. This is crazy."

Jake nodded. "I know."

"I shouldn't. We shouldn't. I can't ... stay." She looked over his shoulder toward the exit. "I have to get out of here."

He nodded again. She was right. This would mess up their professional relationship big time. "I know."

Ella didn't move. It didn't matter how many times she told herself he was backwards, her body was screaming for his touch. For the magic she knew he had in his fingertips, his mouth, the rock of his hips. She made one last appeal.

"Please, just send me away."

Her entreaty had the opposite effect. There was a note of desperation, a husky tremor in her plea that clawed at his gut, stroked along his muscles as surely as if she'd trailed her fingernail across them. And God help him, he wasn't strong enough to do what she wanted.

"Shit, Ella," he groaned, stroking her face, cupping her cheek, rubbing his thumb over the plump contour of her bottom lip. "I can't." And then he lowered his head and captured her mouth in a kiss that was out of control from the first touch.

All Ella could do was hang on as the kiss exploded around and inside her. She rose on her toes, her arms circling his neck, a hand snaking into his hair, bringing him closer, nearer. Jake's hands found her ass, squeezing her cheeks, pulling her in and then lifting her, until she was sitting on the edge of the table.

She tore her mouth away, staring up at him dazedly, his mouth smeared with moisture, his green gaze as infused with lust as hers, as bewildered by it as hers, his chest heaving air in and out like an ancient bellows. He looked so goddamn lust-drunk and confounded she felt a rush of pure feminine power knowing she was responsible.

Jake swooped again, his pulse ratcheting another notch as her tongue pushed into his mouth. He eased her back against the table, pushing balls out of the way as he went. His lips left hers, travelled to her neck, the spot behind her ear, her collar bone. The V-neck of his jersey tickled his chin and he was overcome with the urge to get the bloody thing off. Now!

He straightened and looked down at her, the light spilling over her, her breathing harsh, her chest expanding emphasizing her assets. He placed a hand on her belly and watched her breath hitch. Then he grasped the hem and pushed it slowly up exposing her stomach and belly button, her ribs and then the ultimate prize. Two purple satin mounds of pure woman.

He lowered his head to her stomach and buried his face in the soft skin there. He inhaled and she smelled like beer and he wanted to lick her all over. Her stomach muscles tightened and he moved slightly as she curled up to remove the jersey.

Ella threw it on the ground and kissed him full on the mouth.

"Now you," she requested, grabbing his T-shirt from behind and pulling it up over his head.

There were a few seconds when they both just looked at each other, their hungry gazes devouring the playgrounds before them, remembering them, anticipating them. And then they were on each other. Ella pulled on Jake's shoulder, yanking him down as she fell backward. He climbed onto the table with her dragging her further up as he went, pressing her into the felt as his lips plundered the sweetness of her mouth. His hand groped behind her to unhook her bra, then moved to her waistband as she put her hands on the fly of his jeans and tugged it open.

His skin felt warm and smooth beneath her hands, the muscles bunching enticingly as she played her palms across them. She'd forgotten how broad he was, how perfectly her hips cradled his, how his stubble grazing the aching tightness of her nipples propelled her closer to orgasm. His hands were everywhere, his mouth hot and wet, blazing trails and leaving devastation and pleasure in equal measure in its wake. Her hand reached for his erection and the groan that tore from his throat was so base, so male, Ella practically purred her satisfaction.

She was vaguely aware of the jukebox singing 'Lay Back in the Arms of Someone', vaguely aware of the scratchy felt pressing into her back as she wrapped her legs around his waist. "Now," she demanded.

Jake chuckled. "Patience," he said and bent to suck an impossibly taut nipple into the heat of his mouth.

Ella moaned and her eyes rolled back in her head for a moment before sense returned. She tugged his head from her breast and yanked his face close to hers. "I need you in me. Now."

"But—"

"I don't want the fancy stuff. Not now. All I need is this." She grasped him with rough hands and squeezed. "Inside me now." Ella didn't care that she still had his sweat pants caught around one knee or her bra wrapped around one wrist or that Jake had one shoe on and his jeans barely off his hips. All she cared about was Jake finding his wallet, putting the condom on and pounding all that hardness into her over and over.

For his part Jake was past caring about everything too. Not about the carpet burns he was sure as hell going to have on his elbows tomorrow or the fact that he was going to have to make up some half-arse excuse for Pete when he sent the pool table away for a professional clean.

Because once he pushed inside Ella everything else ceased to exist. There was just her and her breathing and her smell and her *yes, yes, yes* every time he thrust like his own private cheer squad and the tight grip of her muscles around him. He'd forgotten how good she'd felt under him and how responsive she was to his every movement.

Ella could feel the edges of her orgasm slowly coming together as Jake went from long, slow, teasing strokes to quicker, shallow ones, hitting that spot he was so good at finding. The spot that only Jake seemed to know existed.

"God, Ella," Jake panted, "you feel so good."

He gripped her already bent knee and pushed it back further, lifting her foot off the table, and thrust again.

Ella cried out as the different angle went deeper and pulled down hard in all the right places. Heat coalesced in her stomach, then bubbled and finally rippled out in ever increasing waves. She shut her eyes, trying to hold it back, wanting him to stay here forever, do this to her forever.

But then Jake groaned and she could feel the tremble of his biceps beneath her hands. Knowing he was near pushed her over the edge and she fell into a pool of such intense pleasure she didn't think it was possible to survive it.

Until Jake joined her, and they drowned together.

# CHAPTER TEN

Jake woke the next morning to a hand sliding up his chest. He cracked his eyes open as Ella draped a leg over his thigh and snuggled her head into his shoulder. Her hair brushed his chin and he shut his eyes again. He'd only been asleep for a few hours and the post-coital buzz had set firmly in his marrow, leadening his bones and eyelids.

A smile touched his lips as his mind drifted back to their brisk walk from the pub to her place as the first blush of dawn streaked the sky. They'd slipped into the darkened house like teenagers late home for curfew and hit her mattress, Ella's hand over his mouth, smothering his laughter, finally kissing him to shut him up. And then passion reigniting, racing to shed their clothes and do it all over again.

And then again. And again. Before finally falling asleep from sheer exhaustion. Ella Lucas was insatiable. To prove his point her hand drifted south and his smile grew wider. Very insatiable.

"You asleep?" Ella murmured as her hand stroked over his flat belly.

He grinned. "Not anymore."

Ella trailed her finger across the soft vulnerable strip where belly met groin, his appreciative purr encouraging her to stay and play a little longer.

"Mmmm," Jake sighed, his dick currently wide awake. Even the brief, loud knock at the door before it opened wasn't enough to kill its interest despite Ella withdrawing her hand like a child who'd been caught with her hand in the cookie jar. His cookie jar.

"Ella, are you awake?" Rosie whispered loudly into the gloom as she approached the bed. "I've been worried about you."

Jake chuckled and Ella dug him in the ribs as she raised herself up on her elbows. "I'm fine."

Rosie heard the chuckle. "Jake? Is that you?"

Jake lifted his head off the pillow and gave her a brief salute before flopping back again. "Morning, Miss Rosie."

Rosie grinned and raised an eyebrow at her best friend. "Well, well, well."

Ella blushed and held the sheet firmly under her arms. "Rosie, it's not—"

"What it looks like?" Rosie interrupted, still grinning like an idiot. "I see you took good care of her then, Jake."

"Yes, ma'am. I'm a man of my word."

"I didn't mean seduce her."

Jake smiled. "What makes you think *I* seduced *her*?"

Rosie snorted. "Twenty years of friendship. Ella thinks too much."

Jake laughed, remembering the moment she almost backed out. "That she does."

"Hey, smart asses, I'm right here," Ella grouched.

"I'm making bacon and eggs," Rosie said. "You must both be famished?"

Jake was starving. But now Mr. Woody was involved, food was low down on his list of priorities. "No."

"I do some mean mushrooms."

"No."

"And grilled tomatoes to die for."

Jake laughed. "Go away, Rosie. Ella needs some more TLC."

Ella was starving and Sunday breakfast was Rosie's forte. She knew seven-foot bearded bikers who wept at Rosie's breakfast table. "No. I'm fine."

"Really?" Jake asked sliding a hand up her side and cupping a breast.

Ella swallowed. "Well ..."

Jake brushed a thumb over a nipple that seemed more responsive to his suggestion than Rosie's. "Really?" he murmured again, lower this time.

Ella collapsed back against the bed as her abdominal muscles twisted. "Maybe I'm having a relapse."

Jake smiled. "Another time, Miss Rosie."

"Okay, okay," Rosie said, backing out the door. "But you know you're passing up one of the best experiences of your life."

Jake smiled into Ella's eyes. "No I'm not."

The door clicked shut and Jake rolled himself on top of her. She spread her legs and he settled into the cradle of her pelvis.

"Rosie really does make the best Sunday breakfast in Australia."

He kissed her eyes, her nose and her mouth. "That's okay. I make the best Sunday love on the planet. Bet I can make you forget all about food," he whispered as he nuzzled her neck.

Ella shut her eyes as his tongue traced her collarbone and a wave of goose bumps marched across her body. "Hmm, that good, huh? Think you're up to it?"

Jake ground his pelvis against hers. "What do you reckon?"

*

Twenty minutes later, having thoroughly succeeded in wiping Ella's brain of not only food but even more basic things like speech and the ability to name simple objects, Jake rolled onto his back, dragging in ragged breaths. Ella lay beside him in a similar state of breathlessness.

For the first time, as he lay struggling to return his breathing and pulse to normal, he took in his surroundings. In the dawn hours he hadn't paid any heed to her room. Only her and her naked skin and the mattress behind her had entered into his tunnel-visioned world. And it had been too dark. But the mid-morning sun pushed its bright fingers around the drawn blinds illuminating the space. He looked from side to side. Ella's room was very *girly*.

Purple ceiling, pale pink walls, a purple-and-pink striped quilt. A large framed print featuring van Gogh's *Starry Night* was pride of place on the wall opposite her bed. Then he noticed the little dolls stuck on bamboo sticks adorning the frame and anchored at other points around the room. They were everywhere. He'd seen them before of course, at the Ekka. Every little girl in Brisbane walked around the annual show carrying one of the damn things with their glittered hair and bodices, tulle skirts, netting wings and too-wide eyes—no doubt from the stick being jammed so firmly up their backsides. But it was kind of freaky to have so many wide kewpie doll eyes staring down at him like he'd been sullying their owner all night.

"Wow," he said. "What's with the dolls?"

Ella turned her head to face him. "Fairies," she corrected.

Jake raised an eyebrow.

Ella shrugged. "I was never allowed to have one as a kid. Every year the show would come to town and girls like Sarah Charlton and Deidre Hillman would bring their fairies on sticks to school and I wanted one so badly. Rachel said they were unnatural but I just loved them. They were so sparkly and pretty."

Jake thought Rachel had a point. They looked almost evil with their plastic mouths frozen in a little red Marilyn Munroe pout. He guessed it was a chick thing.

"The night Rosie and I left town she gave me one. She knew how much I adored them and, being a carnie kid, she had access to boxes of them. And then she gave me one for my birthday that first year together and it became a bit of a tradition. Now Daisy and Iris do it also. And of course the word went out to the extended family and they just show up from time to time."

Jake rolled up on his elbow and looked down at her. "Doesn't it … freak you out to have them watching you like that?"

Ella laughed. "No."

Jake kissed her shoulder. "Your room's not what I imagined."

Ella raised an eyebrow. "You imagined my room?"

He grinned. "Well, only insofar as you being naked on the bed." She laughed again.

"So what did you imagine then?"

Jake lifted his head. "Not so … pink."

Ella smiled. "Does it offend your masculinity?"

He smiled back. "Absolutely not. But have you ever thought how good a big-screen television would look on that wall?" He moved his head, indicating the framed print.

Ella gave a horrified gasp. "That's a van Gogh, Jake."

He shrugged. "You could hang it in your office. Or, better still, have it as a screen saver."

She shook her head. "Philistine."

Jake looked around a bit more and was hit by a fragment of a memory. "Actually, Deidre Hillman had a pink room. Pinker than this. Frilly too." He shuddered. "The whole catastrophe."

Ella arched an eyebrow. "Really?"

Jake grinned. "Hey, just because Roger was a dickhead didn't mean his sister was. Deidre was a very accommodating girl."

Ella felt the bitch in her roar to life. "So I believe. Let me guess. She let you touch her breasts?"

Jake smiled at the memory before throwing her a look. "How do you know?"

"She did it for everyone, Jake, it was her specialty." Ella pulled the sheet a little more firmly under her arms. "And they called Rachel a slut."

"I have a lot to thank Deidre for," he said, tugging on the sheet covering Ella's breasts. "I've been a breast man ever since."

Ella clamped down harder with her elbows, resisting his tug. "Did you and she ...?"

Jake watched her worry her bottom lip with her teeth; she couldn't quite meet him in the eye. He grinned. "Jealous?"

She shrugged unconvincingly. "Curious."

"No."

Now she'd started she couldn't stop. She wanted to know which of Huntley's bitchy bigoted girls had been lucky enough to deflower Jake. "Who was it? Your first?"

Jake gave her a stern look. "Ella, a gentleman never divulges that sort of information."

Ella was surprised at his coyness. If only half the boys in Huntley hadn't been so eager to kiss and tell about Rachel. "Okay, okay," she said. "How old were you then?"

"Fourteen."

"Fourteen?" Ella squeaked. Bloody hell. Cameron was fifteen and she couldn't even begin to imagine him being sexually active. He was flat out stringing a sentence together most days let alone something witty to convince a girl to do the nasty with him. What an articulate girl like Miranda saw in him was a total mystery.

But she *was* eternally grateful.

"I was an early starter. Plus, if it helps, I was really bad at it."

Ella snorted. She had a feeling bad sex with Jake would still be better than a lot of the "good" sex she'd had since she'd become sexually active at the decrepit age of twenty.

"Don't tell me the great Jake Prince finished a little early?"

Jake laughed. "You could say that. But I was lucky—she was more experienced and very patient. Plus ... I'm a fast learner."

Ella gave him a half smile. "And I bet your teachers always said you had difficulty concentrating."

Jake laughed. He tugged on the sheet again and flashed her a knowing smile when she let him have his way. He dropped his head to nuzzle the swell of her left breast, as his hand stroked down her body.

A loud banging on the door intruded before he reached his target.

"Jake. It's Pete."

Jake reluctantly released his mouthful, placing his forehead against Ella's chest. He looked up at her. "Jesus, it's like Grand Central Station here, isn't it?" And then he turned to face the door. "Go away," he called.

"Rosie invited me for breakfast. She says last chance."

Jake rolled his eyes and threw himself back against the mattress as Ella muffled a laugh. "No, thanks."

"She says you'll be sorry. She says it's like an orgasm for your mouth."

Ella laughed again and Jake shook his head. "Does the kid not realise that I'm trying to score a real one here?" he murmured. "Pete," he said, louder this time, "I hired you, I can fire you. Go away."

"I hope we practiced safe sex."

Jake reached over the side of the bed, groped around for one of his shoes and hurled it at Ella's door. It connected with an almighty thud.

"Jeez, okay, I'm going, I'm going."

Ella laughed out loud this time as Jake rolled up on his elbow again.

"Now. Where were we?"

Ella cupped his cheek. "What does 'a hand up' mean?"

Jake frowned. "A hand up?"

"Last night you said you gave Pete a bit of a hand up."

"Ah." He flopped back against the mattress. He was silent for a moment. "I paid some school fees. Found him a place to live."

Ella could hear the dismissive note in his voice and could tell he wasn't comfortable talking about it. She turned her head and studied his face. He was scrutinizing her ceiling like it was a Michelangelo masterpiece. "That was a good thing you did," she said.

Jake waited a beat or two and shrugged. "Just paying it forward. If Sergeant Peters hadn't given me a chance at thirteen, I'd have probably ended up in juvie. Or stayed in Huntley, become a loser drunk like my father."

Ella rolled on her side, pressing her body down the length of him and snuggled her head into his shoulder. His arm came up around her and she said, "You did him proud."

Jake shut his eyes. On the football field maybe.

Ella snuggled closer, halting the sudden rise of the sordid memories from his past. He stroked his fingers up and down her arm and smiled at her contented sigh.

Lying with women after sex had never been his thing. It didn't usually take them long to get to the hard sell, the when-can-I-see-you-again speech. When he'd been younger, the hey-baby-sure-I'll-call lies had been easy. The older he got, the more gnawing his arm off in the middle of the night appealed.

But being here with Ella, escape was the furthest thing from his mind; he could stay for hours. He opened his eyes, twisting his head from side to side, looking for a clock. He spied a set of large digital numbers on a bedside table draped in a purple gauzy fabric. Nearly eleven.

A flash of red caught his eye as he looked away and he turned back. Two little red vases sat on the table as well. A stray beam of sunlight pierced a path through swirling dust particles and struck one of the vases, throwing a deep ruby glow on the wall behind.

It triggered a memory. "Hey," Jake said. "Aren't they the vases your mother had in her room? High on that window ledge, opposite her bed?"

\*

Ella had been drifting away to the deep rhythm of Jake's heart beat when his comment ripped her by the roots of her hair back to consciousness. For a few seconds everything stopped as his words sank in.

How in the hell did he know that?

She pushed herself away from him, anchoring the sheet firmly under her armpits. Her heart was beating so hard it felt like bullets hitting her chest at close range.

She looked at the vases and for the first time in her life they revolted her. They'd been the only thing she'd taken from the house after she'd packed Cam up. A fragile link to her mother—not Rachel, *her mother*. The woman she'd loved and known before the ugly truth had infected the memories, eating them away like a cancer.

Ella felt a rising tide of heat. The urge to hurl the vases against the wall and watch them smash into a pile of ruby shards shook her to the core. Damn Rachel to hell.

Jake frowned. Ella had gone really pale and was looking at him like he'd just sprouted fangs. "Ella?"

"Yes, Jake," she said, her voice trembling with roiling emotions, "they are."

Jake looked at them again. "Yeah. I thought so. I always thought it was pretty cool how they refracted that weird red light around her room."

"Oh God. Oh God. Oh God," she moaned. The vain flicker of hope that maybe he'd just heard about the vases through grubby boys' talk was brutally snuffed out.

She leaped out of bed, her mind scattering as she searched for something to put on. Jake's coyness earlier about the experienced woman who had taken his virginity set ice running in her veins. Roger Hillman's words from last night—*Come on, Jake, you know what Rachel was like*—caused a pain in her chest so severe she thought she was having a heart attack. She rubbed at it, trying to ease it.

She threw on Jake's jersey. "Get out," she said, crossing her arms around her middle to stop her hands from shaking. How could he have done this to her? How could he have touched her, made love to her, when he'd slept with her mother first?

Jake vaulted up. Jesus Christ, what had just happened? "What the hell?"

"Oh, Jake." Ella fought against the urge to let her face crumple and bit back the emotion that rose on a high tide of despair. "Don't be so bloody obtuse. The vases, Jake. The *vases*."

It took a few more seconds of her bitter accusatory glare for it to click. Her horrifying assumption crashed over him. *She thought that he'd …*

"Oh, hang on," he said after a moment, ripping back the sheets and scrabbling for his own clothes. "This is insane, Ella."

Ella, her chest a cold block of ice, watched as Jake stepped commando into his jeans and reached for the zipper. She prayed his dick would get stuck in the vicious teeth, maybe then he'd know a bit of the pain that was tearing into her flesh. But he yanked it up without incident.

Ella's breath hissed in and out of her lungs. "Just get out," she commanded.

Jake couldn't believe that they'd gone from post-coital bliss to bitter recrimination in a matter of seconds. "You think I slept with Rachel?"

She barely heard him, her brain too busy conjuring images that made her want to retch. She needed a shower. Even hearing him say the words was like an ice-pick to her heart. "Damn right I do, Jake."

Jake raked a hand through his hair. He pulled his T-shirt over his head and stalked toward her. She seriously thought that of him? After everything they'd shared these last weeks? "This is bullshit, Ella."

A noise came from the back of Ella's throat that defied description. It was guttural and ugly, a cross between a roar and a mortally wounded whimper. "You have to have been in her room to know about the sunlight on the vases, Jake."

It was one of the happier memories from her childhood, from when she was really little: lying in bed with her mother in the morning, waiting for the sun to get high enough to strike the vases. The sense of wonder as the room took on a mystical garnet hue. Her mother laughing with her, telling her how she had laid with *her* mother as a little girl, waiting for the very same thing.

She gave Jake's chest an angry shove and he rocked back on his heels. "What do you think, Jake?" She shoved again, harder this time. "How do you rate me?" Another shove, which made no dent to the solid wall of his chest. "Was I as good as her? Was I?"

Jake reared back as if she'd struck him across the face instead of the rather paltry pushing. Her face was red, her eyes wild, her hair flying around her face with each enraged push she administered. She looked ... crazed.

Unreasonable.

A little like that day in Huntley two years ago when she'd come to him, grieving for her mother and angry at the town over the vicious rumor surrounding her departure.

Jake grabbed her hands, which had fisted into his T-shirt, and pulled them off him, stepping back. Everything inside him froze. Everything that had been warm and loose just moments ago was now cold and tight. She seriously, seriously thought that he'd slept with her mother.

Surely, she knew him better than that?

Obviously not.

A white hot anger flared to life in the pit of his belly. The solution was an easy fix—just open his mouth and deny it. But the heat became a burn that licked through his veins and pride kept his mouth firmly shut.

If Ella could believe him capable of that, then he didn't want anything to do with her. "I don't have to put up with this crap," he said softly.

He turned and gathered the rest of his belongings, hardening his heart to the tiny whimpering noises he could hear gurgling at the back of her throat. But when he turned back she looked so devastated that his earlier resolve faltered. He couldn't leave her like this. She was trembling all over, standing in his jersey, her arms around her waist pulling it higher till it barely reached her thighs. She was sniffing and biting her lip.

Then he sighed, stepping closer. "Ella."

She retreated a step, but forced herself to look at him. The man who had done something he'd known she'd never forgive him for but had gone ahead and slept with her anyway. "Just leave the money on the table on your way out."

Jake sucked in a breath and his lips flattened into two thin slashes in his face. He opened the door without a backward glance and left.

Ella's legs collapsed beneath her and she slid down the wall. Tears came to her eyes but she suppressed them. They clogged her throat, tingled like a thousand needles in her nose but she pushed them back. She would not cry twice in as many days. So she hugged her knees to her chest, laid her cheek against them and rocked.

*

Jake was watching the Demons do drills on Thursday afternoon. He'd been working them hard all week, having brought them down from the high of their first win on Monday morning with brutal honesty, hammering in to them that the comp would get harder—and the Schools Cup would be hardest of all.

They'd looked at the video from the match over and over, pointing out each player's weaknesses and strengths, their errors, and he and Pete had spent the week running endless drills targeting specific areas. The fact that he'd been pissed since storming out of Ella's house on Sunday had certainly kept the fire burning in his gut. He'd seen her only a few times at a distance and frankly, he didn't care if he never saw her again.

So, they fucked like they were made for each other? Sex he could get—with uncomplicated women. Women who wanted to say they'd screwed a legend and didn't give a shit about the piss-ant town he'd grown up in nor who he'd bedded while he lived there. He didn't need someone from his past messing up his future. He was the coach and she was the principal. It was a line they should never have crossed.

He tracked Cameron around the field for a bit as he worked on his passing. The boy had loads of stamina, but he was a ball hogger, relying on his bulk to bust through the opposition's front line instead of using his brains and his team members. He watched some of the other guys working with Pete on their tackling. They needed some training machines.

Hanniford High had no equipment and no budget to buy any. The Demons' training sessions seemed archaic compared to the high-tech sessions during his professional career. It put them at a disadvantage and, God knew, they were already handicapped enough. He could probably apply for a disabled parking space for the team bus. Not that they had one of those either. *Fuck!*

"Pass the goddamned ball, Cameron," he shouted from the sidelines.

He made a mental note to start getting some basic stuff. What the hell else was he going to do with his money? The teams they were up against had equipment, top-class equipment, he'd wager. If Ella wanted to win, wanted him to coach Hanniford High to victory, then he needed the right tools.

"Jake!"

Jake turned to find Miranda bounding along the sideline with all her usual indefatigable vigor. Honestly, if he hadn't had seen her feet as she'd emerged into the world fifteen years ago he'd swear she'd been born with springs instead.

She enveloped him in her usual enthusiastic hug as Trish brought up the rear. "Miranda. Stop it. You know you're not supposed to hug Jake at school."

Jake grinned at Trish, an older version of her daughter, her step still springy despite the march of time. He kissed her on the cheek and they chatted briefly about the debut game before Miranda spat out what it was that had her shifting from foot to foot like a Cocker Spaniel on speed.

"I want to form a cheer squad."

Jake glanced sharply at Trish. The years fell away between them and he could see her in her little bitty skirt, her ponytail bouncing as she did the splits in midair, the team logo emblazoned across her tight blue and white shirt. "You okay with this?" he asked.

"Course she is," Miranda jumped in. "Mum even said she'd train us."

Trish held up her hands and shrugged. "I've tried to talk her out of it."

Jake looked at Miranda again, not comfortable with the idea of her flashing her legs and shaking her chest in front of a bunch of horny teenage boys. As a professional, he understood that a cheer squad was all part of the showbiz of the game. The razzamatazz. But cheerleading wasn't all pom-poms and routines. He and Trish knew that better than anyone.

He'd hate to see history repeating itself. Hate to see Miranda crushed like her mother had been. But he didn't have the heart to tell her no. He'd never been able to say no to her. Then a sudden thought had him smiling. Ella could do his dirty work for him.

"Okay. But you have to get Ella's permission first."

Miranda squealed and grabbed him around the neck. "Oh thank you, Jake. Thank you, thank you."

Jake chuckled as he pulled her arms off his neck. "Yeah, well, don't count your chickens."

"Could you come with me, Jake? Ms. Lucas has been a real grouch all week and she likes you."

Liked him? Liked to castrate him, maybe. "Grouchy, huh?"

"Cameron thinks she might be, you know … going through the change."

Jake saw Trish roll her eyes and threw back his head as a huge belly laugh escaped. Considering Ella was two years younger than him and still in her thirties, he doubted her ovaries were in any immediate danger of ceasing to function. "Best not mention that to her."

"So you'll help me? Tomorrow before training?"

It was on the tip of Jake's tongue to tell her no. He doubted whether his presence would do much for her cause. But wasn't that what he wanted? He sighed. "Okay. Sure."

"Yes." Miranda squealed again. "You're the best, Jake." And she ran back to a group of girls who huddled together and then all started squealing together.

"Oh God,' he said to Trish. "I've created a monster."

\*

Ella, already well and truly shitty with the world, was tearing up another letter that had arrived in an ominous yellow envelope when the knock came. "Come in," she called.

She looked up to see Miranda Jones entering and smiled. Jake followed her in and the smile died. She hadn't spoken with him since Sunday and had, frankly, been dreading the prospect.

Which, apparently, was now.

She'd lived that moment over and over in her mind, that dreadful sinking moment when she'd realized Jake had been in Rachel's room. Men had gone into Rachel's room for one reason only—and Jake had been one of them. It didn't matter how hot he looked right now in his grey Nike singlet, screwing her mother was unforgiveable. She didn't know why she held Jake to a higher standard. She just did.

Miranda shifted nervously in front of her and Ella dragged her mind away from the weekend's humiliation. The young woman gave her a shy smile and Ella wondered where peppy Miranda had gone.

"Can I help you with something, Miranda?" She saw Jake flinch a little at her deliberate snub. She only wished it made her feel better.

"I asked Jake yesterday if we could form a cheer squad and he said you had to give your permission first. So I'm here to ask your permission."

Ella frowned. Her gaze cut to Jake. What the hell was he playing at? He knew how she felt about cheerleaders. "Oh. I see," Ella murmured looking back at Miranda, steepling her fingers, buying some time.

"My mum said she'd train us," Miranda added into the growing silence. "We can train in the afternoons on the oval."

"Your mother?"

Miranda nodded her head enthusiastically. "She was a professional cheerleader. That's where she met Jake."

Ella saw Jake close his eyes briefly and her fingers collapsed. She scrutinized his face and he looked guilty as hell. Aha! She'd always wondered about their story. Had Trish and Jake been lovers?

She got up and sauntered over to the window, wondering if there were any women on this planet—*and their mothers*—who hadn't ended up between his sheets. A train was waiting at the station opposite and she studied it for a second, choosing her words carefully, before turning.

"I have to be honest with you, Miranda. I'm not in favor of this. At all."

"Oh but, Miss—"

Ella held up her hand. "Have you heard of Emmeline Pankhurst, Miranda?"

Miranda looked affronted. "Of course. She was a British suffragette," Miranda expanded. "She rocks."

"And how do you think she'd feel to see young women prancing around in itty-bitty costumes providing sexual entertainment for males at sports events?"

Miranda frowned. "I know there's a huge debate about cheerleaders and feminism, Ms. Lucas. I'm a feminist, just ask Mr. Deacon—he gave me an A for my *Beyond the Female Eunuch* essay. But I like to think that feminism came about to fight for our right to make our own choices."

Ella blinked at Miranda's eloquence. She even felt a rush of optimism that young women were still thinking, still aware of the issues. In her peripheral vision she saw Jake hide a smile with a stubble rub.

"But what about the message cheerleading sends to younger, less informed girls? That women are just there to prop up male egos while they chase a stupid ball around a ground—"

"Field," Jake interrupted. *Field. For the love of God.*

"Because," Ella continued, ignoring him, "they're too delicate or uncoordinated or stupid to play themselves?"

Miranda blew her fringe off her face with a huff. "I know we have a long way to go. I know that the glass ceiling still exists. That some men still think it's okay to rape and beat up women and make sexist jokes and discriminate against us. But this isn't about that. This is about what we can do to support Hanniford's cup bid."

Ella opened her mouth to speak but Miranda ploughed through, on a roll.

"Look at the Bullets last weekend. Their cheer squad was amazing. And right off the bat they had a mental advantage over us because they had all the bells and whistles and we didn't. With every chant, they were saying our team's better than yours because we have all the luxuries, like a cheer squad. Think of it as a stare down. Like the Hakka. We want every team in Brisbane to know that we're a school to be reckoned with."

Miranda fell silent. Jake caught Ella's eye, shook his head and mouthed, *No*, at her.

Ella frowned. Jake didn't want it either? She bit back a snort. She'd have thought Jake would be all for it. She pictured him munching a cigar and saying, "Sure, babe, stick them in tassels and thongs and let 'em shake their tushes all over the ground."

*Field.*

Jake could see Ella was hesitating and he shook his head at her, firmer this time. *No*, he mouthed again. Jesus! What the hell was there to prevaricate about?

He was glaring at her now and Ella felt all the bitterness from Sunday rise in her like mercury in a thermometer. She opened her mouth to say something but Jake got in first.

"I think Miss Lucas has made herself clear, Miranda," Jake said. "I don't think we should take up any more of her time."

"But" Miranda protested as Jake grabbed her elbow.

Ella narrowed her eyes. "Wait right there!" What the hell was *his* problem? Whatever it was, she was sufficiently angry with him that she was perfectly happy to sacrifice her feminist principles just to piss him off in any way she could. "I think Miranda's made some very salient points."

"Ella."

She arched an eyebrow at his clearly irritated voice. "We don't want to come across as the poor cousins or second-class citizens."

"What about Emmeline?" he asked through gritted teeth.

"I'm sure Emmeline would have approved of Miranda's daring to stand up for something she believes in."

Jake looked at her smug face and knew instantly this wasn't about a long-dead suffragette. This was about Sunday. "Yes," he agreed, "but would she approve of your actions?"

Ella gave a harsh laugh. "You really want to debate disgraceful actions?"

Jake's teeth ground together so hard he suddenly knew what it must feel like to have lock jaw. Damned if he was going to do this in front of Miranda.

Miranda was looking from one to the other, frowning. "Er, excuse me?" She broke the tense silence. "I am still here."

Ella dragged her gaze away from a grim Jake and forced herself to smile at Miranda. "I'll ring and talk to your mother this afternoon."

Miranda quirked an eyebrow. "Is that a yes?"

Ella gave a brief nod. "That's a yes."

"Oh my God. Oh my God!" Miranda turned to an immobile Jake and hugged him. She turned back to Ella and beamed. "Thank you. Thank you so much."

Ella laughed at Miranda's enthusiasm. "There are conditions."

"Name them."

"I don't want to walk around the school grounds and feel like I'm in an *Archie* comic."

Miranda furrowed her brow. "Huh?"

Ella sighed. "No beauty pageants, no popularity contests—all comers regardless of size, sex and nationality are welcome to be in if they want."

Miranda nodded. "Diversity. Check."

"The uniforms are to be modest. No short skirts, no bare bits."

Miranda nodded again. "Functional. Check."

"No sexually suggestive or male ego-stroking chants. It's about the school, okay?"

"Hanniford chants only. Check."

Ella smiled. "Alright, then. Keep me up-to-date."

"I will. I will.' Miranda grinned and then bounded out of the office.

Which left Jake and Ella glaring at each other.

Jake shook his head. "All you had to do was say no."

"This felt better," she snapped. They glared at each other for a few more moments. "Is that all?" she demanded.

Jake huffed out an irritated sigh and turned on his heel, yanking the door open. He stopped, looked back over his shoulder and contemplated talking to her about Sunday. But she was still glaring and he was too pissed off to bother so he slammed the door on his way out instead.

At least having this wall of resentment between them made keeping their professional distance easy. It also helped dampen the urge to tear her clothes off and do her on her desk.

Because, despite everything, he really, really wanted to do her on her desk.

# CHAPTER ELEVEN

Looking around the grounds of her beloved school as she sat in her very own Demons jersey nervously awaiting the referee's whistle, Ella couldn't believe what a difference six months had made.

The Hanniford oval had undergone a complete facelift. The grass was tended to lovingly by a retired groundskeeper. New undercover stands lined each side of the field. The goalposts had been replaced and the score board had been repaired and repainted and towered, pride of place, over the proceedings. All this was thanks to the hard work and fundraising efforts of the newly established P&C. Two years ago when she'd had the principal's job thrust upon her, she'd tried to get a P&C up and running, tried to engage parents, but she hadn't been able to attract a single one.

My, how things had changed.

She glanced at Jake. He was already prowling up and down the sideline like a caged beast. Even in his regulation dark glasses and baseball cap, he was all hard muscle and sleek lines. Everything he'd worked for—they'd worked for—was riding on the outcome of this match. The Hanniford Demons were battling it out with the Stafford Sabers for the last spot on the finals board. They'd come a long way and gotten here by the skin of their teeth.

They had to do it. They just *had* to.

A short, decisive trill pierced the electric hum and the crowd roared as the Sabers kicked the ball toward their goal post.

"I'm going to throw up," Ella said to Rosie.

"You say that every match," Rosie murmured, her gaze firmly glued to the action.

"Yeah, but this time I think I mean it."

"They're going to be fine, babe." Rosie turned to Ella and gave her hand a squeeze. "They're going to kick some Saber ass."

Ella looked at her friend and smiled. The change in Rosie had been rather dramatic too. Gone was the studded dog's collar and the blood red lips had been replaced with demure clear lip gloss. There was color in her wardrobe—blue jeans, some pinks, purples and oranges. The eyebrow piercing had been removed. Even her language had been cleaned up. She'd morphed into Doris bloody Day—with black hair.

Simon sat beside Rosie, his hand on her knee, his fingers drumming. She liked Simon, she really did. Rosie was in love with him and his support for the Demons had been unwavering. But Ella wasn't so sure it was good idea to change so dramatically for a man.

Another blast from the whistle brought her attention back to the game as a penalty was awarded to the Sabers. Ella buried her face in her palms. The game had been going for five minutes and already she couldn't watch. She just couldn't.

"Come on the Demons!"

Ella turned and looked behind her up into the crowded stand, witnessing another miraculous change. The Hanniford supporters, a sea of black and red complete with their signature red horn headbands, had turned out in force. As the season had progressed and the Demons had won more games, the stands had gradually filled with Hanniford families until it was a must-attend weekend event.

A lump rose in her chest as she gazed upon the entire school community packing the stands at this, their final home game. The sense of pride and accomplishment Ella felt glowed like a furnace deep inside her, warming her soul. Hanniford had finally found its mojo. And she wasn't about to let it go.

As she scanned the crowd she still couldn't believe the changes the last six months had wrought had also managed to filter through to the student body. She'd hoped that they'd win a few footy matches and save their school from closure, maybe show her students that hard work and determination could pay off. But she'd never expected this.

It seemed the entire male student population had undergone a magical transformation: every one of them had traded their awful, shaggy hairstyles for sleek number twos. It had been a gradual change to begin with, subtle, not something she'd noticed. But slowly, as the Demons had crept up the points ladder, more and more boys had joined the ranks. And, sitting here today, it was a sight to behold. She could see eyes again, faces.

And then there was the gradual decline in her truancy rate and the spring in everyone's step, from the teachers to the students. Her staff was energized and kids who used to mope around with the weight of the world on their shoulders were walking tall, smiling at her, greeting her with enthusiasm. With respect. Greeting her like she was principal of the year.

But perhaps the biggest change of all had occurred in her. For a start, she never would have believed that she'd be voluntarily spending every Saturday perched on a hard wooden seat, watching a football match—not in a million years. Six months ago, she'd have rather had root canal every

Saturday. Actually, not much had changed. In fact, she'd upgrade to electric shock therapy if it got her out of having to watch their most important game to date. She still thought football seemed ridiculously macho and kind of pointless but she couldn't deny its positive effects.

She would be forever grateful to it—to Jake—for giving her back her school.

The crowd in the stand opposite started to roar and Ella turned back to see what the excitement was about. One of the Sabers was storming toward their try line. Cameron and several Demons were hot on his heels and Ella felt like her heart was in her mouth. *Go Cam. Go Cam. Go Cam.*

Even her relationship with Cam had come a long way. Cameron was the happiest, the most settled she'd seen him since she'd dragged him out of Huntley and brought him to live with her. He attended school, he trained hard, he'd become polite and respectful. More talkative.

She knew that "close" was a ways off, but for the first time in two and a half years, Ella actually felt it was a possibility. He and Miranda, however, had become quite close, and it was encouraging at least to see that he had the capacity to form human relationships. He'd always been so distant; it was a relief to see him engaging finally.

Cameron reached out and grabbed the wiry halfback's jersey and yanked on it, wrapping the speeding Saber in a bear hug and pulling him to the ground. Everyone in the stand rose to their feet, cheering.

"Good tackle, Cam," Jake called.

Ella watched as Cameron untangled himself from the wildly kicking Saber and stood, turning to Jake with a huge grin on his face. Ella's heart lurched in her chest. He adored Jake, hero worshipped him. She owed Jake a lot. It rankled but it was the truth. Their personal stuff aside, he had helped her connect with her brother.

A scrum was being formed as Ella continued to watch, her fingers gripping the edge of the narrow wooden bench she was balancing on. It was a Hanniford feed so it was important they got it the hell away from the opposition's try line.

The Demons had the ball for ten seconds until a tricky intercept put the Sabers frighteningly close to their line again with a full six tackles to go.

Oh God! She couldn't watch.

She looked away, her gaze falling on Miranda and Hanniford's diverse cheer squad cheering on the sidelines.

*Hanniford, Hanniford we are the best*
*Better, much better, than all the rest.*
*You wanna, you wanna, put us to the test?*
*You're gonna be sad, you're gonna be sorry*
*Cos we're gonna win, don't you worry.*

Plump red and black pompoms flashed through the air as the squad shook them high above their heads. Ella had to admit, despite her initial misgivings, the squad was a credit to Miranda and Trish. A melting pot of genders and sizes and ethnicities, they had become an integral part of the Demons' matches. They entered into another chant and Ella compared them to the Sabers' cheer leaders: tiny green and yellow outfits with micro skirts, plunging necklines and green Lycra hot pants with Sabers stamped across the ass.

The Demons, boys and girls, had red cotton leotards with mandarin necklines and black cargo-style pants that ended below their knees. They all wore the red devil-ear headbands. An image in black of a devil complete with pitchfork graced the front of the leotards. "Hanniford Demons" was emblazoned beside him.

On the back of the leotard, and this was what Ella loved the most, it said, "Hanniford Demons Say No to Violence Against Women."

Even better was how the entire school, rallied by Miranda, had united to produce them. The senior textiles students had made the uniforms as part of their assessments and the art students had enthusiastically taken on the project of the leotard design from logo conception right through to the screen printing. And the P&C had paid for them.

Ella had been blown away by the way the project had been embraced by the students. Even now a lump rose in her throat thinking about how everyone had pulled together. And they looked amazing. Not cutesy-pie like the Sabers but fit and strong and, with red and black stripes slashed on each cheek, warrior-like.

Miranda had even roped Cerberus into the team spirit, making him a doggy coat with "Hanniford Demons" hand-stitched across it. And, so he wouldn't feel out of place, she'd modified a headband to give him his own pair of red horns. Jake had taken one look at Cerberus that first time and rolled his eyes. But, like a true stray, Cerberus loved the attention and when he wasn't sitting by Simon's feet, he prowled the sidelines, barking encouragement at his team.

A roar came from the Sabers' stand and Ella didn't have to look to know the opposition had just scored their first try. "Oh no," she wailed and clutched Rosie's hand.

"Don't worry," Simon said. "Plenty of time. It ain't over till the last hooter sounds."

Ella knew he was right but still her insides felt like they'd been scrunched in a tight ball and she watched the first half through the cracks of her fingers when she could bear to peek out. When the half-time siren blew, the Demons were scoreless to the Sabers' twelve. Ella went to the toilets and threw up.

When she ventured back, Pete, Jake and the team were huddled together. Seventeen sweaty teenage boys were drinking water and eating orange segments while Jake strategized, encouraged and praised in equal measure.

Ella approached. After assuring Jake she wouldn't say break a leg again, it had become a tradition for her to talk to the team at the start of the match. But she wanted them to know that no matter what happened in the second half, she was proud of them.

"Ella?"

She hated how formal it was between them now. It was for the best, she knew, drawing a definitive line through their past, both distant and recent. But it seemed impossible to believe now that he'd looked at her with such blind lust not that long ago. That he'd pushed her onto a pool table and pounded into her until she'd had burn marks on her ass.

"Don't be discouraged, guys." She gave them all a big smile, letting it linger on Cameron. "There's another forty minutes. Anything can happen. Just remember, I'm so happy that we even got this far. You've done me and Hanniford proud."

The whistle blew and the team ran back onto the ground. Miranda lead the squad in a cheer and the Hanniford crowd yelled, "Go Demons," and "Demons rule." Ella stood beside Jake and watched them get into position, her gut twisting harder.

Jake glanced down at her. "You okay?" he asked.

"Fine."

"You look like you're going to throw up."

She gave him a weak smile. "Already accomplished." There were a few moments of silence and then she asked, "They've been playing well though, haven't they?"

Jake chuckled. "How would you know that? You've been sitting there with your hands over your face."

"I can't bear to look!"

Jake nodded. "I know the feeling."

This was the most personal conversation they'd had, just the two of them, since that night. It gave her courage to say what had to be said.

"Look, Jake, I know there's some ... stuff between us—that we have our ... issues." She looked up at him, gauging his reaction but he was watching the field, his dark shades giving nothing away, the shadow from the brim of his cap throwing his face into hard-to-read lines.

"But I just want you to know that I'm more than aware you've given this your all. I know you were coerced into it and this wasn't how you planned to spend your retirement. And it's okay that we didn't make it. You gave it your best shot."

Jake removed his glasses and looked down at her. Her words were like a stiletto between his ribs. Not only had she accused him of sleeping with Rachel, she also thought the game was over.

*She'd given up.*

Jake had contemplated strangling her on many occasions over the last six months but never more than at this moment. Not even that awful morning. "Listen to me carefully. We're going to win this match. And then we're going to win the finals. And then we're going to take out the Schools Cup. I may not have wanted this in the beginning, Ella, but I'm in now. And I play to win."

Ella was captured by the blaze of conviction in his green eyes and the growl of menace in his low voice. She really, really wanted to believe him. Wanted to believe they could win.

"Jake. They're ahead by twelve points."

"Ella," he cautioned. "Have some faith." He replaced his glasses and turned his attention back to the field.

Dismissed, she returned to her seat. Trish Jones had joined Rosie and Simon and Ella smiled at her absently while she stewed on his reprimand. They'd been moving on the peripheries of each other's worlds for so long now she'd forgotten how much of an impact he had close up.

The desire to communicate with him after that fateful Sunday morning had been non-existent. So they hadn't, other than what was absolutely necessary, using a good-natured Pete as their intermediary. Their relationship had been strained at first but had moved to polite over the intervening months. Today was the first time he'd said anything of a personal nature at all.

In fact the only times she saw him these days were at the matches. Maybe an occasional glimpse around the school. He was courteous at these times and always allowed her a few minutes for her pep talk before each match but that was where it ended. She'd have to have been blind to miss the major keep out signs posted in his impersonal green gaze.

Fine with her; she'd asked him to coach her team to success and so far he was bang on target—the rest was immaterial. And if, late at night, she still woke with a throb between her thighs and an empty ache in her gut, then that was too bad. So he'd ruined her for other men—some things couldn't be forgiven.

Although her thoughts on what he'd done had mellowed somewhat. God knew she'd turned it over in her mind a thousand times. Jake had been fifteen when he left Huntley. A boy. A testosterone-driven, screw-anyone-who-said-yes teenager. And the entire town knew that Rachel was Huntley's favorite yes-woman. Most of the guys Ella had gone to school with had paid Rachel for sex—God knew they weren't going to get it any other way. Why should Jake have been any different?

Just because she'd felt some feeble connection with him back then, didn't mean he had. But she'd have bet her life on the fact that he'd felt it too. Why else would he have kissed her that night of the dance? Maybe that's what made her so mad? Okay, it hadn't been much of a kiss—much of anything, really. It certainly hadn't meant undying love or eternal fidelity. But it had meant something to her. The fact she was cut up about something that had to have happened over twenty years ago told her how much. Could the lips that had touched hers so gently, so tentatively, at that high school dance really have touched Rachel's first? Had she tutored him in how women liked to be kissed? Where they liked to be touched? All their secret places? Did she have her mother to thank for that thing Jake did?

Ella shuddered and dragged her attention back to the game. Such thoughts were futile. She'd already let them torture her enough, had already given them too much power.

Thankfully Hanniford chose that moment to score a try and thoughts of Jake and Rachel and Huntley and her screwed up personal life were completely obliterated as the crowd surged to their feet and she joined them.

She spent the next half-hour on the edge of her seat, hiding behind her fingers as the game progressed. With two minutes to go, Hanniford was trailing by four points. The crowd behind her were stomping their feet on the wooden floor of the stands and her heart thundered along in time.

Sixty seconds out, Hanniford scored a try, leveling with the Sabers, and the supporters went wild.

"So, if they convert the try, we win, right?" Ella asked Trish, trying to convince herself more than anything. Because of the comp points system, they had to win, not draw, to progress to the finals.

"That's right.' Trish grinned.

"Oh God. Tell me what happens," Ella burying her face in her hands.

Rosie gave her knee a squeeze and the sudden silence after so much noise was preternaturally eerie. Everyone held their breath as the Hanniford center lined up his kick at a very tricky angle.

"What's happening?" Ella whispered as the silence stretched.

"He's taking a moment," Trish assured. "It's a lot of pressure."

"See, it's at times like this I wish I was religious. I guess it's a bit hypocritical to pray?"

"Jesus," Rosie murmured. "Do you want the poor kid to convert the goal or be struck down by lightning?"

And then a boot sent the ball flying through the goal posts and the crowd went crazy.

"We did it?" Ella asked, rising to her feet with everyone else. "We did it."

"Yes," Rosie yelled crying and laughing all at once. 'We did it."

"Oh my God!" Ella wailed as Rosie and then Trish hugged her, "Oh my God! We did it. We did it!"

She turned to the field to see Jake and Pete running on and the team huddling together in a big group hug. "We did it," she whispered, tears filling her eyes and streaming down her face.

The boys picked Jake and Pete up and carried them off the field. The Hanniford supporters surged forward, the cheer squad swarmed around and Ella, Rosie and Simon got swallowed by the crowd, reveling in the love. Cameron gave her a bear hug that lifted her off the ground.

"We did it," he said, grinning down at her.

Ella almost fell over from the shock at such a show of affection and was glad he was still hanging on to her.

"*You* did it," she said, beaming.

# CHAPTER TWELVE

Half an hour later Jake found himself standing in a circle with Cameron, Miranda, Rosie, Simon, Pete and Ella.

"Well that does it," Rosie announced. "I'm making curry—you're all invited."

The only one of them to look enthused was Cerberus, who had grown fat on Rosie's curry treats that appeared regularly under the table from anyone who dared to sit and attempt it. He gave an ecstatic little shudder and whined appreciatively at her.

"Ah, count me out," Jake said.

Ella glanced at him and he felt the tension between them again. He hadn't set foot in their house since she'd kicked him out and she didn't look all that keen for him to do so now either.

"Oh no. No, no, no." Rosie shook her head vehemently. "It's not a celebration without the coach."

"She's right," said Pete.

"Yeah," said Cameron. "Please, coach."

"Please, Jake," Miranda said, her arm around Cameron.

Jake looked around at the eager faces knowing that part of their motivation was how much less curry they'd all have to consume with one more at the table. Ella's face, however, was carefully neutral and, today, it irritated him more than usual.

"Please, Jake," Miranda said again. She was bouncing from foot to foot like she always did when trying to suppress her excitement, and he knew he was beat. One of the women in his life was probably going to stick arsenic in his curry but he'd never been very good at saying no to the other. He gave a grudging nod. "Looks like I'm outgunned."

"Hah!" Rosie whooped triumphantly. "I've sourced this great new spice that adds that little extra zing. You're going to love it."

Jake glanced at Simon who was looking more than a little alarmed. If Rosie's curry had any more zing it'd need to be classified as a poison.

"I'll go and get it started," she grinned, and dragged Simon with her toward the car park.

"I'll stop off and buy yoghurt," Pete offered.

"Buy extra," Jake ordered.

They all nodded, despite knowing not even yoghurt was going to save them from death by curry.

*

The sun was dipping below the skyline, gilding the violet-blue with streaks of fiery tangerine as everyone sat to eat. The chatter and screech of hundreds of rainbow lorikeets drowned out the collective gasps as the first tentative nibbles had a predictable effect. Simon took a large gulp of his water and passed around the yoghurt bowl for second helpings.

"Delicious." He smiled at Rosie.

Miranda and Cameron excused themselves, taking their meals into the lounge room to play the Wii. Cerberus followed them in and Ella wondered how long it'd take before the curry found a canine host.

Daisy, a light cardigan covering her inked arms, shoveled a large spoonful of curry into her mouth. Iris, rugged up even further, tucked in heartily too. The two sisters were the only people Ella knew who could stomach Rosie's spicy food. Daisy always said growing up in a circus had given the Forsythes cast-iron constitutions.

Iris asked about the game and the conversation turned to football. "I still can't believe it," Ella said, shaking her head. A part of her was sure she was going to wake up to find it had all been a fantasy conjured up by the anxious principal that lurked just beneath the surface.

"Believe it." Pete grinned. "We did it."

"Just," she clarified. They were in last position on the finals board.

Ella had to remember that while they were another step closer to their goal, they were still a long way off. Even if they did win, they still had to go on to play in the Schools Cup. It wasn't the end, she had to remind herself. But it was the end of the beginning.

Pete shook his head. "Doesn't matter. We wipe the slate clean now and start all over again."

Ella wanted to hug him. His glass-half-full optimism was just what she needed. Jake, on the other hand, sitting opposite her brooding into his curry, was not instilling confidence at all. He was in his pub clothes—jeans and a black T-shirt—ready to skedaddle off to work at the first opportunity. The shirt, as usual, showed off his magnificent biceps and she wondered absently if he was cold. Not that it was remotely possible for any of them to be so at the moment. The heat from the thermonuclear reaction of the curry was likely to keep them warm to the end of their days. Ella wondered if Rosie secretly laced it with plutonium. Maybe she should get Iris and Daisy to see if they could win a Geiger counter; the last thing this place needed was glow-in-the-dark residents.

The neighbours thought there were enough freaks at number twenty as it was.

"But we go in as underdogs," Rosie pointed out.

Simon shrugged. "That can work in our favor."

"What do the cards say, Iris?" Pete asked.

Iris jumped like a small animal caught in the headlights of a very large all-terrain vehicle. After a moment of everyone looking at her expectantly, she put down her fork, moved her bowl aside, shuffled the worn, ever-present pack and laid out a twelve-card spread. She pursed her lips.

"The cards are favorable," she murmured. Then she tsked. "But it's going to come at a cost." She gave an involuntary shudder.

Ella knew Iris and Daisy had been worried for months now. Between the screws being turned by the council and the developer hounding them with offers, they'd been earnestly searching for answers in the cards. None of the answers had satisfied them. And the mysterious dreams of yellow gold still taunted Iris her with their elusive meaning.

Ella knew deep down that Iris's unease came from a gut feeling that was far from frivolous and she felt a corresponding itch up her spine. She trusted Iris's intuition—she'd trust it with her life. As someone who drew the eight of swords on a freakishly regular basis, Ella the math geek had learned that there were some things you just couldn't quantify. But for now she chose to latch onto Iris's statement about the cards being favorable.

"You should both come to watch the final matches," Pete said to Daisy and Iris. "The Demons need all the support we can muster."

Daisy cackled. "I'm sure Cam would love that, his two freaky old pseudo aunts showing up."

"We could rustle you up some jerseys, couldn't we, Jake?"

Jake nodded and took a long gulp of his frosty beer. "Sure."

Iris shook her head. "Can't."

"We need to stay put," Daisy elaborated. "The council is sending around some inspector."

"What the fuck?" Rosie interjected. She saw Simon's mid-eyebrow crinkle and ignored it. "Why didn't you tell us? What now?"

Iris and Daisy traded a look. "It's nothing. They say they've had complaints about the structural integrity of the house. They claim it may not be safe for habitation." Daisy waved a dismissive hand. "They're clutching at straws."

Ella wasn't so sure about that. In the years she'd been living here the house had become more saggy; the floorboards shifted alarmingly and the kitchen seemed to sink a little each year. The house was always needing something repaired—a leaking roof, recalcitrant plumbing, dodgy wiring—which they could keep up with, but major renovations were beyond them, financially. The double mortgage was crippling even with two incomes. A prickle of alarm burst the precarious bubble that had formed around her since the big win. First her school and now this. What on earth had she done to the universe to bring two such ugly threats down on their heads?

"That's harassment," Rosie fumed. She turned to Simon. "Can't you do something about this?"

Simon, who'd been surreptitiously feeding a returned Cerberus, looked at her, alarmed. "Rosie …"

"Your father works for the mayor, for God's sake! You must be able to pull some strings."

Simon looked at her. Rosie had come to mean so much to him. But he couldn't compromise his integrity. He just couldn't. "Rosie … I can't … everything my father does has to be above board. Above reproach."

He squirmed in his seat a little. He'd never hated being a part of a high profile family more. But being raised in a political dynasty and, in particular, by a scandal-phobic mother, had entrenched certain absolutes.

"Some journo would find out and the papers would have a field day." Not to mention his mother breaking out in hives. "My father could lose his job. Not to mention any whiff of impropriety could be used against me in the future."

Rosie could see that she'd put Simon on the spot and felt immediately guilty. "Sorry," she said, putting her hand on his sleeve. The sensual side of her, seduced by the softness of his cashmere knit, overruled the carnie chick who was demanding Simon man up.

Simon gave her a gentle smile. He knew how much her aunts, this crazy old house meant to her. "Do you think they have a case?" he asked Daisy.

"Well, it can't be denied, the house could do with some work."

Jake glanced at Ella. "I take it there's no money to fix what needs to be fixed?"

Iris shook her head. "We stopped taking in boarders when the girls arrived. The house has been mortgaged twice since. Thank the stars for Ella and Rosie. They pay that."

Ella rolled her eyes. "The only reason you have it is because of us." The way she saw it, she owed them big time.

Iris waved her suggestion away. "That's only part of the reason. Don't forget little Stevie's treatment cost a bomb and anyway, you both needed an education."

Simon frowned. "What about the competitions? If you don't mind me saying, you ladies are extraordinarily lucky. Why don't you enter some money-based ones?"

Iris, whose attention had been snagged by Cerberus scratching at the patch under the wattle tree again, snapped her head back, looking at Simon as if he'd just sacrificed a lorikeet at the table.

"We never enter cash comps," she said, utterly scandalised. "It's very bad karma. Very bad." She picked up the deck and rubbed the top one with her thumbs. "We don't want for anything. We have a roof over our head and food in our bellies. We only enter the competitions the cards tell us to."

Simon blinked. The cards told them to enter for twelve refrigerators, five big screen televisions, hundreds of clocks and three sets of ceramic flying ducks? "Maybe if you entered some car comps? Then you could sell them?"

Daisy's brow wrinkled. "But we don't drive."

Rosie gave his thigh a squeeze beneath the table. She knew better than anyone that her aunt's logic was more mystical than practical. "So when are we expecting these council dudes?" she asked.

Daisy shrugged. "They don't tell you. But we're going to be here when they do. If they're going to erect razor wire and keep out signs, they've got to drag us out kicking and screaming first."

"It won't come to that," Ella said vehemently. "I promise. If we can save a school ..." She glanced at Jake and saw him watching her with his steady green gaze. She couldn't have done it without him. "We can save a house."

*

Half an hour later Jake stood to leave. He didn't want to, he was enjoying himself too much. The company was great, laughter flowed. Daisy had put on an old Ella Fitzgerald record and now the colorful parrots flown away for the night it was just "Mack the Knife" and the crickets. It was decidedly mellow. After three beers, the mood fit the buzz quite nicely.

But Ella hadn't stopped chewing on her damn lip and it was driving him nuts. Her hair was loose, her skivvy tight. Just because he was still pissed at her didn't mean he didn't want to take that bottom lip between his own teeth and devour it.

Libido had no pride.

He needed to get the hell away. He made his goodbyes nodding to Ella as he left.

"Wait up. I'll see you out," she said.

Jake stiffened a little, giving a mighty internal groan before gesturing for her to precede him. Her bottom swayed all the way up the hallway in front of him. The same bottom he dreamed about—soft and smooth beneath his hands in this very house. Dragging his thoughts back, he called goodbye to Cameron and Miranda.

Ella flipped off the sensor light on her way out the door and they walked to the front gate. The night was darker beneath the loom of the towering poincianas. There were things to say and she didn't want to say them in the full glare of the spotlight. Jake stopped at the gate and she knew he was waiting for her to say something.

Jake could hear the faint strains of "A Fine Romance" reaching around to them from the back of the house. He had the craziest urge to take her in his arms and waltz her along the darkened path. He curled his fingers into fists. "Ella Fitzgerald, huh?"

Ella nodded. "They play it for me. They know Rachel named me after her, that she was a huge fan."

It was on the tip of Jake's tongue to tell her he knew. How many times had he been to Rachel's while Ms. Fitzgerald crooned the blues? But given what had happened last time he'd mentioned being at the house, he didn't feel so inspired.

"You didn't have to walk me out."

Ella gathered her wits. His voice was low in the quiet shadows and he smelled just like she remembered. "I know. I just wanted to say … thank you. I didn't get a chance to say it after the match."

Jake nodded. "There was a bit of a crush."

"Well ... thank you. You don't know how much this means to me."

Jake paused for a moment. "Oh, I think I do." If he hadn't before, he did after tonight.

Ella glanced at him. His face was in complete shadow making him look even more forbidding than he had in the previous months. But there was something else she needed to tell him. "I also wanted to say that I'm okay with the ... you know ... the Rachel thing. It was a shock ... I never thought ... Anyway. You were a teenager and ... that's what teenage boys in Huntley did."

Ella was surprised, even years later how much the knowledge still hurt. Trying to reconcile the woman who had danced with her to the dulcet strains of Blue Moon when she'd been little to the woman the town knew her as, was a conundrum she'd never really wrapped her head around.

Jake stiffened, even more insulted now than he'd been six months ago. He looked down at her for the longest time before reaching for the gate. "Goodnight, Ella."

*

As if Ella's mood wasn't flat enough, Bernie delivered another yellow envelope to her on Monday morning. Her fingers shook as they opened it and she took a deep breath before unfolding the single white page.

*Dear Ms Lucas—blah blah. We note your numbers have dropped by a further six—blah blah. You need to present to Education HQ in two weeks—blah blah. Show cause as to why Hanniford shouldn't be shut at the end of the year. Blah, blah, blah, blah.*

Ella's heart thundered in her chest. No praise for her vastly improved truancy figures. No mention that the reason her numbers had dropped was that two of her families had parents who were in the armed forces and had moved to another post.

Before she could fully think it through she lifted the phone. "Bernie, can you find me a number for the *Western Suburbs Post* please."

She'd promised Jake no press but this was just a local free paper, not big enough to make a fuss though popular with the locals. It was time to tap the fledgling support the Demons had birthed and get the wider community involved.

It was time to go public.

# CHAPTER THIRTEEN

As soon as the *Western Suburbs Post* was delivered to the school on Wednesday morning, Bernie brought it through to her. The first period bell had gone and Ella was sitting at her desk relishing the peace.

"I think you're gonna love this." He smiled, holding it up to reveal the front page headline.

THE LITTLE SCHOOL THAT COULD said the bold black type and then under it in smaller print but still readable from across the room—EDUCATION DEPT THREATENS TO SHUT DOWN LOCAL SCHOOL.

"Front page?" Ella practically leaped off the chair. "Oh my God! Much better than I hoped for."

Ella took the paper from Bernie and he departed. Her hand trembled a little as she cleared a space in front of her and laid it flat. A large picture of the jubilant team carrying Jake and Pete off the field with the Hanniford High scoreboard in the background dominated the article. Ella smiled again at the memory.

She devoured the article which spilled over to page three. Suzy Barton, the young reporter who had obviously seen *All The President's Men* a little too often had been most eager to listen to what Ella had to say. Given that she probably spent her time covering the fluffy bunny stories Ella was happy to play Deep Throat to her Bernstein.

*Whatever rallied the local community worked for her.*

And it was a very good, very comprehensive article. Everything she'd discussed with Suzy was there. The Education Department's threats to close the struggling school and the desperate measures Hanniford High was employing to stay open. The BSFC bid was outlined succinctly with a great summary of all the Demons' successes concluding with Saturday's win.

Suzy Barton went on to trumpet Ella's coup in landing Jake Prince as the coach, mentioning that they'd gone to school together. She also raved about the school spirit and how the cheer squad, tutored by Trish Jones, herself once a professional cheerleader, had become a whole school project, applauding their anti-violence message. There were also mentions of Cam and Miranda, to demonstrate how Hanniford High was one big family and praise for Ella herself, for leading the charge and standing up to the Man.

The piece ended with a diatribe on heartless beaurocrats who were ripping the soul out of a severely depressed socioeconomic area to pinch a few pennies. Phrases such as "denying poor kids access to free education" and "discrimination" leaped off the page.

It was exactly what Ella hoped it would be: a stirring piece of journalism to inspire even the most apathetic in the community to rally to the cause. She made a mental note to nominate Suzy Barton for a Pulitzer Prize—or whatever the Australian equivalent was.

It may not be Watergate but Ella hoped it'd have Donald Wiseman on the run. Or silenced, at least.

She leaned back in her chair, reveling in the buzz of a job well done, until a loud knock on her door startled her out of the glow. Before she could open her mouth to say come in, the door was flung open and Jake strode in to her office.

"What," he asked, holding up the paper, "the hell is this?"

Ella blinked and the glow disappeared like a genie in a puff of smoke. Damn it! Sadly she'd had post-coital moments that hadn't been this good, so she'd been hoping to prolong it.

Needless to say his interruption was irritating in the extreme. She raised an eyebrow and then made a point of looking at her watch.

"Good morning to you too, Jake. Bit early for you, isn't it?"

"I run a pub," he snapped. "You know, in my real life? I don't get home until three a.m. So imagine my annoyance when Pete bashed on my door at eight this morning." He slammed his copy of the paper on top of hers. "Didn't I say no press?"

Ella stood. "Yes, I know you did but—"

Jake gave a loud snort, raking a hand through his hair. "Damn it, Ella, I think I was fairly specific."

"The department's demanding I show cause. I just thought this might drum up some support."

"I don't care what you thought," he roared.

Ella glared at him. "Look, Jake, I know you didn't want any media attention drawn to you, that you wanted to stay anonymous, but I think you're overreacting here."

Jake closed his eyes and pressed his thumb and forefinger hard against them. He dropped his hand and opened his eyes. "Overreacting? You don't have a clue, do you?" he yelled.

"It's only the local rag, Jake. It's hardly *The Age*."

Jake gave another snort, stalking over to the window. He slapped his palm hard and high against the frame. "There's no such thing as local, Ella, especially not now with the internet. People will bloody blog and tweet about it, for fuck's sake. Every national paper, every TV station and radio station will see this story—they pay people to comb independent newspapers looking for juicy stories."

Ella secretly perked up. Some local radio would help spread the word a little further. And if their story went national? And they won the grand final? Surely they wouldn't dare shut Hanniford down if that happened?

"Your name's barely mentioned," she rationalized. "You can't even tell it's you or Pete in the picture."

Jake took two steps toward her desk, flipped the paper over and stabbed his finger at the photo of himself gracing the back page. "Wrong."

Ella gawked at the headline: THE PRODIGAL PRINCE. The back page as well—Suzy had outdone herself. In this shot, Jake was in the foreground in his Demons jersey, standing arms crossed on the sidelines. Not even his dark glasses and baseball cap disguised his enigmatic presence.

On the bench in the background were Trish Jones and herself, their blank gazes that appeared to be locked with the camera were actually glued to the action. And beside them, Rosie and Simon, ignoring the game totally, pashing like two horny teenagers who had been grounded for a week. Even Cerberus had been captured in his Demons coat and horns.

She shrugged. "It's just the back page, Jake. No one reads the back page."

Jake thumped his fist down on her desk. "I bloody did. And here's a newsflash, Ella, so do a lot of other people. It's only you who considers sports beneath her dignity." He glared at her for a moment. "Where were you hiding him anyway?"

Ella frowned. "Hiding who?"

"The photographer."

Ella folded her arms. "I wasn't hiding anyone," she snapped. "The reporter who interviewed me made arrangements to send someone to take some shots of you and the guys training on Monday but then she rang to say that, coincidentally, their sports photographer had snapped some pics at the match on Saturday and they were going to use them."

Jake rubbed the nape of his neck a few times. He must be getting old. He hadn't seen anyone with a telephoto lens on Saturday. A couple of years ago he'd been able to sniff out a cameraman or a journo from a hundred paces. But then he had been quite preoccupied with trying to win a match.

Maybe some time out of the spotlight had made him complacent, had lowered his guard. Not that this was about him. Rekindling interest in his messy exit from football was nothing compared with the story he'd managed to keep under wraps for almost two decades.

*Until now anyway.*

He shook his head, his temper barely suppressed. "You have no idea what you've done."

Ella rolled her eyes. "Oh please. Do you really think anyone cares about a washed-up footballer? I mean, really?"

Jake's jaw clenched. He had the sudden urge to pull her over his knee and smack her backside. Who did she think she was to be playing God with other people's lives? And then a really ugly thought wormed its way into his head.

"Oh my God. You did this on purpose. You did this to get back at me for Rachel."

Ella blinked, Jake's statement momentarily stunning her. "Don't be ridiculous, Jake. How could you even think that of me?"

"Yeah. Ironic, isn't it?"

Ella snorted. "More like moronic."

Jake took a step closer and leaned over the desk. "Listen up," he growled. "I'm only going to say this once. I. Did. Not. Sleep. With. Rachel."

He retreated into the chair behind him, resting his elbows on his knees, and looked up at her. "My father was one of her clients. Sometimes he was too drunk to get home and Rachel would ring the pub and I would go and pick him up. That's how I knew about the damn vases."

Ella stared at him, his fervent denial and explanation seeping into the cracks of her frozen gray matter. *He hadn't slept with Rachel.* She sank into the chair behind her. He looked part pissed off, part exasperated, and tired as hell. "You didn't—"

"No," he said tersely.

And she believed him, his face a picture of absolute honesty. "Why didn't you say something?" she demanded.

"Maybe I hoped you'd had a better opinion of me?"

Guilt bloomed in Ella's chest. "I'm sorry, I—"

"Forget it," he dismissed.

"But—"

"Jesus, Ella." He stood. "It doesn't matter. Not compared to this mess."

Her phone rang and Ella was grateful for the reprieve from his accusatory stare. "Yes, Bernie?"

Jake crossed his arms as he watched Ella murmur into the phone, smiling.

"The phones are ringing off the hook," she said, replacing the receiver. "Some radio station wants to talk to me."

Jake nodded. *And so it begins.* There was only one way he could think of to put the genie back in the bottle. Or at least take the heat off him and make the story be about Hanniford. "I quit."

Ella shot to her feet. "What?"

"Hey," Jake snapped pointing at her. "I told you I'd walk if the press became involved."

Ella couldn't believe what she was hearing. "You can't do this to the team."

Jake rubbed his eyes. "They have Pete. They'll be fine."

Ella walked around the desk and stood directly in front of him. "It's not Pete they're doing this for. It's you." She poked him in the chest. "They look up to you." Another poke. "You can't walk out on them now. Not when they have the finals to go. You'll devastate them."

"Well, maybe you should have thought about that when you went to the press." Jake turned to the door.

"Oh no. No, you don't," Ella snapped. "You're not putting your desertion on me."

He stopped. "I knew this was going to be trouble. Right from the beginning. I just knew it."

God, he sounded like Iris now. "Jake, please." She put her hand on his shoulder and he reluctantly turned to face her. "Look, I'm sorry about thinking the worst of you and I'm sorry I took this to the media. But you can't just walk away. You made these kids believe in you. Kids who didn't believe in anything. The whole school believes in you. Don't walk out on them when the going gets tough like every other adult in their life has."

Jake hadn't thought it possible to feel worse than when he'd read that headline this morning. He'd been wrong. "Go and do your radio, Ella. Milk the publicity for all it's worth. Just leave me out of it, okay?"

He turned, opened the door and walked out.

Ella reached out and laid her hand against the door, her heart drumming wildly, her chest rising and falling, as agitated as the rest of her.

What had she done?

*

Ella was on the oval as soon as the final bell sounded. It had been a busy day. She'd done a couple of talk-back radio slots and a journo from *The Courier Mail* had interviewed her. The photographer was due to show any moment. She'd avoided Jake's name as he'd requested but it did seem to be the one thing they were the most interested in.

Only Pete was there when she arrived. The knot of nerves in her belly tangled tighter. She couldn't believe Jake was serious. Surely he wouldn't pull out on them? He was mad, she understood that, but he wouldn't do something so damaging, would he?

"Ella." Pete nodded.

She smiled at him and forced herself to be light. "Jake running late?"

Pete returned her smile with a grim one of his own. "He's not coming, Ella."

Ella heard the tenderness in his tone and knew he was trying to let her down gently. She nodded. "He'll be here. Tomorrow," she said. "After he's had a chance to calm down."

"He's pretty pissed. I think Chernobyl's nuclear reactor has a greater chance of cooling down before Jake does."

"He can't just walk out on the team, Pete," she said. "Can you talk to him?" she asked. "Please?"

"If I thought it would make a difference, Ella, I would. But he won't listen to me. I'm sorry."

When the Heroes had asked him to go quietly and resign from professional football, Jake had stubbornly refused, forcing them to sack him. Forcing them to publically defend the transparency of their decision. Jake Prince could be one bloody-minded son-of-a-bitch.

Ella could see the honesty in Pete's gaze and swallowed a lump in her throat. Damn Jake to hell.

"It's okay," she said, patting Pete on the arm. "He'll be back tomorrow. Just do me a favor? Tell the team he's not well and he'll see them tomorrow."

"What happens when he doesn't show?"

"He will," she said with a confidence that was only wafer thin.

\*

Thursday was as crazy as Wednesday. Crazier. The phones ran hot. Everyone wanted a piece of her. The community was getting together a petition. A letter-writing campaign to the state member and the Education Department was being organized. And the cherry on top came in the form of Donald Wiseman from the education review panel ringing to express his displeasure at the negative press she was generating for the department.

Ella embraced all comers, grateful for something to occupy her mind, to keep it off this afternoon's practice session. Would he be there? She wished she could be sure. He hadn't returned any of the umpteen messages she'd left on his mobile since yesterday afternoon. She'd barely slept for fretting about it. Was it possible to develop an ulcer overnight?

A last-minute phone call kept her from being early to the oval and she arrived with the rest of the team to find Jake was another no show. The boys looked around, searching for him.

"Coach still sick, Pete?" Cameron asked.

Pete looked at Ella and she gave him a slight nod. "Yep. You know these old blokes. Can't keep up. He asked me to work you guys extra hard though."

The team grumbled but hit the oval for their warm-ups in good spirits. "Thanks, Pete," Ella said.

"They're going to have to know sooner or later," he warned.

Ella chewed on her bottom lip. "I know. I know. Did he tell you he wasn't coming?"

Pete shrugged. "Couldn't get hold of him. He hasn't been in to work either."

"At least the finals comp doesn't start for a few weeks," Ella murmured. Last week the thought of prolonging the final series even by a day had been pure torture. Today Ella was prepared to get on her knees and praise the football gods.

Her life had officially gone to hell.

"What's his problem, Pete?" she demanded, watching the Demons go about their drills. "Why's he so damn media shy? His face was on practically every tabloid and magazine in the known universe during his career. He picked a really bad time to do a Howard Hughes on me."

Pete shook his head. "It's not really my place to say, Ella. I think it should come from Jake."

There was a strange note in Pete's voice and he was looking at her like she'd just dropped one hundred IQ points. But if he thought she was going to go crawling to Jake for an explanation then he had another thing coming. Not when she could consult a far greater authority. All hail the great god Google.

# CHAPTER FOURTEEN

Rosie, dressed in demure grey skirt, pink blouse and kitten heels, didn't even stop to pat the dogs as she flew up the front steps and followed the smoke plume around the verandah.

"I knew it. I knew it," Iris said to her, holding out an official-looking envelope. "It's all coming to a head. Jupiter's in retrograde."

Rosie, who had received an urgent phone call from Daisy at three o'clock, snatched the offending letter off the table and sped through the official jargon.

"Those fuckers," she said, flopping into the nearest chair as if she'd been hit with a taser.

"They were so smug when they left here yesterday," Daisy muttered, pouring Iris and herself a healthy splash of sherry.

"A week? A week to address all these things?" Rosie pressed her coral-coated lips together as she read down the list. It was extensive. God, they were living in a death trap.

Iris nodded. "Or they'll condemn the house."

"Evicting us in the process." Daisy took a swig of her drink.

A lot of the things wouldn't require much money or effort but a full re-stumping was major. "They can't do this to us," Rosie wailed. "This is our home."

"They're evicting us over my cold, dead body," Daisy muttered, draining her mug. "Might be time to bring out the old 303."

Rosie looked at her eldest aunt in alarm. "We have a gun?"

"Course."

"And you know how to shoot it?"

"Of course I know how to shoot it. I'll have you know I hold a duck-shooting record."

"Daisy," Iris said softly, worrying the back of her cards with her thumbs. "Metal ducks do not count." She turned and looked at Rosie. "There'll be no more talk of guns."

Rosie glanced at a suitably chastised Daisy. Iris may be the flaky one but when she stepped up to the mark, no one disobeyed her. She looked down at the letter in utter disbelief. Ella was going to be devastated. If it was possible, her best friend was more attached to this old house then any of them. And Ella certainly had enough to worry about without having to plug one more hole.

The dogs, who'd been lying at the women's feet, perked up their ears and then lumbered off in a pack, racing around the side of the verandah, barking like the Dementors had arrived at their door. Even Cerberus, who was investigating his favorite spot under the wattle tree, joined them.

A voice floated around to them. "Rosie?"

"Simon?"

She leaped up from her seat and raced around the verandah, meeting him halfway and throwing herself into his arms. Everything felt better when he held her close. The dogs mulled around for a bit and Cerberus even scored a scratch behind the ears before they decided no food would be forthcoming.

"Hey," Simon said as he prised her arms from their boa-like hold on his neck. "What on earth's the matter?"

Rosie's hands moved to his shirt. The fabric was rich beneath her fingers, like a tapestry. Had it been sheets, it would have had a thread count. "You didn't get my message?"

"No, I rang your extension to chat and they said you'd already left for the day." He shrugged. "I wanted to see you."

Rosie gave him a hug, burying her face in his collar, which was stiff with starch.

Simon held her for a while longer. "What's up, Rosie?"

She pulled back from him slightly, her fingers finding the perfect Windsor knot of his beautiful tie. It felt luxurious, like she was stroking a silk worm.

"Daisy and Iris got a letter from the council with a list of repairs to attend to in seven days or they're going to chuck us out of our home."

"Ah. I see."

Rosie pushed out of his arms and leaned against the railing. It wobbled a little and she eased some of her weight away. "How can they do this to us?" she asked him.

He shook his head. "I don't know."

Rosie started to pace. "There has to be a way though. There just has to be."

"What about heritage listing?" Simon asked. "How old did you say this place was?"

"Nah, the previous owner apparently looked into it years ago. The place wasn't old enough or of significant enough historical importance."

"Rosie." Simon took a step toward her, placing his hands on her waist. "Have you ever just thought of … selling? The developer is offering good money. Your aunts could live in the lap of luxury."

Rosie couldn't believe what she was hearing. Sell up? *Sell out?* Was he serious?

"It's a viable option," he pressed.

Rosie shook her head. She wiggled her hips so his hands fell away. "These four walls, those two old ladies, Ella, Cam—they're my home, Simon."

She could see the vacant look in his eyes and knew that to Simon, a guy who lived in the family mansion by the river purely because of its convenience would never get her almost pathological attachment to this run-down old house. Never had she felt the gap between them yawn wider but it was suddenly vitally important that he understand.

Rosie hugged herself. "I never had a home—not one that wasn't mobile anyway. I was dragged from pillar to post all my life. Three or four months in one spot, trying to fit in at another school with the same old bunch of stereotypical kids where I was the freaky carnie chick. An outsider. And then we'd be rolling again.

"What'd I have to look forward to? My dad's biggest ambition for me was to inherit his hoop stand. And hey, maybe if I got knocked up by the greasy Bartlett kid I'd inherit the carousel as well. And Ella? Sure, she had a house but she'd never had a home—a place where the people in it made her the number one priority in their lives.

"This place has been our sanctuary. Daisy and Iris have been our saviors, a couple of old spinsters throwing their home open to two teenagers, feeding us, educating us, encouraging us to reach for the stars." Rosie gave him an imploring look. "You can't put a price on that, Simon. And if you think you can, then you're not the man I thought you were."

Simon held up his hands in surrender. "Okay, okay," he said, then rested his hands on his hips.

She watched as his shirt pulled enticingly across his flat abdomen and wished she was pressed against him. She took a step toward him. "What about the media?" she asked.

"Oh, whoa there." Simon took a step back. His mother would have a cow. He still hadn't stopped hearing about the damn picture of them kissing at the footy final. Geraldine did not approve of public displays of affection. Or having the family name dragged into a media scrum. "I think that's a bad idea."

"For who? You? Your mother?"

Simon massaged his temples. "Rosie, please ... I know she's paranoid but she never really got over the scandal that ousted her father."

Somewhere in the back of her mind, Rosie was thinking that the filthy old Tory shouldn't have been sticking his dick in everything with a pulse but her gut was tumbling as the bottom fell out of her world and it just didn't seem important. Not when Simon was choosing his family over her. The thing with going out with seven-foot bearded bikers was that she really hadn't expected anything lasting from any of them. She certainly hadn't expected the finer qualities like loyalty and integrity. But Simon, with his suits and his pedigree? She'd been building a whole future in her head with him. Being without Simon was going to hurt more than all her break-ups combined.

"Fine."

Simon watched her stiffen and visibly withdraw from him. He took a step back towards her. "Rosie."

She held out her hands, warding him off. This was her line in the sand. If he couldn't understand that then there wasn't a future for them. A pain tore through her chest as her heart broke in two. "Just go, Simon."

"Don't do this."

"Why not? I was a fool to think it would ever work in the first place. That I could ever fit in to your world."

Simon ruffled his hair. "I thought you were okay with that."

"I was." *And then I grew some self respect.* "But I'm losing myself. Look at me," she said, inspecting her god-awful blouse. "I'm dressed in *pink*, for fuck's sake."

"I never asked you to change," he said quietly.

"Yeh, but you never said, *don't* change, did you? You never said, babe, what the hell are you doing in that Jackie O shit?" She watched his brow crease. "And you can stop frowning at me. I say fuck—get over it."

Simon ignored the profanity. "But you look beautiful."

Rosie felt a white-hot rage start to broil her stomach juices. It seeped acidic loathing through her system like a faulty nuclear core leaking radioactive waste. Her fingers went to her buttons and before she knew it, she was undoing them.

"I look like fricking June Dally-Watkins," she hissed, peeling the blouse off and throwing it on the ground.

"Okay," he said calmly. Even though he didn't feel it. His heart thumped painfully as the direction of this conversation slowly dawned. Rosie was ending it. Even the thought made him catch his breath.

She kicked off her kitten heels. "This is not me. I'm the freaky Goth chick. I wear black. I have my eyebrow pierced. That's who I am. And I don't want to be looking over my shoulder every time I kiss you in public in case we cause some *scandal.* So just turn around now and walk away—I have a house to save."

Rosie didn't give him time to comply. She couldn't bear to see him go. She turned on her heel and marched in the opposite direction, tears stinging her eyes, tears of loss and lament that came from the depths of her soul. Turning her back on Simon was the most difficult thing she'd ever done. And she wanted to be mad at him—at the world, at his mother, at his philandering, long-dead grandfather. But she couldn't, because the further away she walked, the more she knew she only had herself to blame. He was right, he'd never asked her to change. She'd done so voluntarily. It had been her choice. And if she was angry with anyone, then it should be herself.

She returned to Daisy and Iris in her skirt and bra, her hands shaking, blinking back tears, refusing them an outlet. She'd been stupid—she wouldn't compound it with a fit of girly tears. Not yet anyway.

"What happened to your shirt?" Daisy asked after a moment.

"I got rid of it."

Daisy poured a slug of sherry into her glass and handed it to Rosie. "Thank God for that. It was hideous."

Rosie smiled and flung the contents of the glass down her throat. It burned but at least it made her feel alive inside, not like a part of her had just died.

"Do we own phone books?" Rosie asked.

"Under the pot plant in the hallway," Daisy confirmed. "Who are you ringing?"

"A journalist. Any journalist. Surely there's a story in this?"

Rosie stormed into the house. Iris shot Daisy a worried look as she reached for the smooth comfort of her tarot deck.

*

When Ella arrived an hour later, her head and heart heavy with the information she'd gleaned about Jake with just a few easy clicks, the three Forsythe women were on their third sherry. Daisy took one look at Ella's face and poured a decent slug into a clean mug for her.

"You look like you could do with this," she said.

Ella nodded, taking her inclusion into the Forsythe family for granted. These women may not be her blood but they'd opened their doors and their hearts to her unconditionally, and Ella had felt loved and accepted from the moment she and Rosie had walked through the front gate of this creaky old home.

She looked out over the backyard, still a little dazed from what she'd learned. A riot of fluffy yellow buds caught her eye, the middle wattle still flowering despite the advanced season and the decline of the blossom on the other trees. Cerberus was, as usual, firmly ensconced beneath the yellow-speckled, silvery-green canopy.

"Are you okay, Ella?"

She dragged her gaze from the colorful display to Rosie—a red-eyed Rosie. A dressed in black again, red-eyed Rosie. It was just the impetus she needed to snap out of her inertia. "Oh my God." She reached across and grabbed for Rosie's hand. "Are *you* okay?" Rosie shook her head. "What happened?"

Rosie filled Ella in on all the sordid details. "I'm so sorry," Ella murmured when Rosie finally ran out of steam, pulling her dearest friend close for a hug.

"He's a fool," Daisy muttered, not so quietly.

Iris nodded. "The cards don't lie."

Rosie sniffled as she shook her head and pulled out of the embrace. "No, I'm the fool. But it's okay," she said. "I'll be okay."

Ella squeezed her friend's hand. "Of course you will. You've got us, right?"

"All of us," Daisy said gruffly.

Rosie smiled. "Right." And let Ella hug her again. She pulled away a moment later, blinking back tears. "Enough about me, why are you here and not at practice?"

Ella looked back at the wattles, suddenly not able to look any of them in the eye. Where did she even start? "Jake's quit and it's all my fault."

Daisy glanced at Iris and topped up everyone's drinks.

Rosie reached out and squeezed Ella's hand. "Jake wasn't impressed with the media coverage?"

Ella gave a half-laugh, half-snort as she pulled her gaze back to the three women watching her, ready to dispense their special brand of tea and sympathy. Well, sherry and sympathy, anyway.

She shook her head. "That's putting it mildly. And I couldn't figure out why someone who's had his picture in the paper more often than bloody Princess Di would be so rabidly media shy. Then I Googled him."

"Ooh, that doesn't sound good," Rosie murmured.

Ella gave her friend a grim look. "It seems he was involved in a rape case a couple of years back."

Rosie gasped. "Jake raped someone?"

"No," Daisy interrupted, "Tony Winchester did."

Ella blinked. "You knew?"

Daisy nodded at all the newspapers strewn around the table, great holes hacked into their pages. "We don't just cut competitions out of these, you know?"

"Why didn't you say something?" Ella asked.

Daisy, ever the spokesperson, shrugged. "Wasn't any of our business."

"Who's Tony Winchester?" Rosie butted in.

Ella shook her head to clear it of the exasperation that had formed. She looked at Rosie. "A guy. A footballer. Used to be a teammate of Jake's when he played for a Sydney club. He was accused of raping this woman and protested his innocence, then Jake came forward to say that he had evidence that Tony had raped another woman eighteen years ago when they were both playing for the Seals."

Rosie whistled. "Wow. Gutsy."

Ella nodded. "But his evidence was disallowed because Jake refused to name the first woman."

Rosie leaned forward. "What happened to Tony Winchester?"

"He pleaded to some watered-down charge, got a good behavior bond. He's some hot-shot NRL commentator now."

"And the Heroes sacked Jake," Daisy said, completing the story.

Ella looked at her. "It sure would have been handy to know."

Daisy shrugged again as she lit a rollie. "You spend your life as a circus freak being judged and misunderstood by everyone outside of that world you soon learn not to judge others."

"I'm not talking about judging him," Ella said testily. "A heads up would have been nice."

"It's Jake's story to tell," Iris said, intervening in her quiet yet commanding way.

Ella felt her exasperation boil over. She opened her mouth to protest but knew it was futile. Daisy and Iris had always kept their own counsel; it was just their way. Even if asked directly they were cautious in their opinions but otherwise they accepted the way things were. Like Rosie turning into Ita Buttrose. And Ella's inept attempts at raising Cam.

And after coming from a small town where nobody could keep their mouths shut and everything you did and said and everywhere you went was gossiped about and judged, Daisy's and Iris's quiet support had been a welcome relief for Ella. It was a bit rich to chafe against it now.

"I know," Ella sighed. "I'm sorry."

There was a moment's silence where Ella stared morosely into her drink, Rosie drummed her fingers on the table and the aunts smoked.

Daisy squinted at Ella through the haze. "Something arrived for you today," she said, jerking her head sideways to indicate the television cabinet.

Ella turned, her gaze falling on the long, cylindrical package, knowing instantly what it was. She leaped up, pleased for the distraction, tearing open the lid. Nestled in tissue paper inside was a bronzed glittery kewpie doll head. She pulled it out, revealing the full fairy perched atop its bamboo stick.

Ella smiled as the golden, glitter-encrusted bodice caught the rays of the slanting afternoon sun. She twisted it around, the bright golden wings and yellow tulle tutu sparkling as if they'd been impregnated with drops of diamond dust.

It was perfectly, awfully, garish. "I love it," Ella said, and beamed.

"It's from old Uncle Clem," Daisy said. "They got a new batch in and he didn't think you had a gold one yet." Uncle Clem was in his eighties, dentally challenged and partially deaf from running the dodgems his entire life, but his memory was rock solid.

Ella sat, twirling her gift, remembering the first one that Rosie had given her almost two decades before. She felt absurdly like crying. She looked at Daisy and Iris. "What am I going to do?" she asked.

Daisy looked at her directly through a curling nicotine wisp. "You askin'?"

Ella nodded. "I'm asking."

Daisy crushed out her cigarette and reached for another. "There's two sides to every story," she said.

# CHAPTER FIFTEEN

It was Ella's turn to belt on Jake's door, which she did with relish. There was no reply after a minute so she belted again, feeling her earlier anger at his desertion return.

"I know you're skulking around in there, Jake," she yelled, giving the wide, fancy, frosted glass and metal piece of art another bash. "Answer the damn door."

The door swung open and Jake stood before her. He was wearing jeans and nothing else, his feet bare, a Corona in hand. He hadn't shaved and it didn't look like he'd slept either. She should have been repulsed. She wasn't.

Jake took a swig of his beer. "I do not skulk."

Ella glared at him. "We need to talk."

Jake swallowed his mouthful and concentrated on its bitter flavor against his tongue. She was wearing that cream peasant blouse from their first training session and treacherous thoughts of how sweet she tasted roared to life.

He leaned a shoulder against his door frame. "Nope. That's one of the advantages of having quit."

The belligerence in his voice stung. Ella held on to the slender thread of her patience. Luckily she'd had plenty of practice with hundreds of sullen teenagers. "Do you think I can come in and we could discuss it?"

Jake straightened. "I have company."

A well of disgust bubbled up and any feelings she'd been harboring for him shattered inside her chest.

"You're having sex?" she asked incredulously. "You have got to be kidding me." Ella was aware her voice was getting higher but she didn't care. How dare he answer the door with his post-coital beer, nearly naked and fresh out of bed with another woman when he should be at Hanniford.

"Jesus, Jake, surely you can keep it your pants for a couple of hours each afternoon?"

"Jake? Who's there?"

Ella tensed and pulled her bottom lip between her teeth. She didn't want to come face to face with Jake's latest. She didn't want to see that I've-just-been-in-bed-with-a-sex-god look she knew would be on the woman's face. But mostly Ella didn't want to see her, because she wasn't entirely sure she wouldn't scratch the bitch's eyes out. Shit!

Since when had she given a rat's ass about who Jake slept with?

Shit, shit, shit.

Jake's gaze fell to her bottom lip, moist from the ministrations of her teeth. Working closely but keeping himself distant the last six months after one night in her bed had been damn near impossible. Having her on his doorstep in that smokin' blouse wasn't helping.

God knew he wanted to suck that lip into his mouth so badly he could barely see straight. His gaze drifted up. She was watching him. He didn't take his eyes off it as he called, "Wrong number," over his shoulder.

Trish Jones appeared from behind Jake with a puzzled expression and Ella almost bit her lip. He was bonking Trish?

She'd always wondered if there was something between them. Had they been lovers? Were they lovers still?

"Ella! Hi, did Pete send you to talk some sense into Jake too?" Trish smiled then gave Jake a playful slap on the arm. "Jake, don't leave the poor girl standing on the doorstep." She grabbed Ella's arm and ushered her inside. "Go and put a shirt on," she ordered.

Jake stood in the doorway for a moment longer watching the two women who, apart from his aunt, had been pivotal in his life. Ella's hips swayed in her long brown skirt and he could see her bra strap as Trish led her away. Her ponytail swished from side to side with each swing of her hips.

*Fuck.*

He was in serious trouble. Both of them here, ganging up on him, Trish and their history, Ella and all their stuff—both modern and ancient.

And that damn blouse.

Ella followed Trish through Jake's open-plan apartment. It was the epitome of rich, single man. Soaring ceilings with exposed ducting gave it an industrial feel and sleek chrome fixtures added to it. A staircase with wire railings and metal treads more at home in a factory than an apartment twisted up to a mezzanine level. Black leather couches, smoky glass tables and gun-metal grey rugs sparsely furnished the cavernous space. Ella winced. She knew it would be like this. About as far removed from kitsch central as you could get.

Trish led her straight to the massive kitchen and opened the stainless steel fridge door. As much as she liked Miranda's mother, a tiny part of Ella hated that she knew her way around Jake's apartment so easily. That she could open the fridge door like she'd done it a thousand times before.

"You look like you could use a drink," Trish said.

Already well lubricated with sherry, Ella didn't argue as the other woman pulled out a bottle of white wine and placed it on the black marble top of the central island. She opened a cupboard, produced a glass that twinkled in the chrome down lights and poured a generous slug of Chardonnay.

"C'mon," Trish said handing Ella the glass. "We're on the deck."

They passed a theater area with black leather recliners and a TV screen that could have been right at home at an Imax, before stepping onto the deck. The railing consisted of smoky glass panels topped with tensile wire. There was more smoky glass for the table surrounded by ten aluminum chairs. A welcome wall of greenery cheered up one high grey boundary wall and attracted Ella like a bee to a flower. Hibiscus plants in a long terracotta planter had been trained into a low hedge and centered strategically. A large potted red chili plant butted against the hedge at the end closest to the railing and at the opposite end a dwarf lemon tree groaned with bright yellow fruit. She guessed that was a smart investment for someone who drank as much Corona as Jake.

Several small shelves had been erected haphazardly on the wall above the hedge and were cluttered with pretty pots full of flowers: pansies and sweet peas, geraniums and fuchsias. Two massive staghorns hung higher on the wall and dark ivy crept decoratively over the spaces in between. It was the only corner of Jake's apartment that looked like it hadn't been decorated by the Australian Metalworkers Union. Ella fingered a red chili and admired its organic beauty.

"You like my handiwork?" Trish laughed. "Miranda and I keep buying him plants. And of course tending them, otherwise they'd be dead. This place is so bloody austere, don't you think? All chrome and glass. I feel like I'm in a factory."

Well that figured. The only part of Jake's place that felt human and it belonged to Trish. "Yes, it's very ... masculine."

Trish laughed. "That's one word for it. I prefer too much money not enough give-a-shit."

Ella laughed with her as she moved to the railing and took a sip of her wine. The sweeping view over the river was breathtaking and it would no doubt have delighted her at any other time but the words she wanted to say to Jake were churning over and over in her head and she'd hoped not to have an audience when she did it. Especially if it was Trish. Her relationship with Jake was making Ella crazy and she really, really wanted to hate the diminutive ex-cheerleader. But Trish Jones was just too damn nice to justify such a potent emotion.

"Let's get this over with."

Ella turned at Jake's announcement. He had thrown on a black button-up shirt shot with a fine silver stripe. It blended effortlessly with his black and chrome furnishings and she disliked it on sight. He hadn't bothered with the buttons and the river breeze tugged at its tails and his tattoo played peek-a-boo.

Okay, the shirt had its good points.

Jake pulled up a chair. "So is this going to be good cop, bad cop?"

Ella watched as he took another swig of his beer, his Adam's apple bobbing as he swallowed. He placed the bottle on the table and it made a harsh tapping noise. He was looking at her belligerently and she couldn't stand how he could be so unaffected when she was fighting for the life of her school, for her kids—and when that damn tattoo was lighting a fire in her knickers that was threatening to burn for the term of her natural life.

She turned to Trish. "You wanna be good cop?"

Trish shook her head. "Nope."

Ella put her hand on her hip and turned back to him. "Looks like it's just bad cop, bad cop."

Jake sighed as Trish pulled up a chair beside him and Ella followed suit, sitting opposite. "Look, I can save you the trouble. Nothing you can say, either of you, will change my mind."

Ella wanted to dump his beer over his head. "You can't just quit, Jake. Not now."

"Yes, I can. I did."

"Jake," Trish chided. "Miranda's going to be very disappointed in you."

"Well, Miranda's going to have to get used to being disappointed. It's a big, bad world out there."

Trish raised an eyebrow. 'You think *I* don't know that?"

"You know why it has to be this way, Trish."

Ella watched them, not quite understanding but growing impatient. She wanted to cut to the chase. Deal with the situation she'd created and get Jake back on the field.

"I know what happened all those years ago," she said, earning a startled look from both Trish and Jake. "I've been Googling." She shrugged. "And I'm sorry I went behind your back and called the paper and stirred it all up again."

Jake closed his eyes and expelled a breath as his past rushed out, swirling around him in all its vivid, sullied glory. He stared at his beer sullenly. Somehow the fact that Ella's loathing of sport had kept her ignorant to his sordid decline had been refreshing. It had meant something that she didn't know. Almost twenty years later the shame still clung and a part of him hadn't wanted her privy to all the murky details. He wasn't sure if he could bear to see the judgment in her eyes.

Ella frowned. Jake suddenly looked decidedly worse than when he'd opened the door to her ten minutes ago: pale and every one of his thirty-eight years. She thought her being aware of the situation would make things better.

"I can't undo it, Jake. I would, if I could. But I can't. And those boys, the team, shouldn't be punished for a mistake I made. Please come back and finish the job."

Ella watched, her heart pounding, as Jake drained his beer and set it gently back on the table with grim resignation. He didn't speak for a while and Ella thought she might just blow a blood vessel as her pulse boomed through her head.

"I can't," he said, glancing at Trish. "I need to lie low while this thing blows over. I can't be out there."

Ella looked from Jake to Trish and back to Jake. "I don't understand."

He sighed. "It took a long while for the media furor to die down two years ago. There was a lot of pressure on me to name the mystery woman and that is not an option. She's been through enough without the media beaming her nightmare into every living room in Australia."

Ella nodded slowly. "And by bowing out you're hoping it'll remain a non-story."

Jake nodded wearily. "Give the woman a cigar."

What could Ella say to that? He was protecting a woman who had been sexually assaulted from being abused all over again by the media. It was decent and honorable and right. Hanniford's fate seemed petty by comparison.

"Pete will manage," Jake added.

Ella nodded. "Of course. I'm sorry ..."

Trish stood, the chair moving back with a harsh metallic scrape. "This is utterly ridiculous." She looked down at Jake. "I'm tired of this. It's time, Jake."

Jake looked up into Trish's fierce face. "No."

Trish nodded. "Yes. If John bloody Wells figures it out, then too bad."

Ella frowned. "Who is John Wells?"

"A journo," Jake muttered. "A very clever, very persistent journo. He's almost connected the dots. He just doesn't realise it."

"Then so be it," Trish said. "Miranda's older now and I'm not the same scared little mouse I was back then. It was a long time ago. Maybe it's time I got to tell my side of the story and hang the confidentiality agreement."

Jake shut his eyes as Trish turned to Ella. "Jake is protecting me. Tony Winchester raped me."

For a moment after the startling announcement, Ella didn't know what to say, what to think. "Oh, Trish ... I'm so—so sorry. That's awful, just ... terrible." The words seemed hopelessly inadequate for the ordeal Trish must have been through.

The photo on the back of yesterday's paper flashed through her mind: Jake in the foreground, her and Trish behind him. If this John Wells character was as determined and clever as Jake seemed to think, no wonder Jake had gone ballistic.

"Jake ..." She shook her head. "I'm so sorry. I really ballsed it up, didn't I? Especially after all you've gone through to protect Trish—"

Jake's harsh laugh cut her off. "Don't put me on a pedestal, Ella. Eighteen years ago, Tony Winchester raped Trish while I stood by and did nothing."

Jake's bitter words fell into the space between them like boulders into a shallow pond. Ella gasped.

"Jake," Trish chided.

Jake shrugged. "As good as."

Ella looked from Jake to Trish and back to Jake. It couldn't be true, surely? The Jake who'd voluntarily coached her team to a finals spot? Had spent a small fortune on uniforms and equipment? Had taught Cam some respect? Taken in Pete and Cerberus? Had defended her honor against Roger frigging Hillman? *Her* Jake?

"No, Jake," Trish said, grasping his shoulder. "How many times do I have to say this? By the time you heard me screaming, it was already done."

Jake picked up his empty bottle and absently rolled it between his palms, staring at the lemon wedge. "If I'd been more sober I would have realised what was going on."

Trish squeezed his shoulder. "He was my boyfriend, Jake. How could you have known?"

He shook his head. "I shouldn't have let those goons stop me from breaking the door down."

Ella could see guilt, remorse and shame warring for top billing in his green gaze as a picture of what must have happened that night started to form in her brain. "Oh, Jake," she whispered.

Jake looked away as pity and something else warred in her gaze. Was it distaste? Reproach? There wasn't any look she could give him that hadn't stared back at him from the mirror for the longest time. But it still scratched deep into the murky swamp of his guilt pulling at the crust, lifting the ugly scab a little, making it bleed all over again.

"Jake was amazing," Trish said, rising to his defense as she ignored his scowl. "Confronting Tony, wrapping me in his jacket—taking me home."

Ella frowned. "Not to the police station?"

"I didn't want to. Not right then. I was a mess. I was crying … shaking so hard. I just wanted to get away, go back to my house where I felt safe. Jake wanted me to go the next day but who was going to believe me, Ella? Tony and I were in a relationship. I went into the room with him more than willingly. Fooled around quite happily. I'd had a couple of drinks. I knew how these things went down. It's never the guy who ends up looking bad, Ella."

Ella wished it wasn't so but she had to admit Trish's concern had been more than valid. Part of the reason she detested big money sport so much was the unforgivable behavior of some of the men who played it. She may not have been big on keeping up with sports news but she'd seen enough headlines over the years to know sports stars got away with all kinds of despicable, not to mention illegal, behavior.

Trish shrugged. "I guess I was in shock. I loved Tony. We'd only been going out for a month but I think I fell for him the first time I laid eyes on him. He was so big and strong. He had this curly blond hair—I swear he looked like an angel. I couldn't believe he was capable of that. I knew he was impatient with my decision to wait before taking our relationship to the next level but I never thought he'd just take what he wanted."

"So the next day I went to the club instead," Jake said grimly. "Told them everything. Demanded a police investigation. Demanded Tony be sacked." He looked at Trish. It was hard to believe now he'd ever been that naive.

Ella looked from one to the other as they both fell silent. "I take it they didn't quite see it your way?"

Jake snorted. "After a cursory investigation they closed ranks, offered Trish money to go away quietly. Had a confidentiality agreement drawn up."

"They threatened Jake, too," Trish said. "Told him he'd sit on the sidelines all season. That he'd be dropped from the team. That he'd never be picked for an Origin side. That he'd never play for Australia."

"Hardball," Ella murmured.

Jake nodded. He'd broken the code. And there's one thing he'd learned early, you don't break the code. In times of trouble the clubs closed ranks around their players and you get on board with that or you get mown flat.

Trish grinned. "Jake told them they could stick their club and their agreement where the sun didn't shine. That he'd rather never kick a ball ever again than play for a club that protected a rapist."

Ella looked at Jake as he continued to inspect the bottle. "That was very noble of you."

Jake looked up. "No. Noble would have been me kicking down the door in the first place."

Trish shook her head. "I think it's time you stopped beating yourself up about it," she said impatiently. "I'm the aggrieved person here, Jake. Not you. Let it go. I have."

Ella could see they cared for each other; there was affection and familiarity. They'd obviously been through a lot together. It would be easy to condemn Jake for his inaction. But if Trish had forgiven him, who was she to judge?

"*I* signed the agreement," Trish reminded him. "*I* took the money. I started a new life for myself. We both did."

Ella's heart banged to a standstill temporarily as another thought occurred to her. Had their solidarity spilled into their private lives? Had Jake fathered Miranda? It certainly made sense now she thought about it.

She couldn't deny that a part of her had rejoiced when Jake had denied being with Rachel. She hadn't really had a chance to figure out what that meant for them. But now it seemed kind of moot; he and Trish obviously had something special.

She looked at Jake. She had to know. "Are you Miranda's father?"

Jake spluttered into his beer as Trish laughed at the question that had come from left field. She raised her hand to her mouth trying to smother her hilarity.

"Good grief, no. Jake and I aren't … we don't have that kind of relationship. We're friends. Good friends. But there's nothing romantic. Never has been. Miranda's father was someone I was with briefly. He ran a mile when he found out I was pregnant. He was a jerk." She shrugged. "I seem to attract them."

Ella felt heat in her cheeks, embarrassed that she'd gotten it so wrong. But the relief was overwhelming. Jake was watching her with unfathomable eyes and she almost squirmed in her seat. "I'm sorry. It's just you seem so—I thought—" Jake's gaze was unnerving and Ella lowered her eyes. "I'm sorry," she ended lamely.

"Don't worry about it," Trish assured her.

Ella nodded and was silent for a moment or two as she contemplated everything she'd heard today. Her heart went out to Trish. She looked at the diminutive blond woman sitting tall and straight opposite her like an Amazon.

"Doesn't it stick in your craw to know that Tony Winchester got away with it?"

She nodded. "That's why I couldn't stand by two years ago and watch him walk over another woman. If I'd spoken up when he'd raped me, maybe she'd have been spared what I'd gone through."

"So Jake spoke up," Ella said softly.

Trish nodded her head slowly. "I couldn't stand how the media were going on like Tony was this bastion of respectability: a happily married man, a great father, a stalwart of the community, blah, blah, blah. And that's when I realised that clubs were always going to defend their legends no matter what they did and I just couldn't sit by and let them crucify her without them knowing he'd done it before."

"But you couldn't say anything because of the confidentiality agreement?" Ella asked.

Trish nodded. "Jake entered the fray for me, with all guns blazing. He went to the police and the media and told everyone that Tony had raped a woman in the past and the Seals had covered it up."

Ella looked at Jake, a stupid welling of pride stretching the confines of her chest. She mightn't know much about professional footy but it sounded like a suicide mission to her. "I take it that wasn't exactly the way to win friends and influence people."

He shrugged. "I couldn't let her go through with it. Apart from the agreement, she was exposing herself and Miranda to intense media scrutiny, the very thing we'd avoided all these years."

"The media went into a frenzy," Trish recalled. "The Seals closed ranks again. The Heroes' management were furious." Trish looked at Jake. "They gave him an ultimatum. Quit or be sacked."

Jake pushed out of his chair and headed for the railing. The breeze blew his shirt back as he leaned heavily against the glass panels and stared unseeingly at the river.

Trish's gaze settled on his back. "Jake refused, forcing them to sack him, forcing them to have to publically defend their decision to get rid of the captain of one of the best teams in the NRL. Someone who was not only honorable but who, despite his age, was still playing brilliant football."

She turned to Ella. "You should have been paying attention, Ella. You would have been so proud of him."

Ella glanced at Jake. Or his back anyway. Two years ago? Around the time Rachel had died. That must have been why he'd been back in Huntley. Not his groin at all.

She looked at Trish. "Thanks for filling me in. And please, I understand why Jake doesn't want to push this. I really don't want to bring any more crap down on your head. You've been through enough."

"Nonsense," Trish dismissed. "There are some things more important, bigger than me. I've brought Miranda up to believe in fighting for what's right, sticking up for the underdog. And that's us. We're the underdogs. It's time to stand up and fight."

Jake turned around. "Trish."

Trish shook her head. "What will happen, will happen, Jake, but you can't walk out on those boys. Not now. And I know you don't want to either. You've got them this far—you need to take them the rest of the way." Trish gave him a look dripping with steely determination as she stood, pushing the chair back. She turned away from him and bathed Ella with the same look.

"Convince him for me," she said and left.

Jake and Ella stared at each other. "Well, I don't know about you but I need another drink," he said, pushing away from the railing. He picked up her half-finished wine. "I'll top you up."

Ella followed him into the kitchen and stood quietly while he busied himself. He passed her the refilled glass and popped the top on a Corona. He took a swig, leaning his bottom against the granite bench top, his gaze never leaving her face. "Well? Go on, say it. You must be dying to."

The bitter edge to his voice prickled against her skin. What did he want her to say? That she was disappointed in him? That she was saddened by his inaction? That he wasn't the guy she thought he was? Because the truth was, she'd heard too much good stuff about him just now to justify grilling him over a stupid error of judgment that was ancient history.

"I'm sure there's nothing I can say that you haven't already thought yourself." She didn't have to be a psychologist to see that what had happened that night to Trish still ate at him.

Jake threw his bottle cap into the bin on the other side of the kitchen with the precision of a trained athlete. "Damn right about that."

"I think Trish is right. If she's moved on, then perhaps you should too? Maybe it's time to stop hating yourself, Jake."

Jake stared at his bare feet for a while, then he lifted his head and said, "Do you hate me?"

Ella felt tears prick the back of her eyes. He looked so anguished, like a little boy, and she wanted to gather him close and stroke his head. And the truth was she loved him, warts and all.

She sucked in a breath. "No. Of course not. I think you got into a situation when you were young that wasn't of your making and you couldn't stop even though you think you should have. I think it made you feel angry and powerless. I think it still does."

Jake gripped the side of the bench and expelled the breath he'd been holding. She was right. All these years later he still wanted to bring Tony Winchester down.

The silence between them grew and he couldn't remember a time when he wanted her more. It'd been months since he'd touched her and he wanted to rip that blouse of her so badly his fingers itched.

"You still want me to coach the team?"

The huskiness of his voice did funny things to Ella's abdominal muscles. He'd lost that little boy look. His abs were laid bare to her gaze and her thoughts were far from maternal now. She ground her feet into the floor as she felt a sharp tug toward him.

She nodded. "They need you, Jake."

"And what about you, Ella?" he asked. "What do you need?"

Ella felt the question slither straight to the ache between her legs. "That doesn't matter."

Jake reached out for her, snagging her hip and dragging her to him. She held herself back from him as much as possible within the confines of his arms but their thighs met and she was close enough to smell him—beer, lemon and sex. It infused her senses and she actually felt a little dizzy.

"Of course it does, Ella. You need to start thinking about number one."

He raised a hand and gently lifted a section of fringe that had worked loose from her ponytail. He pushed it behind her ear and then cupped her cheek. He stared at her mouth. "I wish I didn't want to kiss you so much," he groaned before kissing her anyway.

Her lips were hot and she whimpered into his mouth as he flayed her with a passion that exploded full roar from his loins. She matched his ardour and he was instantly hard, instantly aflame. He deepened the kiss further, pressing her closer. She opened to him, grinding her hips into his, squashing her breasts against his chest, snaking her arms around his neck, raking her fingers into his hair.

Ella broke off, dragging in much needed air. Her heart was pounding like speakers at a rock concert. He filled her up too much. Made it hard to breathe. He reached for her again and she placed a stilling hand on his warm, muscled abdomen, her head spinning.

"No. Wait." She heaved in another breath, "I take it this is a yes. You'll coach the team."

Jake also sucked in lungfuls of oxygen. "Yes," he said.

He put his beer down on the bench behind him and reached for the hem of her peasant blouse, lifting it over her head in one swift movement. "Paradise," he said, staring at the pink bra and the luscious bits it held in check. He cupped them, kneaded them, lowered his mouth to them.

Ella dragged herself back from melting into a puddle on the floor. "Stop," she panted. She put her forehead on his chest, reaching for sanity. She hadn't come here for this. The fact that it was happening gave her hope but she needed to focus right now. She lifted her head and looked at her watch. "There's still three-quarters of an hour left of training."

Jake ignored her, reaching for the twinkling diamante clasp taunting him from the depths of her cleavage. He flicked it and her breasts sprang free.

Ella looked down at her chest. "Is there some place you go to study that?"

He grinned. "Sure. Got myself a PhD." He traced the ridge of her collar bone with his index finger and then headed south over the swell of a breast to the tip of a rapidly hardening nipple.

"Jake," she whimpered, grabbing for his shoulder, trying to keep her head. 'Training."

"Tomorrow," he dismissed as he bent his head and let his lips retrace the path.

Ella shut her eyes and arched her back. She was so going to hell.

# CHAPTER SIXTEEN

Ella, who hadn't left Jake's bed since he'd thrown her on it the day before, reluctantly prised herself out of it to get to school—she made it just before the bell. Bernie raised an eyebrow when he noticed she was wearing the same clothes she'd worn the day before and Ella felt her cheeks flame as he gave her a wink.

The day flew and she was heading to training before she knew it. Seeing Jake back at the Hanniford oval was a sight for sore eyes. The team greeted him like he'd risen from the dead and Ella winced as Cam gripped his coach in a rib-crunching bear hug. Jake laughed and ruffled Cam's hair in the manly way sports stars seem to have perfected and got straight down to the business of putting the Demons through their paces. Considering the man had had no sleep last night, he was firing on all pistons, which was just as well, given the final series was only a few short weeks away.

When Jake drove Ella and Cameron home after training, there wasn't any question in his mind that he wouldn't follow her inside. He was totally hooked. A more manly man might have cared that she had him firmly by his testicles. Jake didn't.

After years of musical girlfriends, he was more than ready for the One.

The dogs greeted them enthusiastically as they walked up the front path. Cerberus almost wriggled out of his skin, he was shimmying so much, and Jake gave him some extra attention. They detoured around the verandah, following the aroma of cigarette smoke and found Daisy, Iris and Rosie in their usual spots at the chipped linoleum table.

Daisy watched him through the thin smoke curl of her cigarette. "Well, look who the cat dragged in."

"Jake!" Rosie leaped up from her chair and gave him a big fan-girl hug. She raised her eyebrows at Ella over his shoulder and Ella gave her an I've-been-in-bed-all-night-with-a-sex-god grin. "We missed you around here."

Jake pulled out of her embrace and inspected the black miniskirt, black army boots with long black socks pulled all the way up to her knees, black *Drac Sucks* T-shirt, blood-red lips and studded dog's collar around her neck. "Hey Miss Rosie, we missed you too."

Rosie and Simon had been to every Demons' game and Jake had watched her go from scary semi-Goth chick to an even scarier Stepford-wife with suppressed semi-Goth tendencies over the course of the last six months. He knew which Rosie he preferred.

Rosie gave him a sad smile. "Never change for a man, Jake. Never."

He nodded. "I'll take that on board."

"So," Daisy said, dragging on her cigarette, "haven't seen you around here for a while."

Jake glanced at Ella. "You will now."

Daisy stared for a moment then gave a nod of approval. "Good."

Jake grinned and switched his attention to Iris. "Hello, Iris. Are we all still doomed?"

She gave him a solemn shake of her head, gripping her tarot deck hard. "I'm afraid so," she murmured. "It's getting closer. The cards never lie."

He put his arm around Ella's shoulder. "We'll get through it."

They sat on the verandah with a light breeze blowing and chatted for a while. They talked about the footy competition and the house and scrupulously avoided talking about Simon.

Ella was excruciatingly aware of Jake's gaze on her. On her face. Her mouth. Her cleavage. She wondered how long they'd have to sit here. All she could think about was excusing themselves and picking up where they'd left off at dawn. In a million years she never would have pictured herself with a Huntley native, someone who was privy to her past, warts and all. And certainly never with Jake, though he'd been a life-long fantasy—a sexy man way out of her league.

But instead of running scared, suddenly she was pleased for the shared background, pleased that they understood each other because they both knew what the other had been through. Pleased that she didn't have to explain or justify herself and knew that if they could overcome their pasts, they could certainly have a future.

Suddenly the dogs who'd been lying placidly, tongues lolling, became alert at the very faint creaking of the front gate and they were off, barking as though a poltergeist had arrived on their doorstep.

"Oh crap," Rosie said standing. "That'll be the journalist."

"Journalist?" Jake and Ella said simultaneously.

"*Rosieee.*"

Rosie froze as Simon's shaky voice carried toward them, just audible above the row of canine disapproval. The dogs had obviously bailed him up and, as she'd spent all last night maligning him in their presence, it didn't sound like they were about to let him pass.

"Simon," she murmured.

"*Rosieeeeee?*" The plaintive call came again.

Rosie looked at her aunts and then at Ella and Jake. She didn't want to face Simon alone. It was too soon.

Ella stood and held out her hand. "I'll come with you."

"Me too," said Jake.

"We all will," Daisy and Iris said in unison.

They cut through the cool, central hallway of the house and emerged into the late afternoon sunshine to see Simon pinned on the ground by Genghis, his big paws on Simon's chest, his top lip lifting in a don't-think-I-won't-do-it growl.

The other dogs had adopted their alpha stances. Except for Cerberus, who did a dithering wiggle between wanting to be with the pack and loyalty to Simon, who'd fed him countless tidbits from the table. Once a stray, always a stray.

"Rosie," Simon called, so relieved to see her he almost let go of the tenuous control he had on his bladder muscles. "Thank God."

Rosie stood on the steps. Her arms were crossed and she drummed her fingers against the sleeve of her T-shirt. Jake, Ella, Daisy and Iris stood behind her.

"He's not going to help you."

"Please, Rosie. Call them off. I need to talk to you."

"So talk."

Simon's head fell back against the grass. "Rosie."

Rosie gave it a moment or two more before she called the dogs away. They backed off but sat alert at Rosie's feet on the step below, putting themselves between her and Simon.

Except for Cerberus, who continued to dither in the middle.

Simon picked himself up and brushed at his jeans and shirt to remove the grass. Rosie watched him with a heart that was thumping like a clanging bell. He looked so gorgeous. So Simon. All neat and pressed—ironed jeans, for crying out loud—in his obviously designer clothes.

But she wanted him anyway, even though he was out of her league, even though he was her total opposite. Even though his mother was a heinous snob with way too much influence and he lived in an ugly monolith by the river.

Oh God—she sucked at being strong where men were concerned. She reached behind for Ella and drew strength from the grip on her hand.

Simon looked up at Rosie, taking in the posse behind her. "Do you think I could talk to you alone?"

Rosie shook her head. God, if they were alone, she'd jump his bones no question. It had been just over twenty four hours but her libido didn't care that she wasn't the woman he wanted her to be. "Anything you want to say to me, you say to all of us."

Simon paused. "You look good," he said.

"I know."

Simon swallowed. "It was wrong of me to watch you changing and not speak up."

Rosie knew she couldn't let him take the fall for that one. She shrugged. "It was my choice. It was wrong but it was still my choice."

"It was wrong of me to let my family crap interfere in our relationship."

Rosie nodded. "Yep. That was wrong." She tapped her foot. "What else?"

"I'm sorry for not understanding about the house. I've never had this," he said, gesturing to Rosie's silent family. He shifted uncomfortably—they should have all been wearing black, with SECURITY stamped across their fronts. "It's a new thing for me."

Rosie nodded again, giving him another concession. Simon's place, his family, were colder than permafrost.

Encouraged by her nod, Simon took a few steps forward until his foot rested on the bottom tread. Genghis growled. "I used my contacts and spent all night in the council archives." He looked at Daisy and Iris. "The woman who sold the house lied. I can only guess that a devout Christian woman like her, who'd been running a respectable Christian boarding house for six decades, didn't want anyone to know the origins of the house. It's significantly older—late eighteen hundreds. A woman called Anne Palmer had it built. Purpose built as a brothel, called Annie's. It was quite well known at the time, by all accounts."

Simon paused and waited for the news to sink in. Everyone was looking at each other.

"Oh God," Ella whispered clutching at her throat as the irony smacked her hard in the face. She leaned heavily against Jake, his arm automatically encircling her waist.

*She'd run away from one whorehouse to seek shelter in another?* "Apparently there were rumors that a famous bushranger, Slippery Shamus O'Grady, frequented the establishment and used it to stash his hauls. He and Annie had a thing but apparently she double-crossed him, took off with his loot. She and the loot were never seen again."

Jake frowned as his brain sorted through the information. "So this means …?"

Simon nodded. "If this house…" He paused and looked at Rosie. "*Your home…* can't get heritage listing, then no building is safe." It took a minute, but Simon watched the transformation on the faces in front of him as realization dawned.

Rosie wanted to leap off the stairs straight into his arms but it all seemed too good to be so. "Really?" she asked.

Simon smiled. "Really. I have the papers in the car to get the ball rolling."

Rosie did a little jig that looked like Riverdance meets Marilyn Manson. Her eyes filled with tears. "Thank you," she whispered. "Thank you so much." And she put out her arms, saying, "Genghis, heel," before falling straight into his.

Everyone was talking at once and hugging each other, standing on the steps, making plans, just being happy and grateful and thankful that their beloved home was safe. It wasn't until the dogs started barking that any of them tuned into the car doors slamming and the gate opening and a small crowd of people surging toward them.

"What the fuck?" Rosie said, staring at the eight people that Genghis's pack had bailed up. Several of them had kick-ass cameras with long lenses that were madly clicking away. She'd been expecting a journalist, not the paparazzi.

"Genghis, heel," Daisy commanded. The dogs retreated to their original position on the stairs in front of their humans.

"Oh, this is bad," Iris murmured. "Very bad. It's beginning."

A flash flared and then another. "Can I help you people?" Daisy demanded as she clutched her sister's hand.

Ella felt Jake's arm around her waist grow tighter as the reporters drew nearer all shouting questions at once and she turned in time to see his mouth flatten into a thin line.

Genghis growled.

"Whoa!" Rosie said above the hubbub, holding up her hand. "One at a time. I'm expecting a Steve Pennyworth from the *Brisbane Herald*."

A middle-aged man stepped forward. "That's me."

"Well, who the hell are the rest of you?" Rosie demanded.

"Blake Abrahams, *Brisbane Herald* sports desk. How does it feel to be heading back into a finals series again, Jake?"

"Jenny Jones, gossip columnist. Is this your girlfriend, Mr. Lewis, sir?"

"John Wells. Investigative journalist for the *Sydney Mail*. Long time no see, Jake."

Jake gave John Wells a carefully neutral look. The other reporters were like dogs straining at their leashes. John, however, was cool and calm.

Ella watched as four sets of reporters thrust mini tape-recorders at the group and their photographers, who it seemed weren't important enough for introductions, continued to snap shots. John Wells? Wasn't that the name of the reporter Jake had told her about? The persistent one?

"Mr. Lewis, sir." Jenny leaped into the pause after the intros. "It's a matter of record that you aren't seeing anyone yet there was a rather intimate photo of you and this woman," she indicated Rosie with a slightly distasteful air, "in a local paper the other day at a football match and here you are together again. There are many women out there who would be interested to know your relationship status."

Rosie bristled at the journalist's disdain. "Now hang on a moment."

Simon placed a calming hand on Rosie's arm. He knew how this went. He knew Jenny was baiting him and that the wisest thing to say was no comment. He'd grown up around media advisors and could have recited the correct response in his sleep. But today was not the day for political correctness. Not anymore.

"Rosie and I are seeing each other. We have been for six months. In fact, we're getting married."

Rosie's head just about spun of her shoulders as she blinked up at him. "We are?"

Simon nodded. "Just as soon as we can."

Rosie grinned and then turned to the reporter. "We're getting married."

More clicking of cameras as the other journos, even Steve Pennyworth, who'd come here about the battle for their home, sniffed a bigger story. A political story.

"And where do you plan on settling?" Jenny asked.

"Well, seeing as how his mother's going to disown him when she sees this, he better come and live here."

The reporters laughed. It was patently obvious to them all that Simon Charles Henry Lewis, political royalty, would never live in such a rundown dump.

Except John Wells didn't laugh. And that made Jake even more nervous. They needed to stop this now.

"What about you, Ella?" Blake asked. "You must be pleased with how the Demons are going, making the finals. This is the kind of publicity your beleaguered school needs, right?"

"Don't answer that," Jake murmured.

Ella squeezed his hand. "It hasn't hurt," she admitted.

"Quite a coup for an acting school principal," Blake continued. "You must be looking forward to the finals—you have a lot riding on it."

"Don't answer that," Jake repeated. He'd gotten too close to these people over the last six months and he loved them and their quirky ways but they were like lambs to the slaughter. No idea how the media machine could twist things. He glanced at Iris rubbing her arms, eerily tuned into her foreboding.

"I'll just be pleased when it's all over and we've hopefully won. I'm not really into sports, deep down I'm just a math geek who's trying to keep her school open for the kids."

"What do you say to that, Jake?" John Wells butted in. "Is she just a maths geek? You and Ella go back a long way, don't you?"

Jake felt a finger of fate crawl up his spine but kept his face appropriately grim. "No comment."

"I don't suppose while I'm here you'd like to name the woman who you alleged Tony Winchester raped all those years ago?"

Jake watched all the other journalists lean in a touch closer. "No comment," he repeated.

"What about you, Ella? You and Jake are obviously close, any pillow talk you care to share?"

If Jake hadn't been holding on to Ella he may just have stormed down and shoved John's photographer's camera right down John's smarmy mouth. He heard her gasp and gave her waist a squeeze for reassurance. "No comment," he repeated, his voice rough with contained anger. "Press conference over."

The reporters all surged forward again yelling questions, well and truly on the scent of something big as Jake retreated dragging Ella with him and ushering Daisy and Iris away too.

Genghis growled and they faltered.

"Mr. Pennyworth, you can come up," Rosie said over the din and then moved back into the house, a bemused reporter and his photographer following in their wake.

\*

Ella woke to the drift of Jake's hand on her hip, stroking down her thigh and then wandering back to her waist. She smiled and murmured, snuggling her bottom into his groin against his already impressive erection. "Are you the Energizer Bunny?"

Jake chuckled, his hand drifting higher, capturing the swell of a breast, brushing across her nipple. "Pretty ever-ready yourself," he murmured, nuzzling her neck. She smelled like clean linen and him and he wanted her.

She turned in his arms but a thundering belting on Ella's door interrupted them.

"Ella!" Rosie called and pounded again.

Jake groaned into her neck. "Rosie, I swear to God," Jake called. "I don't care how good your mushrooms are, I'm not letting her out of bed."

For the first Saturday in months there was no footy match and they intended to stay right where they were until Jake's presence was required at the Demons' training session later this afternoon.

"You have to get up," Rosie called. "It's the papers. It's … pretty awful."

Jake's hand stilled on her breast. Ella's eyes flew open, the post-coital fatigue vanishing. Iris's fretting last night returned and settled like a lead weight in her stomach. She sprang out of bed, threw Jake's clothes at him and hastily pulled on some of her own, shoving her hair into a shabby ponytail.

Jake reached for the door handle and she covered his hand with her own. "Before we go out there, I just want you to know that I am truly sorry about bringing this down on your head. If I could go back and undo it, I would. Do you think John Wells has uncovered Trish?"

Jake brushed her cheek with the backs of his fingers. He looked into her dark brown eyes. "I don't know. It's done now, anyway. Maybe, as Trish says, it's time."

Ella nodded, a knot of dread twisting in her stomach, knowing it was all her fault. Jake was going to be raked through the muck again and she'd been the instigator.

They hurried down the hallway and walked out onto the verandah, cigarette smoke and despair embracing them in equal measure. Four faces looked back at them in varying shades of grimness.

"Oh God," Ella said, her heart thumping as she saw Rosie's red-rimmed panda eyes. Simon couldn't even maintain eye contact. Daisy and Iris already had a slug of sherry in their glasses. She sank into a chair and her hand shook as she took the *Sydney Mail* from Daisy.

The massive front page headline said SUBURBAN SECRETS and then underneath in slightly smaller print, THE COACH, THE GEEK, THE GOTH AND HER LOVER. A full-sized photo of them all standing on the stairs took up half the page. Ella felt sick as her gaze dropped to the first paragraph in smaller but still bold print. The byline read, "John Wells".

*In a run-down house marked for the scrap heap in an inner-city suburb of Brisbane, an urban pantomime plays out. The cast of characters? Interesting to say the least. An ex-footy star, an up-and-coming member of a political dynasty, two aging circus freaks, the daughter of a small-town hooker and a wanna-be Goth.*

Ella gasped. "Oh. My. God. I don't believe this."

Jake, who was reading over her shoulder, was slightly less wordy. "Fuck."

The report went on, in the vilest details, about their lives under the rather loose guise of fallen celebrity and political deceit. It chronicled Ella's connection to Jake through Huntley and her mother's sordid history, making much out of the irony of Ella trading one brothel for another. It repeated the old rumor that Ella had run away with her high school principal and questioned her moral integrity. It challenged the appropriateness of her being a role model for school children and her ability to raise her fifteen-year-old brother.

Simon was slammed for keeping his relationship with Rosie, "a third-generation carnie with Goth tendencies", to himself. "What kind of political wife would she make?" it questioned. "At least she could attend all the state funerals." The article also speculated on Simon's connections. Would he use his influence to save his fiancee's home?

Daisy and Iris were painted as some feed-the-birds, grumpy old ladies turning down multi-million dollar deals to buy their property just to piss off their neighbours. But Wells hadn't stopped there. He'd done a little more digging and found that the sisters had never lodged a tax return. Suddenly they were tax evaders in the order of Al Capone.

Ella looked up. "You two seriously haven't ever lodged a tax return?"

Iris and Daisy traded a look. "Never could wrap my head around those damn forms," Daisy said, pouring herself another slug of sherry.

Ella returned her gaze to the page to discover that even their beloved animals had copped it. Apparently the reporters had been menaced by "a pack of mangy, unruly, unregistered dogs". Ella looked at the picture with Cerberus mid-wriggle, obviously ecstatic at the attention and wanted to cut John Wells's heart out.

She threw the paper on the table. "I feel sick."

"Fucking. Bastard," Rosie said stabbing her finger at Wells's byline.

"He's good," Simon said. "It took me well into the night to dig through the archives to find out the stuff about Annie's."

Jake shook his head. "He's probably just gotten it off Pennyworth." The Huntley stuff, however, would have taken some digging.

They all sat and stared at the paper like it was a toxic stain. "Can he—can he say that stuff?" Ella asked into the growing silence. When Rosie had alerted them to the paper this morning Ella had been prepared to pick up the pieces for Jake. She'd had no idea that the media machine she'd embraced would turn around and kick her in the teeth.

Jake nodded. "Unfortunately. Most of the facts are essentially true. And he's been really careful to wrap the more outrageous things in phrases like 'it's rumoured' and 'sources say'."

"I don't care," Simon said. "I'm going to sue him anyway. And when I've finished with him, my mother will move in for the kill—if she hasn't put out a contract on him already."

As if on cue, his mobile rang for the fifteenth time that morning and Rosie didn't have to look at it to know who it was. "How does she know to ring right after you've uttered her name?" Rosie asked him.

Simon shrugged and hit the end button.

Jake plonked himself in the chair next to Ella and put his hand on her shoulder, his thumb stroking her collar bone. "Are you okay?" he asked.

Ella felt like her head was going to explode. Prior to today, the only people outside of Huntley who knew her story were the people sitting at the table; now the whole nation knew her shame.

"Not really." She cradled her face in her hands for a moment and then looked at him. "I don't think I've got anyone but myself to blame though."

"No," he murmured, shaking his head. "This stuff is inexcusable. I'm really sorry you got dragged in." His hand moved to her nape and he drew her head onto his shoulder. "I'm really sorry everyone here got dragged through the muck," he said, addressing the table.

Ella lifted her head. "What does he hope to gain from this?"

Rosie frowned. "Notoriety?"

"Circulation," Simon said.

Jake shook his head. "He's hoping to flush me out. Piss me off enough that I'll give him what he wants in exchange for him backing off."

Ella looked at him. "He doesn't know you very well." But she did. She knew Jake Prince was his own master and didn't dance to anyone else's tune.

"What are you going to do?" Daisy demanded.

"Nothing. For now. I'm not going to feed this monster any more morsels." Jake stood. "I have a finals series to win and the Schools Cup to claim. And I will not let a slimy toe-rag like John Wells distract me."

But after that was done, he wouldn't rest until John Wells was writing the fluffiest cat in show stories for some two-bit rag in outer Woop-Woop.

# CHAPTER SEVENTEEN

Ella was not prepared for the impact of the newspaper article. It started when journalists began gathering at their front gate late Saturday afternoon and were still there Monday morning as Rosie, Simon and Ella left for work. It continued on talk-back radio in her car. She, along with Simon, were hot topics. People were talking about her morals—*her morals*—and her suitability to run a school.

Hanniford supporters rang in too, with their rather colorful ways of telling the wowsers to butt out. But by the time she got to school she had several messages from concerned parents and one from head office. By midday, five families had announced their intentions to pull their kids out of Hanniford and the phone calls from the media were relentless.

And then the phone call she'd been expecting—dreading—the most came from Donald Wiseman. "Ms. Lucas, this is unacceptable. I hate it when any of my schools are dragged into disrepute."

"Mr. Wiseman, I can explain."

"I've had media and angry parents on my phone all morning."

"Join the club."

"By my reckoning, if the number of people who say they will pull their kids out of your school actually do, then your numbers will no longer be viable."

Ella's grip tightened on the pencil she was flicking in her hand. Was that gloating she heard in his voice? She'd worked so hard to keep Hanniford open and the change in the school and the students over the last six months had been truly miraculous.

"I'm sure after this has blown over in a few days parents will realize it's all been a media beat up and everyone will calm down."

"So, it's not true what they're saying? About your mother, about the affair with your high school principal?"

Ella gritted her teeth. "What I'm saying is that it's nobody's business, and give it a day or two or some other juicy news items and it'll all be forgotten."

"And if it doesn't?" Ella could hear his pompous splutter and pictured the phone receiver covered in his spittle. She shuddered. "It might be just as easy to affect an immediate closure. At least the publicity will be deflected from the school on to you."

Ella, usually calm and professional, felt that all snap at his preposterous statement. The rage that had been building since Saturday coalesced with the rage she'd felt all her goddamn years in Huntley. She stabbed the pencil into the fake leather inset of her desk, snapping it in half. She rose to her feet and her hand shook as she gripped the phone wishing it was Donald Wisemans' testicles instead.

"*Don't you bloody dare,*" she hissed. "I'm telling you, pretty soon this will have blown over and no one is going to give a damn who my mother slept with or how many times I supposedly porked my high school principal." Ella gave a disgusted half-laugh. "You think this is a media storm? This is nothing, *nothing*, compared to what you'll have on your hands if you try to shut me down now. You might like to remember, Donald, that I have nothing left to lose. And you better believe that makes me a completely loose cannon."

Ella slammed down the phone. And for a moment felt so alive, so invigorated, she could fleetingly understand why people took drugs.

And then her legs gave way and she flopped into an unceremonious heap in her chair.

*

On Wednesday, things were still manic and Ella felt like she'd been on the rack for months. Iris's prediction had come eerily true—everything was a mess. Her entire urban family had been dragged through the muck.

The negative publicity had taken a toll on the students and teachers alike and the Demons, in particular, were finding it distracting. None of it was conducive to their training, to putting them in the zone to win their first finals match on Saturday.

Her phone rang not long after the bell for the first period had gone and Ella picked it up with some trepidation in case a journalist had somehow managed to get her private line number. It was Gwen, Cameron's biology teacher.

"Cameron's not here," Gwen said.

Ella frowned. "Oh." Cameron hadn't missed a day's school since Jake had picked him for the Demons. None of them had.

"I thought you might like to know."

Ella thanked Gwen and hung up. Where the hell was he? He'd been quiet the last few days but then they'd all been a little preoccupied. She rang his mobile and it went to his voicemail. She left a terse get-your-ass-to-school message, then she texted the same for good measure.

Over the course of the day, she rang and texted Cam dozens of times, but she wasn't overly worried. She was pissed off, sure, but she knew where he'd be come three o'clock.

But he wasn't on the oval for training after school.

"Cam not joining us?" Pete asked.

Ella frowned. "Apparently not."

"Everything okay?"

Ella gave a half-laugh, half-snort that sounded like an asthmatic horse. "What do you reckon?"

Pete nodded. "Some of the guys said Cameron's been copping it a fair bit the last few days from the other kids, teasing him about Rachel."

Ella bit her lip as tears sprang to her eyes. Goddamn it—the woman had lived a thousand miles away and was *dead* for crying out loud but still managed to cause Ella and Cam grief. "Thanks, Pete."

She left the oval and rang Jake, who was attending to pub business. Jake hadn't seen him. She rang Trish. Not there. She rang a couple of the boys he used to hang with before football had set him on the straight and narrow. Not there. She went to the arcade he'd frequented during his truant phase. Not there. She went home. Not there either.

By now it was late afternoon and Ella was imagining him dead on a road somewhere or kidnapped by a serial killer. He'd never done this before. He may have been, sullen, rude and hard to get along with but she'd always known where he was—even when he'd been playing hooky. And they'd been making such progress.

It was almost dark and Ella was pacing the front verandah, her thoughts shunting from worried sick to irrationally angry. When he got home Cam was going to wish Ted Bundy had picked him up. The gate squeaked and the sensor lights caught Cameron ambling up the path.

"Where the hell have you been?" Ella demanded, coming out of the shadows, making him jump.

"Jesus, Ella, you scared me half to death," he grumbled.

"Well good. Maybe you'll know how I've felt all afternoon."

Cameron went to push past her. "I don't want to talk."

Ella stood her ground, placing a hand on his chest. Two years ago, the pissed look he was sporting now would have scared the hell out of her, had her backing down, but they'd grown closer in the last six months and she was surer of their relationship.

"I don't give a good goddamn what you want. Where the hell have you been all day?"

"Places."

"Who were you with?"

"No one."

Ella curled her fingers around the nearby railing in case her temper got the better of her. "Have you forgotten your promise to Jake when he put you in the team? What about your practice session? What about your teammates?" Ella knew she was pushing him but the adrenaline that had been pumping through her system needed a release somewhere. "Jeez, Cam, can't you think of somebody else once other than yourself? What about the Demons, about Hanniford?"

"What about them?" Cameron roared.

Ella startled at his sudden vehemence. She could feel his anger but she also heard the crack in his voice and could see tears shining in his eyes.

"They don't give a shit about me. Jesus, Ella, why'd you have to go and open your mouth to that reporter? For the first time in my life, I was living someplace where no one knew all my dirty secrets," he yelled, putting his face right up in hers. "And now the entire school does. Fuck! The whole bloody *country* knows that my mother was a whore."

Ella gasped as he spat the word with such contempt it blew her fringe back. She didn't even think about her next action, just raised her hand and slapped him hard across his face. She'd put up with boys from Huntley calling Rachel a whore for years and she sure as hell didn't have to hear it come from her brother.

"That's a despicable thing to say."

Cameron blinked and cradled his cheek as tears spilled down his face. "Goddamn it, Ella, I'm not some kid you have to protect from the truth." He was crying hard now, his breath choppy and gasping between sobs. "I knew who she was two years ago. I knew who she was from very early on. You can go on saying things like, oh Rachel liked to entertain or Rachel had a lot of men friends, to protect me for as long as you like, but I'm not an idiot."

Ella reached for him, a sob choking her throat, horrified at her actions, but he took a step back. He was right, she had done that, made excuses for their mother, tried to pretend she wasn't who she was. She had tried to protect him from the truth, just like she had tried to protect herself for so many years. Trying to justify and absolve Rachel of her actions.

"And now the whole bloody world knows. How could you?" he demanded. "How could you?"

Cameron whirled around and ran back down the stairs.

"Cam, wait," Ella cried. How was she to know this would happen? That talking to one piss-ant paper would lead John Wells to Huntley and their sordid past?

Ella was shaking all over and crying so hard she could barely see her mobile screen as she located Jake's number and pushed call.

"Hey."

Ella could only just hear him over the background noise of the bar but she sobbed at the sound of his voice anyway.

"Jake? Jake ... it's so ... we yelled and ... Cam was so mad ... and I—I slapped him and—" Ella stopped, the thought of what she'd done, of slapping him, choking her up further, rendering her incapable of coherent speech.

"Ella? Stop. What's wrong? Are you hurt? Where are you?"

"At h—home," she wailed.

"I'll be there in ten."

He made it in eight by running all the way from the pub. She was sitting on the front steps, her head in her hands, sobbing her heart out when he sat beside her and pulled her into his arms.

"Oh, Jake," she cried.

"Hey," he said, "hey. It's okay. I'm here."

"No ... please. Go find Cam," she said, shrugging his arms away. "He's so angry ... go after him ... I'm worried about him ... don't know what he—"

"Cam can wait," Jake murmured. "He'll be fine for a few minutes. Tell me what happened."

Ella opened her mouth to tell him but her face crumpled instead and she reached for him.

"Hey, sh," he crooned, stroking her hair, his heart pounding from his run and from her scaring the life out of him with that phone call. He pulled her onto his lap like he had that night in his office and they sat for a few minutes while Ella's tears subsided.

"What happened?" he murmured when she'd grown silent and all that could be heard were the hum of insects, the squawk of lorikeets and the drone of an occasional distant engine.

Ella raised her head from the comforting curve of his neck, hiccupped, took a deep breath and the whole messy argument tumbled out.

"Damn it, Jake. How can Rachel still be causing this much trouble so many years down the track? I thought we were both putting it behind us but it just won't let us be. Why can't

Huntley just let us be? It's always there, between us. *She's always bloody there.*"

Jake rubbed his cheek against her hair. "Maybe she's always there because you've never let go of the anger. Maybe Huntley keeps sucking you back because you keep trying to erase it from your memory banks instead of confronting it."

He dropped a gentle kiss on her head. "You never even grieved her passing, Ella. Maybe it's time to just let all that anger go?"

Ella's heart beat filled her head. She knew he was right, even as the rejection came to her lips. "No."

"Yes," he whispered, looking directly into her eyes. "Instead of railing against your origins, maybe you need to embrace them? Whether you like it or not, whether I like it or not, Huntley's part of us. Rachel's part of you. And Cam. Just like my drunkard, gambling father's part of me. Like them or loathe them, they made us who we are today." He brushed his thumb across her mouth. "Stronger. And better."

"What about you?" Ella searched his face, looking for an out. He was asking too much. "Have you let go of your anger?"

Jake nodded. "Over Huntley? Sure. I had to, years ago. It was interfering with my game too much."

Somewhere amid the storm of emotions the irony that the meathead footballer was more emotionally evolved than her was a major comeuppance.

Jake placed his forehead against hers. "Have you ever thought that maybe Rachel was just doing the best she could with what she had?" He paused. "I think by and large, people just do the best they can. Even my father. They're not all strong like you, Ella."

Ella gave a little laugh, her voice wobbly. "I'm strong?" She'd cried three times in the last two years and Jake had been there for each one. Frankly at the moment, she felt like she was going to break into a thousand pieces.

Jake grinned, easing away from her again. "You're one of the strongest women I know." He stroked her cheek. "It's okay to have loved her, Ella."

Ella felt a lump in her throat. "I did. I did love her."

"Of course you did," he murmured. "She was your mother. It's okay to miss her and to grieve for her. It's also okay to admit you didn't like her. You don't have to make excuses or atone for her sins, no one's asking you to do that. She was a grown woman and her actions were her own. But you do have to find a way to make peace with them, with her. Or you're never going to be able to move forward. Neither will Cameron."

Ella's eyes filled with tears. She knew he was right. She'd spent the last nineteen years in a knot of conflicted feelings about Rachel. She'd always thought admitting she loved her mother was tantamount to approving of her. But maybe she could love Rachel and not like her all at the same time and that was okay.

"She used to dance with me. When I was little. She'd put on 'Blue Moon' and she'd pick me up and waltz me around the room."

Jake smiled. "She used to feed me," he said. "When I came to pick Dad up. I think she knew with my aunt gone there wasn't a lot of routine. She'd say, 'Jake, you must be starving. I've made some choc-chip muffins for Ella, help yourself.' Then she'd whiz up this thick shake with honey and ice-cream and she'd sprinkle the top with Milo and she'd sit and chat with me while I ate." He rubbed his forehead against her hair. "She asked me about school. About footy. She talked about you. A lot. She was proud of your achievements, Ella."

Ella's face crumpled again as she remembered the garnet glow in her mother's room, the choc-chip muffins that had been such a staple of her childhood. When she'd cried in his office that night after the Roger Hillman debacle, she'd been crying for herself, for the sucky hand that life had dealt her.

But now she was crying for her mother, mourning the person Rachel was beneath the label Huntley had given her. The real person that no one, including her, had bothered to see.

Ella sat up, wiping her eyes. "Better?" he asked.

She lowered her head and kissed him. "I love you."

Jake smiled. "I love you too."

Ella felt her heart skip a beat at his admission. "So this isn't just sex?"

Jake shook his head. "Nope. This is the real thing."

Ella grinned. Then she laughed and hugged him. "Thank you, Jake."

Jake shut his eyes and squeezed her tight. "Come on then, let me go find Cam." He helped Ella off and rose to his feet.

"I don't know where he'll be," Ella said, worrying her bottom lip.

"I think I do." Jake dropped a kiss on her mouth. "Sit tight."

*

Jake pulled up at the Hanniford Oval fifteen minutes later. In the glow cast by a nearby street light he could see a human shape sitting in the stands; he'd bet the pub it was Cameron. He'd always gone to the field when he'd needed to think. He unbuckled and got out of his car, jumping the fence with ease, and headed toward his target. It was evident as he drew close from the waft of rum that greeted him that Cameron was drinking.

"Cam."

Cameron took another swig out of the bottle. "I suppose my sister sent you?"

"She's worried about you."

"Probably shit scared I'm going to dob her into the child protection agency for abuse."

Jake ignored the jibe. He could hear the bitterness in the teenager's voice and tried to remember that they weren't that different, Cam and he. He took the wooden steps two at a time and sat down next to Cameron. "Getting drunk?"

Cameron shrugged. "You gonna dob?"

"Is it helping?"

Cameron held the bottle up to the light, inspecting the line of amber fluid sloshing against the glass. "Give it another ten minutes."

"So, what? You're just going to drink that till you pass out? Is that your way of getting back at her?"

"Got a problem with that?"

Jake held onto his temper, forcing an air of nonchalance. "Well, it's not particularly smart."

"Oh, right," Cameron sneered. "You telling me that you've never drowned your sorrows before?"

"Nope. I'm telling you as someone who's drowned his sorrows a little too often that it's a dumbass thing to do."

Cameron glared at him. "I'm the laughing stock of the school. I thought I'd gotten away from all that crap when she took me away from Huntley. She should have just left me there."

Jake nodded and stayed silent for a few minutes. "You know what I learnt a long time ago, Cameron? You can't control what people say about you. You can only control how you react to it. Now, you can get mad, hell, you can even get drunk, or you do what I do."

Cameron eyed him with suspicion. "What's that?"

Jake held his hand out for the bottle. "You get even."

Cameron regarded his open hand for a moment. He took one last swallow then handed it to Jake. "I choose even."

Jake grinned. "Good choice." He tipped the bottle upside down until the last drop of amber fluid had drained away and soaked into the grass beneath the stand.

"Now let's go win this comp."

# CHAPTER EIGHTEEN

Ella stood in front of the glass door simply labeled LAWYER, conscious that Huntley was, as always, watching her. She couldn't believe she was back. She almost turned around and told Jake to forget it.

Jake squeezed her shoulder and the urge to flee subsided. He was right. She needed to find some peace. She took a deep, fortifying breath. It didn't stop her hand trembling, though, as she pushed the door open, the blinds swinging slightly from side to side with the movement. The door shut behind them and she was aware of the rattling as their momentum settled.

Ella blinked as her pupils adjusted to the low light inside Mr. Levy's wood-paneled office, unchanged in forty years. There was no pretentiousness in here—no highfalutin' secretary, no gilt-framed art, no leather Chesterfields. Just Sol in his three-piece suit sitting at his big old mahogany desk with real leather inlay, framed by a bank of mahogany bookshelves crammed full of leather-bound texts, as he always had.

"Ah, Ella, how lovely to see you my dear."

Jake's warmth behind her was welcome as the elderly lawyer peered at her over the top of his bifocals and half stood, acknowledging Jake with a nod of his head. "Please, sit, both of you," he said, indicating the chairs opposite him.

They sat. "Thank you for seeing me, Mr. Levy," Ella said.

Sol smiled at her. "I'm pleased you decided to come." He reached down beside him, opened a draw and extracted a thick, cream-colored envelope. "I believe you're after this." He handed it to her.

Ella took the envelope she'd refused two years ago. Back then, she'd instructed Sol to shred it—she was grateful he hadn't. She sat looking at it for a moment or two. What did it say? Did she want to know? Would it help?

"Your mother came to me about a year before she died," Sol said, finally giving voice to the words Ella hadn't wanted to hear two years ago. He watched Ella finger the envelope. "She'd had a premonition she wasn't going to be around for much longer."

Ella glanced at him sharply. She hadn't known that. Of course, blind Freddy could have seen that Rachel was walking a dangerous line and the good folk of Huntley had had a few premonitions of their own. None of them had involved the rather pedestrian heart attack that had killed Rachel at fifty-three. Ella was pretty sure Huntley had been waiting for a much stickier end for Rachel. Lord knew there were any number of scorned women who hadn't shed a tear when the town tramp had collapsed in her front yard and not been able to be revived. Ella certainly wouldn't have put it past a bitter wife or an angry girlfriend to extract revenge.

Sol steepled his fingers and pursed his lips. "There are things in there she desperately wanted you to know."

Ella nodded, coming out of her reverie. She slipped it into her handbag. "Thank you."

Silence descended upon them, broken only by the tick of a clock. It reminded Ella of the clocks at home and she stood, wanting to be gone, wanting to be back in Brisbane with Iris and Daisy. With Rosie.

Sol and Jake stood too. She held out her hand. "Thank you, Mr. Levy."

Sol shook it. "Your mother was a good woman, Ella," he said gently, releasing Ella's hand. "She always had the time of day for me. People tolerate me here because I'm the only lawyer. But even after forty years, none of them really go out of their way. Rachel wasn't like that."

Ella heard the affection in the older man's voice and was reminded that despite the way the town had painted her, her mother had always possessed an innate kindness. It had been an easy fact to forget growing up in a community that hadn't cared about the finer points of Rachel's character. But Jake obviously hadn't forgotten and neither had Sol Levy.

"Thank you," she murmured.

Jake waited for Ella to say something more but she just stood there looking awkward. He placed his palm on the small of her back. "I think we'll be on our way now," he said to Sol.

The lawyer nodded. "Of course. Nice seeing you both."

*

Ella stood in front of the non-descript tombstone. Just a name and two dates. No lament. No words to usher Rachel's spirit into the afterlife. No flowers either. All around them, neatly kept graves boasted vases of freshly cut blooms. Only weeds grew where Rachel lay. Huntley would probably think that was fitting. In fact Ella wouldn't have put it past the town to deliberately infect her mother's final resting place with such ugliness.

Rachel, who'd always had an eye for beauty, would have hated it.

Ella fell to her knees and started yanking at the scrawny weeds, her movements agitated as she clamped down hard on the rising block of emotion threatening to blind and choke her. Her hands were cold despite the bite of the sun at her neck.

"Hey," Jake murmured, kneeling beside her, one hand on her back. He placed his other hand over hers, stilling the frantic movements. "Let me do this. Why don't you read the letter?"

Ella rested back on her haunches and looked at him. "She'd hate them," she said.

Jake nodded. "I know." And he took over where she left off.

Ella watched him for a moment or two before she slowly opened her bag and located the cream envelope Sol Levy had given her. She turned it over a few times before summoning the courage to open it.

The paper was beautiful—expensive and delicately perfumed—so very, very Rachel. But the shock of seeing her mother's flowery handwriting again rocked Ella and she was gripped with a sudden sense of foreboding.

"You're never going to know unless you read it."

Ella looked up at Jake, who had stopped weeding and was looking at her with his calm green eyes.

"Read it," he murmured. "I'm right here." And then he returned to his job, throwing another weed in the pile near his right knee.

Ella settled cross-legged on the grass, took a deep breath and started to read:

*My Darling Ella,*

*I guess if you're reading this then the prayers of every spoken-for woman in Huntley have been answered. They've had their rosary beads and voodoo dolls out for a lot of years and it's nice to know, for them at least, that persistence pays dividends.*

*Don't be mad at them, darling. Or at me, for that matter. You're a long time dead so life shouldn't be wasted on things that you can't change.*

*I know you don't understand why I do what I do. It was so much easier, darling, when you were little and would look at me with those huge blue eyes of yours and say, "You look so pretty, Mummy," and not care about the whys.*

*But then of course, you grew up and I couldn't protect you from the truth. Nor Cam. Please know that if I could have, I would have. But gossip is rife in small towns and it was only ever going to be a matter of time.*

*I'm truly sorry, darling, if I could do something else, be something else, I would. But the truth is, I'm good at what I do.*

*And I love it.*

*You've always made me so proud, darling, but I'm not like you. I didn't have much schooling nor the brains or patience to work for someone else. I never really had any ambition other than falling in love and being loved and being surrounded by beautiful things.*

*It's why you always gave me so much joy and why Cam continues to do so—you two are the most beautiful things I've ever done.*

*I've been lucky that men have loved me and allowed me to live in beauty. People in Huntley can call it whatever they like—I know the truth.*

*I give love, darling—and what is more important than love?*

*Even the young boys, so cocky and full of bravado, leave this place knowing that. They arrive wanting only one thing but leave knowing how to love a woman—truly love her. How to touch her. How to read her. How to appreciate her.*

*I know that I've made you ashamed, but please, darling, don't be ashamed on my behalf.*

*I'm okay with what I do. What I am.*

*Huntley, I guess, will be breathing a sigh of relief knowing that I can now be relegated to the annals of history—the dark years when Rachel Lucas preyed on their men.*

*For that I am sorry. I've always held my head up in this town and the thought that I will be judged harshly doesn't sit easily. But, as I said earlier—time shouldn't be wasted on things you can't change.*

*It is my fervent wish that history will treat me kindly but even I'm not fool enough to believe that. I shall have to settle for being notorious—for that is better than slipping from this life without no-one ever having known you existed.*

*I'm sorry, my darling, that I'm not the Brady Bunch mother you and Cam yearned for and deserved. But I hope you know that I love you and that I'm happy you have the life now that you always wanted.*

*I know you will take good care of Cameron. He has perhaps suffered even more than you for what I am. I rejoice, knowing that you'll finally be together.*

*Be happy my darling. Remember, life is short.*
*Your loving mother,*
*Rachel xxx*

Ella wasn't sure how long she stared at the letter after she finished. She was angry and confused and sad. So very sad.

"Hey." Jake had finished weeding and plonked himself down next to Ella. "You okay?"

Ella shook her head as the sadness overwhelmed her. She handed him the letter and he read it without comment. When he finished, he folded it up. "Pragmatic to the end," he said gently, tugging her close.

Ella nodded and they sat in the blazing sun for a while longer, lost in the tranquility of a late spring afternoon.

"Back to Brisbane?" Jake asked eventually. Ella had done what she'd needed to do and he'd dropped in and seen his old man. They were square with Huntley.

Ella shook her head. "Back to Levy's."

*

"Ella?" Sol rose to his feet, surprise at seeing her again so soon written across his face. "Is everything alright, dear?"

Ella nodded. "I'd like to set up a Rachel Lucas University Scholarship for disadvantaged students at the high school."

Ella couldn't change the past but she could see to it that her mother wouldn't slip from this life without anyone knowing she'd existed. Huntley may want to forget Rachel Lucas—but they could all go to hell. She wasn't rich but she could factor a couple of thousand dollars every year into her budget.

Sol smiled. "Good for you, Ella. Good for you."

*

Iris dragged the smoke deep into her lungs and held it until her chest burned. The anxiety seemed to have increased, not lessened, since things had turned around, and she was taking Daisy's advice to practice some deep breathing. The girls would probably have preferred she did it without the aid of nicotine but if she ever needed to smoke, the time was now. She couldn't shake the feeling that something ugly loomed in the future.

And then of course there was the money situation.

Application for heritage status was all well and good; it had given them a stay of execution but an inspection would be part of the process and she knew that they would insist on some major repairs just to make the place safe. Those would take serious cash, especially with the hoops they'd have to jump through now a heritage listing was on the cards—cash that they just didn't have. Not being flush with money wasn't something that had ever bothered her or Daisy. They got by. The girls covered the mortgage and the bills, they had clothes on their backs and three squares a day with enough left over for dog food, sherry and tobacco.

She looked out over the yard. Despite the encroaching shadows of steel and glass, impinging on their space, she loved this house. It may be sagging in the middle and listing a little to the side but owning something after the transience of circus life had meant a lot to them.

Coming to the city, starting anew, had been daunting, but they'd seen the writing on the wall for traditional circus life and had gone with their dignity still intact.

"Here it is," Daisy announced as she plonked herself down at the table, brandishing a full packet of tobacco. She shook her head and let out a loud hoot. "They think I don't know where they hide our supply."

Iris gave her sister a half smile before fanning her anxious gaze back to the yard, her fingers stroking her cards. The middle wattle was finally giving in to the dictates of the season, its yellow flowers turning brown, hardening into little balls and littering the ground beneath where Cerberus was once again digging.

"Cerberus!" Iris called. "Stop that damn digging!" Cerberus looked at them guiltily and collapsed atop his latest hole. Iris shook her head at Daisy. "Honestly, I don't know how many times I've filled up holes under that tree."

Daisy shrugged. "At least he's confined it to one spot. Remember when Genghis was a puppy? Bloody holes everywhere."

Iris nodded. "Nearly broke my ankle falling into one. Laid me up for weeks."

Daisy chuckled, remembering. Good memories here—every one. She opened the pouch and they both rolled cigarettes for a while without speaking.

Daisy eventually broke the silence. "Iris, why don't you say what's bothering you? Reading minds is your forté, not mine."

Iris looked at her sister. "Daisy, how are we going to pay for the building repairs?"

Daisy licked the edge of a fully stuffed paper. "Something will come along."

Iris shot her sister an exasperated look. "How can you possibly know that?"

Daisy raised an eyebrow at Iris's tone but kept on with her job. "It always does," she said mildly.

Iris sighed, instantly contrite. "I'm sorry. I'm not getting much sleep lately."

"Still dreaming about yellow gold?"

Iris nodded. "I can't even remember what the dream is about but I wake up with those two damn words in my head and I know they're our salvation. I just don't know how."

"You will. It'll come. Eventually."

Daisy was a great believer in the universe providing. Iris was too connected with it to be assured. She shook her head. "We're running out of time, Dais."

Daisy put the cigarette down and looked at her sister. She was scrunching a paper into a tiny ball. She'd lost weight the last little while, there were cheekbones, collar bones. "Let me pick a card."

"You'll just pick the four of cups," Iris dismissed. "You always pick the four of cups."

Daisy was not to be deterred. Even if Iris was right, Daisy knew that nothing soothed her sister like connecting with her beloved cards. "Maybe I'll surprise you?"

Iris sighed, shuffled the deck and spread them in a line for Daisy to choose one. Daisy went straight to the middle and flipped one over.

The four of cups.

She hooted. "Still got it."

Iris looked at the card. It depicted a man sitting under a tree, who appeared to be mediating. He was being offered a cup but seemed oblivious to its presence. Daisy to a T: self-absorbed, wrapped up in her own world; totally uninterested in the goings on outside her front gate; unashamedly parochial, not in a mean or miserly way, just family-centric. She knew what was important, what mattered most.

"Didn't help, huh?"

Iris shook her head, her gaze lifting from the card back to the garden, desperately looking for answers from the universe. Cerberus digging caught her eye again. His body was butted up against the sturdy trunk and his exertions reverberated through the wood, shaking the fading blossoms free from the lower branches. They fell on him like confetti. It was hard to believe that only two weeks ago they'd been fluffy yellow pompoms like a new-born chick and now they were darker, like little golden nuggets.

"Stop that, Cerberus!" Daisy called, because she knew how crazy it drove Iris and her sister was anxious enough.

Iris watched as the image seemed to freeze before her eyes. She looked down at the four of cups, the meditating man morphing into the backyard scene, the tree with yellow gold blossoms taking pride of place.

Her heart beat a little faster.

She stood. "The wattle."

Daisy stopped mid-match strike, a cigarette drooping from her bottom lip. Goose bumps pricked at her inked arms. Iris had that woo-woo look about her and Daisy had learned a long time ago not to mess with the woo-woo look. She removed the cigarette. "What about the wattle?"

"Yellow gold," Iris said, her gaze firmly fixed on the blossoms as she moved around the table, heading for the back stairs.

Daisy followed as her twin practically levitated to the tree in question. Cerberus backed up slightly and hung his head, not sure if they'd come to scold him.

"What now?" Daisy asked as they both stared at the tree.

"I don't know," Iris said. "I think we have to dig."

Daisy didn't blink an eyelid. "Right, I'll get the shovels. I told you we'd need 'em one day," she said cheerily as she headed toward the shed. "As you were, Cerberus."

*

Half an hour later, Ella and Jake, just back from Huntley, found two old women with shovels and one ecstatic dog making limited progress into the compacted earth around the base of the middle wattle tree.

"I don't suppose you're digging a shallow grave for our friend John Wells?" Ella asked as they approached.

"No dear, yellow gold," Iris said, as if it explained everything, not bothering to look up from her ministrations.

Jake raised an eyebrow at Ella and she shot him a don't-ask-me look. "Here," he said, stepping forward, unable to watch women in their sixties torture their spinal columns with such back breaking activity. "Let me do it."

Iris surrendered her shovel and stepped back. Daisy also fell back, leaning on hers. Cerberus kept going, barking occasionally as if in encouragement.

"How was it?" Daisy asked.

Ella heard the familiar gruff note in her voice and smiled at the tough old dame with a marshmallow center. "Good." She nodded. "I'm pleased we went."

Ten minutes later, Jake had doubled the depth. He stood and stretched his back, wiping at the sweat on his forehead. "How deep do you want me to go?" he asked.

"You can stop when you get to China," Daisy said, then laughed at her own joke.

The other dogs, who'd had shown only cursory interest in the activity in the backyard, started to bark, and Ella turned around to see Rosie and Simon on the verandah.

"Did we accidentally murder someone?" Rosie asked as she and Simon approached.

Ella laughed. "Yellow gold," she said.

"Oh. I see," Rosie said as Simon took Daisy's shovel and joined Jake. "I think."

Another twenty minutes of digging into the hard earth and significantly deepening and widening the hole hadn't yielded anything. Jake, shoulder deep in the earth, looked up at Iris, sweat pouring off him. "You sure there's something here?"

Iris nodded, absolutely certain for the first time all year. "Our salvation."

Jake glanced at Simon, who shrugged back at him. How could they argue with salvation? "Okay then."

He drove the shovel into earth that still felt like a block of concrete. A loud tink echoed up the hole as he hit something metallic. Iris gasped and reached for Daisy's hand. Rosie put her arm around Ella's shoulder as they all peered over the edge down into the hole. Cerberus, who had been removed from the hole due to lack of room, barked excitedly. In a few minutes Jake had unearthed a plain metal box, not much bigger than a regulation lunch box but reasonably weighty. He handed it up to Iris.

Iris held the box reverently, absently brushing the dirt away. The metal that had felt cold in her palms a moment ago now felt incredibly warm. The energy flowing from it was off the scale.

"Well?" Daisy demanded as Jake and Simon scrambled out of the hole. "Aren't you going to open it?"

Iris nodded. "At the table."

Everyone hurried to the verandah. No one dared to speak as they sat and watched Iris place the box in front of her. Cerberus whined at her side and she gave him a pat as she sat. "Good boy, Cerberus. Good dog." He wiggled happily.

"What do you suppose is in there?" Rosie asked.

"It's Annie's stuff," Iris said, her hand resting on the lid. The realisation had come to her slowly as the hole had deepened. She didn't doubt it; she knew it the way she always knew things.

Then she opened the box and pulled out a couple of small drawstring sacks still remarkably intact. Iris placed them on the table and looked at them for a moment or two.

"You open them," she said to Daisy.

Daisy didn't need to be asked twice. She widened the opening on one bag and emptied the contents onto the table top. An assortment of jewelry slipped out, brooches, rings, necklaces—diamonds, rubies, pearls.

Rosie gasped. "Are they—do you think they're real?"

Simon nodded. "I'd say this is Shamus's loot. I reckon they're the real deal."

Daisy quickly emptied the contents of the other, much heavier, sack. Coins tumbled out, followed by a bundle of old paper currency rolled up and held tight by a piece of string and several dirty-looking irregular-shaped rocks ranging in size from a pea to a marble.

Simon picked one up and inspected it. "I think these are nuggets. Gold nuggets."

Nobody said a word for the longest time as they sat looking at Annie's loot. Or, as Iris had put it, their salvation.

Then Daisy reached for a cigarette. "Looks like we can pay for those repairs now," she said as she lit it.

# CHAPTER NINETEEN

You could have heard a pin drop in the dying seconds of the BSFC grand final as the Demons kicked to convert their score-evening try in the last two minutes. It was a difficult kick, at a crazy angle in the hands of Ned, a skinny, hormonal sixteen-year-old, whose knees could be heard knocking in the next state.

Ella couldn't look—she buried her face in Rosie's shoulder. At the moment just pulling air in and out of her lungs and keeping her stomach contents where they belonged was difficult enough. She didn't have to look at Jake to know how tense he was, his statue-like presence just a few feet from her, radiating an edgy anticipation.

Ella peeked. Ned peered at the middle bar of the goal post and then back at the ball. He repeated the process several times, mentally lining up his kick. Ella pressed her face back again as Ned took his first step toward the ball. Rosie's hand tightened on hers and Ella swore she heard the sound of a collective gasp from the entire Hanniford stand as the sound of a boot hitting leather echoed across the field.

"What's happening?" Ella whispered urgently.

"It's up in the air," Rosie commentated. "It's arcing back down … it's looking pretty good, it's looking … very good. Oh my God! It's dead center."

And then the entire crowd roared and Ella was yanked to her feet by Rosie and she turned to see Jake and Pete running on to the field toward the huddle of Demons, who had lifted skinny Ned into the air and were throwing him up and down like a crowd surfer in a mosh pit.

Rosie was hugging her, Simon was hugging her, some Demons' supporters who were standing behind her were hugging her. It was an orgy of embraces and cheers and excited jumping up and down.

Then the Demons' supporters and the cheer squad were running onto the field and Rosie was pulling her along as well. She stumbled, laughing and accepting congratulations from blurry people as they charged past her to get to the team.

The full extent of what they'd achieved hit her as she stood among the chaos. Hanniford High School, the down-and-out, inner-suburban, hard-luck school, *her school*, had won the BSFC in their inaugural year. They'd done it. She'd done it. She'd notched up the first step in saving her school from the education department axe.

And in the process, the school community had united as she'd never imagined possible. It was as if Hanniford had gone into a chrysalis all broken and defeated and emerged a thing of beauty, cohesive and unified. The students had pride, she could see it in the way they walked and the way they met her eyes. Even the teachers, jaded from years of disillusionment, had a spring in their step and a vigor in their lessons.

They'd done it. They'd really done it. Suddenly she was shaking all over. The crowd pushed and jostled around her but Ella didn't even register it. She searched for Jake in the sea of well-wishers. He was probably only a few meters away—she could see his buzz-cut a head higher than most of the crowd—but he may as well have been on the moon; the mass of people between them was too impenetrable and she was suddenly utterly exhausted.

She turned away from the crowd and made her way back to the empty stand, taking a seat. She smiled at the excited mob still hogging the middle of the field. She watched Jake sign an autograph. He chose that moment to look up and she grinned at him. Damn it! Even half a field away she wanted to tear his clothes off and do him. He gave her a little shrug and waggled his fingers at her. She blew him a kiss. Their celebration could wait. They had all night. Hell, they had all their lives.

It was nice not to have to worry, to just sit and know for the first time in two years that her job was safe, her school was safe. Combine that with their home also being safe and Ella felt so carefree it was as if she'd been filled with helium.

She had an overwhelming urge to lie down on the wooden seat and shut her eyes. The last couple of weeks had been exhausting. Between the media interest, the intense training schedule and her hot sweaty nights with Jake, there hadn't been a lot of sleeping going on. But Ella wouldn't have traded them for anything.

She couldn't say she was the same person now as she had been before the furor but maybe it'd been time to change anyway. Her trip to Huntley had helped. Enrolling Cam and her in counseling—despite his protests—had helped even more so. Jake was right—her anger had been holding her back. Taking steps toward letting it go had been incredibly cathartic. They still had a long road ahead but at last Ella felt as if they were finally on the right track.

It seemed like an age before the crowd let Jake out of its clutches and he didn't waste any time bounding toward her. Her heart beat a crazy little tap-dance as his powerful thighs ate up the distance between them, taking the steps two at a time. He stopped in front of her, placing one foot on the step beside her and gave her a lazy smile as her gaze slowly crawled from his groin to his face.

"I know what you're thinking."

"Really? It's kind of shocking." She grinned.

Jake swallowed at the thought. "Isn't it improper or illegal or something for the principal to be talking dirty to the coach within school grounds? With so many minors around?"

"Not on grand final day."

Jake laughed as he sat beside her and put his arm around her shoulders, looking at the Demons still lapping up praise in the middle of the oval. "You did it. Today the BSFC, tomorrow the Schools Cup."

Ella beamed at him. "*We* did it."

Jake shook his head. "No way. This was all you. I had to be coerced, remember?"

Ella's smile slipped. "I know." She lifted her hand and trailed her fingers along his jaw. "Thank you for changing your mind."

Jake grinned as he bent his head to nuzzle her neck. "It's been my pleasure."

"Hey Jake, unhand that woman," Trish hollered. Jake and Ella looked up at her. "They're presenting the trophy. Get your asses down here."

Jake glanced at Ella. "Later," he murmured and then stood and held out his hand.

*

Monday was a joy to behold for Ella. A steady flow of phone calls in the morning for enrollments for the following year not only put them into the safe zone but looked like it would also garner Hanniford a deputy principal as well as several extra teachers.

An official from Junior Rugby League Australia rang to talk about funding to base a rugby league school of excellence at Hanniford. Six months ago, Ella would rather have burnt the school to the ground, but today she felt a little trill of excitement as the possibilities blossomed in her head.

And, sweetest of all, Donald Wiseman rang to rather stiffly congratulate her and inform her that with all the new enrollments, the education review panel no longer had Hanniford on its closure list.

It really was a bloody marvelous day.

That night they all gathered around Daisy and Iris's table to celebrate their achievements. The aroma of saw dust hung like a blanket of humidity in the air—thick and heavy—and tickled Ella's throat.

After going through all the proper channels, the sale of Annie's loot, arranged by Simon to a private collector, had netted them enough money to clear the mortgage, with plenty left over for renovations, and the heritage contractors had started a few days ago. The renovations were going to take six months but nobody cared. They could live in a construction zone for as long as it took to get Annie's old bordello shipshape.

The household of five had grown to seven now that Jake and Simon had taken up permanent residence with their women. Miranda and Pete, who always seemed to be around as they were tonight, had joined them for dinner. The four-legged residents all lolled on the ground by their feet, except for Cerberus, who was up next to Simon, scoring food.

Dinner—Rosie's curry, of course—accompanied by the low hum of Ella Fitzgerald magic tinkling in the background, was a raucous affair, competing with the lorikeets in the noise department. Watching the proceedings Ella realized she loved Daisy and Iris more tonight than she ever had. She and Rosie had essentially invaded their perfect, spinster-like existence twenty years ago and they hadn't once complained.

"What?" Daisy asked through squinty eyes as she dragged on a rollie, her shrewd gaze resting on Ella.

Ella smiled at the cantankerous old woman. "Nothing."

"Nothing my ass," she chortled. "What was that look about?"

Ella sighed. "I was just thinking how marvelous you and Iris are. You took us in and became our family. You gave us a life."

"Nonsense," Daisy dismissed. "Our lives hadn't begun until you girls came along. You are our life."

Ella's vision misted over at the gruffness in the older woman's voice. She felt Jake's hand give her thigh a squeeze. Daisy wasn't big on personal statements so she took that as a major concession.

"Ah, I think we're going to go and watch some TV," Cam interrupted.

"Not too late," Jake warned. "Early to bed for the next week. Miranda, I'm taking you home in an hour."

"Yes, coach," they chorused as they departed, rolling their eyes in the way of teenagers the world over.

The adults watched them go. "They're good together," Iris murmured. Nobody disagreed.

As dinner continued, conversation turned to their grand-final win. "I'd just like to point out," Simon said, "this whole thing was my idea."

"So it was," Ella agreed.

Rosie slung her arm around his shoulders. "He's brilliant, isn't he?"

"Definitely," Ella agreed. "And for that I give you permission to marry my best friend."

"Ella, don't take this the wrong way." Simon smiled. "But I'm marrying this woman whether you permit it or not."

Ella grinned at her friend. "I see your penchant for dominance is rubbing off?"

Rosie sighed. "What can I say, the man knows too much about democracy."

The conversation soon turned to football and strategy for the Schools Cup, which was to be played against exclusive Chiswick College the following Saturday. Chiswick would be hosting the match and had won the cup eight out of the last ten years.

"I managed to get hold of a DVD of Chiswick's last game." Pete dropped the morsel into the conversation and everyone turned to stare at him.

Jake shook his head. "How on earth did you manage that? The street-urchin network again?"

Pete grinned. "Something like that."

When Jake had first taken Pete under his wing, he'd been amazed at the kid's ability to attain the unattainable, to source the unsourceable. Now nothing surprised him.

"Have you seen it?"

Pete nodded. "They're good."

"Well," Daisy demanded. "Did you bring it with you?"

Pete winked at her. "Of course."

"Well?" she demanded again.

Pete rose from the table, retrieved the disk from his bag and slotted it into the DVD player that sat on top of the television in the veranda's very own entertainment unit. "This is their grand final match."

He pressed play on the remote as all eyes fixed on the television. For forty minutes, only the odd scraping of plates could be heard above the muffled sounds of an amateur taping. But there were good close-ups of the action and Jake knew they'd scored gold.

"Well done, Pete," he said as the half-time hooter went and the person taping the game obviously decided crowd shots and scenery would suffice until the game started again.

They used the break in play to analyse the tape. "There's some great stuff on there," Jake said. "We'll go over it all in more detail tomorrow morning, Pete, and with the team in the afternoon."

"They do look good," Simon commented. "Really good."

Jake nodded, they did. That was irrefutable. But the Demons had come from nowhere, with nothing, and won the BSFC trophy. Chiswick were champions. But so were Hanniford and they had something that Chiswick didn't. They had something to prove.

Ella had been mesmerized by how skillful the play was. She may have been a novice but everything about Chiswick scared the bejesus about her. "They look like they play to win."

"So do we," Pete said.

Ella turned to Jake. She loved him. He'd turned her entire life upside down and somehow in the process managed to turn it right around. She wanted him to know that it was okay to be beaten by a far superior team. That winning this one didn't matter. That they'd proved themselves.

"Jake. The Schools Cup doesn't matter. Not anymore. Hanniford's not under threat of closing. And the boys have nothing to prove. They came from nowhere to beat the best in Brisbane public schools. But these guys—" she shook her head, "they're in a league of their own."

"You hired me to win you the Schools Cup. And that's what I'm going to do."

Ella smiled, surprised that she loved his stupid male pride as much as the rest of him. "Okay, I'm just saying that no one's going to think less of you, or the Demons, if they lose this match."

Jake's jaw tightened. "I'll think less of me."

Ella smiled despite his suddenly serious face. "I mean it, Jake. Chiswick College is the most exclusive boys' education-al facility in the state. They obviously have the best equipment and coaches money can buy."

Jake shook his head. "You have the best coach money can buy."

Ella glared. "You're free, Jake."

Jake grinned. "What can I say? The school principal drives a hard bargain."

"What I'm trying to say," she said with a tinge of exasperation, "is the boys have done their best and I don't want them to get their hopes up too high. It's alright to admit defeat, you know. Sometimes there's even honor in it."

A shout on the video drew everyone's attention back to the television as the Chiswick College boys ran back on to the field. The person behind the camera said, "What do you think, coach?" and swung around for a close-up of a man wearing a shirt that said *Coach*.

The shot was blurry and came slowly into focus as the man said, "Those guys are a pack of limp dick, pansy-assed crybabies. Call themselves an opposition? They play like a bunch of girls. They might as well have their cheerleaders play the game for them. At least we'd have a bit of tits and ass, a bit of girl-on-girl to look at. We've got this one in the bag."

Everyone stared as the speaker came into focus. "Oh yeah, I forgot that bit," Pete said sheepishly over the continuing tirade of abuse. "Tony Winchester's son plays for Chiswick. He's the coach."

Ella stared at the face on the screen as it continued to mouth unprintable obscenities about the opposition like they were brainless zombies and their cheerleaders like they were there for his sexual pleasure. She felt sick. How dare he talk like that about the opposition? About fellow human beings?

A wave of disgust welled up, heating her skin and flushing her face. She already detested the man for what he'd done to Trish but this tirade was hazing her vision with a red fog.

She turned to Jake. "Forget what I just said. I want you to win. Not just win but I want you to crush that smarmy prick into the dust. And then when he's down, I want you to stomp on his neck so he can never utter another vile word. Can you do that?"

Jake grinned. "Yep."

"Good," she muttered and reached across to the table for the remote, flicking a button to switch it off. Tony Winchester had already infected too much of their lives. Damned if he was going to taint them with his vileness on her home turf.

# CHAPTER TWENTY

Ella sat in the plush change rooms at Chiswick College, listening to Jake and Pete give their pre-match talk to the Demons. She could see the impossibly green, manicured field through the open louvers—it looked as if a team of trained leprechauns had individually trimmed each blade of grass. Occasional shouts from the already strong crowd filtered in. The aroma of sweat and Deep-Heat infused her senses.

Her stomach felt like a flock of butterflies had swallowed elephants and were trouncing around inside her. She wanted to win this. Not for her or for Jake or for Hanniford, but for Trish and women like her. She wanted to see Tony Winchester go down.

"Ella?"

Jake and Pete were looking at her expectantly and Ella guessed it was her turn to speak. She enjoyed the tradition of her principal pep talk more and more each time and so, she thought, did the team. Or at least, it was a ritual they'd dare not buck in case any deviation from routine brought them bad luck.

And they called women flighty!

She looked at each of the boys in turn; she could tell they were a little awed by their surroundings. Chiswick College was a physically impressive campus: landscaped gardens, state-of-the-art classrooms and intimidating sandstone buildings that reeked wealth. And they were looking to her to tell them it didn't matter. That how you played the game and the size of your heart trumped money and tradition.

But today she was reluctant. Today she wanted to say things she never thought she'd ever think, let alone contemplate giving voice to. She wanted to say kill them, smash them, play dirty if you have to, gouge their eyes, punch them in the kidneys, spear their rich little heads into the ground if needs be—just win. At any cost.

It went against everything she believed in but it was right there on the tip of her tongue, waging a battle against her political correctness to be heard.

"Ella?" Jake prompted.

She looked at him. He was frowning and nodding at her to get on with it. She stood on shaky legs, her gaze falling on Cameron. He was sitting so tall. So confident. And when he smiled at her she knew she'd come too far with him to take him backward.

She cleared her throat. "I'm not going to say much," she said. "You guys have already done me and Hanniford and Jake and Pete so proud. You've come a long way and earned yourselves a fearsome reputation. I know you want to win today. Well, guess what? I want you to win today too."

The Demons glanced at her with confused looks. Usually Ella spoke to them about might and heart and spirit. What she was saying slowly dawned on them and, one by one, they grinned and then clapped and then stomped their boots on the ground, filling the change rooms with an almighty clatter.

"So go on now," she called out above the din, holding up her hand and waiting for the racket to die down. "Let's get our names on that damn cup."

The team sprang to their feet, cheering and clapping and Ella laughed, caught up in the heady mix of exuberance and testosterone.

"Way to go, Ms. Lucas," Jake murmured as the boys filed out of the room.

Ella favored him with a steady stare. "Annihilate him."

Jake smiled before lowering his lips to hers, bending her head back with a kiss full of passion and revenge. "I love it when you talk dirty," he whispered, flicking a towel at her butt as he followed his team out.

Ella was the only one left in the change room and she took a moment to center herself. It was at times like this she wished she believed in God. Not that it was appropriate, she supposed, to ask a benevolent God to orchestrate a slow, painful death, but it'd be nice to have faith that Tony Winchester would get what was coming to him.

She stepped out into the cool darkness of the tunnel that lead from the change rooms to the oval, surprised to see Cameron lingering. "Cam?" She frowned. "Everything okay?"

Cameron nodded. "Yes."

Ella heard his boot scraping against the concrete floor and wondered what on earth he was doing. "Cam, shouldn't you be on the field?"

"I just want to—I'd like to talk to you for a moment."

Ella frowned again. She looked to the light at the end of the tunnel, relieved to see the game hadn't yet started. "Oh. Okay."

Cameron took a deep breath. "I'm sorry for being such a jerk."

Ella blinked, completely taken aback by his apology, the only one she'd ever heard come from his mouth. "About our argument a few weeks ago?"

"No. Well, yes ... that too. But I mean, just ... generally. I know I haven't been very easy to get along with and you've been nothing but kind. It's just growing up in Huntley was hard, you know? And I dreamed for years my big sister would come and rescue me and when you didn't it was easier to … hate you."

Ella felt tears needle her eyes. "Oh, Cam! I would have, if I'd known, I would have …" She took a step toward him.

Cam took a step back and held out his hand to pause her movement. "I know that now. I do. And I didn't hate you, not really. Miranda reckons I'm lucky to have such a cool big sister. And so do I."

She heard his voice crack and the tears threatened to spill. A lump in her throat grew bigger, stretching her chest to painful proportions. Cameron's admission was shocking—he just didn't do deep and meaningful. Maybe the counseling she'd insisted upon was making bigger inroads than she thought?

"I love you, Cam," she whispered. "We may not have been brother and sister for long but we're part of each other and I love you."

Cameron looked at the ground examining his boot. "I love you too."

"Cam!" Ella jumped as Jake's exasperated command ricocheted around the cavernous tunnel. "What are you doing? It's twenty seconds to kick-off."

Cameron looked at Jake then at her. "Go," she said, giving him a quick, fierce hug. "Go!"

Cameron ran from her toward the entrance, his cleats clacking on the cement, echoing noisily. Jake slapped him on the back as he passed and ran beside Cameron, accompanying him to the field.

Ella followed at a more sedate pace, her mind turning over the things Cam had said and rejoicing in the step forward he'd taken. Sure he'd taken steps before—baby steps. This was one giant leap.

The whistle sounded as she emerged into the full light of the Saturday morning. The sound of boot hitting ball rang like a shot around the field and the packed stands erupted into a hearty cheer. She noticed a large contingent of press roped off to one end with John Wells in the middle, a smug look on his face. This simple high school football match had been significantly elevated in the press, egged on by Wells. It wasn't about the Schools Cup anymore, it was about two old rivals squaring off against each other. As though the pressure on the Demons wasn't already bad enough.

She hurried to the sideline bench, ignoring the media. Rosie, Simon and Trish were already sitting, their devil-horn headbands firmly in place. Pete was standing off to one side, watching the play. Jake was prowling along the sideline, a bedeviled Cerberus at his heels. She plonked herself between Rosie and Trish and grabbed their hands. "What's happening?"

"Nothing yet," Rosie said.

It didn't take long for that to change. And it wasn't a change for the better. Chiswick wiped the field with the Demons in the first half with their superior ball skills, as though it was their God-given right to reclaim the cup. Ella, as per her usual position, spent half the time with her hands over her eyes, begging Rosie and Trish to tell her what was happening.

Tony Winchester spent the first forty minutes on the opposite side of the field yelling at his team despite their exemplary play. A slight fumble, a misstep, and he was hurling insults that would have made Rosie blush from the sidelines.

It was a shame really, because Ella had to admit, looking at him clinically, he was still a very impressive man. He wasn't in Jake's league—but then few men were. Richard Armitage and Hugh Jackman aside. On the surface Tony Winchester still had *it*. She could see why Trish had fallen for him. But as far as she was concerned, his black heart and cruel tongue made him uglier than a hat full of assholes.

After a particularly awful tongue-lashing, Ella turned to Trish, whose fingers had curled around hers like a vice. "Is it hard for you to see him again?"

Trish shuddered. "He's such a tyrant. Where the hell was my head?"

"Hmph," Rosie butted in. "He's a fricking mad man. Aren't there rules against Adolf coaches in children's sports?"

Ella placed her hand over Trish's. "Time has a way of eroding facades."

"And he's just butt-ugly under his," Rosie added.

Trish laughed. "Yes, he is, isn't he?"

*

At half time, Chiswick led by sixteen points, with Hanniford only managing to get one on the board from a field goal before the whistle.

The Demons trailed back into their change room followed by their entire entourage—Ella, Simon, Rosie and Trish. Even Cerberus followed them in, finding Cameron immediately and collapsing on the floor at his feet.

Jake eyed his dejected team, struggling with finding the right words to encourage and empower. He glanced at Ella, who gave him an encouraging nod. He opened his mouth, hoping to God the words that came out were the ones the Demons needed to hear. But before he said a single thing, a string of obscenities from the Chiswick camp next door echoed around the Hanniford rooms.

Jake's mouth shut automatically, stunned by the ferocity of Tony Winchester's pep talk. He was ranting about the field goal. How Chiswick's strategy was to keep Hanniford off the board altogether and how badly they'd fucked up. He was screaming *failure, failure, failure* at them. Calling them morons. Calling them girls.

"Why is he yelling at them?"

Jake tuned back in to his locker room and saw the stunned looks on his team's faces as Ned voiced the question that was obviously on all of their minds.

"They're really good," Ned said. "They're all over us."

Jake looked at Ella standing by the door, her livid face so rigid he was afraid she'd been struck with a case of lockjaw. Trish just looked pale and Jake wanted to go next door and punch the lousy mongrel in the head.

"Yes." Jake cleared his throat. "Yes, they are. Their coach, however, is a monumental dickhead."

A few of the guys laughed but Jake could see that most of them were still tuned in to Tony Winchester's verbal abuse of his team. He couldn't blame them. It was ghoulishly compelling, like hanging around a crash site watching the victims being cut out of their cars; wrong in so many ways but fascinating nonetheless.

Jake belted on a nearby locker, the sound crashing into the morbid stillness and pulling everyone's attention back to him. "Don't listen to him," Jake said quietly. "Listen to me."

He spoke to them about their struggle to get here. About their spirit, their heart, their triumphs; things that Ella usually talked about. He praised their individual strengths and applauded their teamwork. And gradually, Tony Winchester's rant faded and he could see by the expressions on their faces that they were listening only to him.

"Whatever happens today, you boys have made me prouder than I've ever been. Prouder even than when I played for my country. And you have one thing that they don't," Jake said, pointing next door to the room where the rant continued. "Respect. For me. For each other. And that's why, despite what that scoreboard says, we're going to win this."

Jake finished and took a moment to look at each team member and shake their hand.

"Pete?" he asked. Pete declined the floor. "Ella?"

She looked at him and smiled with tears in her eyes. There was nothing she could add. Jake had said it all.

A loud rap at the door alerted them that halftime was nearly over. "Alright," Jake said. "Let's line up outside and run onto that field like we've already won."

The boys sprang to their feet, cheering and high-fiving as they filed out and waited in the tunnel for the signal to take the field. The adults stood behind them. Jake slipped his hands into Ella's and she shot him a you-were-so-hot-just-now smile. Jake could hear Chiswick clattering out of their locker-room and lining up behind them.

'Well, well, well," a voice drawled from behind him. "If it isn't the coach, the geek, the Goth and her lover."

Jake stiffened and turned slowly around. He felt Ella flinch and kept hold of her hand in case she decided smacking Winchester's face was worth it. He sensed rather than saw Rosie's mouth open and placed a stilling arm on her too. He was not going to get into a slanging match in front of his team and the press snapping shots with a clear view from the tunnel mouth. He forced himself to be impassive and kept his voice low. "It's been a long time, Tony."

Tony nodded. "That it has." He flicked his gaze over Trish. "My, my, Trish. Unlike Jake, I see you've gotten better and better."

Cerberus growled, a growl Genghis would have been proud of, and Ella reached down to pat him.

Trish smiled. "How was community service, Tony?"

Tony's laugh echoed in the tunnel, enhancing its creepiness. "Piece of cake."

A figure appeared at the mouth of the tunnel. "Time to rumble," it announced.

Jake turned away and faced his team. "Let's go."

The Demons ran out to the field, followed by Chiswick. Tony stopped by Jake and they both watched their boys line up against each other. Tony's gaze flicked to the Hanniford cheer squad and he smirked.

"What kind of cheerleaders are they?" he scoffed. "You can't even look up their skirts."

Jake gave Tony a hard look. "The minor kind."

Tony squinted. "What does it say on the backs of their shirts?"

"Hanniford Demons say no to violence against women," Jake said. "Not that you'd know what that means would you, Tony?" Jake was satisfied to see Tony's jaw tighten.

"You always were a morally superior prick," Tony spat.

"Better than being just a prick," Jake said and walked away before the urge to beat Tony to a pulp became even stronger.

*

The second half started and it was as if a switch had been flicked. Chiswick looked defeated from the whistle, making simple errors and not capitalizing on a host of opportunities. Tony ranted. The more he ranted, the worse they played.

"I've made up my mind," Trish said to Ella about ten minutes into the second half. "After the match, I'm going to the police to press charges against Tony."

Ella gaped. She admired Trish's guts but she'd didn't think suicide was the answer. "Are you sure? This many years down the track it would be so hard to prove. Even with Jake's evidence."

"It doesn't matter," she said. "If they throw it out of court, it doesn't matter. Anything I can do to see to it that Tony Winchester isn't allowed to coach minors again, I'm prepared to do it."

Ella grimaced. "That's very noble of you but you know how messy these things can get. You may well live to regret it. What about Miranda?"

Trish shrugged. "You and Cameron are still here, aren't you?"

Ella smiled. Yes, they were. And no doubt better for having all their dirty linen hung out to dry.

A cheer exploded from behind her and Rosie leaped to her feet, yanking Ella with her. Trish rose too and they all hugged and cheered as Hanniford ran in another try. When Ned converted it, his third in a row, the cheer became a roar and Ella grinned as a puce-faced Tony Winchester went apoplectic on the other side of the field.

Karma, baby. Karma!

Five minutes later, however, the high they'd been riding took a sudden nosedive. A collective gasp rang around the field at a sickening spear tackle perpetrated on Ned by two of Chiswick's fullbacks. The referee blew his whistle as Ned lay crunched in a heap on the ground.

Simon flew to his feet. "They've targeted him."

Jake and Pete were running onto the field, followed by a stretcher bearer and a medic. Ella looked back to see Ned's parents on their feet, their faces screwed up into anguished masks. She turned in time to see Tony Winchester smiling and patting the shoulder of one of the Chiswick boys who'd been responsible for the dangerous tackle.

A minute later, Ned was on his feet but very groggy, being supported by the medic and Jake. The referee blew his whistle for a penalty but Ella knew that Tony Winchester's mission had been accomplished—they'd taken out Hanniford's best kicker.

They took Ned into the locker room and his worried parents followed. "Is he okay?" Ella asked as Jake joined her and play resumed.

Jake gave a stiff nod. "A little concussed. They'll take him to hospital, probably keep him under observation overnight."

Tactically it was the worst thing Tony Winchester could have sanctioned, because now the Demons were just plain mad and they played the remaining fifteen minutes like they'd been born with their boots on. With one minute to go, the Demons had passed the Chiswick score and knew they were unbeatable.

Ella and Rosie had tears streaming down their faces as the hooter sounded and Ella laughed as the cameras caught Tony Winchester mid-tantrum, stomping off the field in the worst case of bad sportsmanship since a well-known rugby league player had stuck his finger up an opposition player's ass to put him off his game.

This time, Ella fought tooth and nail to get to Jake and Cameron in the scrum of well-wishers. Jake had done it. She'd asked him to annihilate Tony Winchester and he had. And with Trish's second salvo, the man was going to be utterly destroyed.

"Let me through," Ella called, elbowing and pushing, keeping Jake firmly in her sights. "Let me pass."

Jake spotted her battling her way toward him and he surged into the crowd to meet her halfway. He grinned at her as she flung herself into his arms. She smiled.

"Let me be the first to kiss the coach."

"I hate to disillusion you," Pete said, "You ain't the first."

"Oh, yeah?" Ella cocked her eyebrow and pulled Jake's head down for a full-on X-rated smacker.

"Okay," Pete admitted. "You're the first one to kiss him like *that*."

"So, Jake, does it feel good to beat your old nemesis?"

Jake dragged his gaze away from Ella's gorgeous flushed face into John Wells's shrewd gaze. "I thought that was you?"

Wells laughed. "I think you know who I'm talking about."

Jake smiled. "It felt fucking unbelievable."

The reporter laughed again. "Can I quote you?"

Jake chuckled. "I'd be amazed if you didn't."

Later that night, Ella and Jake lay in bed in a post-coital drowse that was better than drugs. "You suppose it's always going to be like this?" Ella mused, stroking her fingers down his arm.

Jake smiled. "Honey, grand final sex is my forté."

Ella laughed. "Well, I guess you're just going to have to stick around and do it all again next year. Sex like that is definitely worth the wait."

Jake smiled again. "For you, I'll make a special effort every night."

Ella's hand stilled, reveling in the warm, solid muscle beneath her palm. "Thank you, Jake. For everything."

Jake heard the wistful note in her voice and shifted so he could roll up on to his side. "No. Thank you. You gave me a direction in my life. You have no idea how much I owe you."

"Well, lucky for you," she said, walking her fingers up his arm, "I have a payment plan."

Jake nuzzled her neck. "I like your thinking."

Ella shut her eyes as his tongue lapped at her neck and short-circuited the nerve supply to her brain. She angled her neck a little further and smiled when Jake's tongue seized the opportunity. "The education department is talking about setting up a rugby league school of excellence at Hanniford. They're talking full funding, new equipment, the works. I'll be able to pay you. And Pete too."

Jake stilled, his lips pressed to the steady beat of her pulse at the base of her neck. He raised his head and looked at her. He laughed. "Well, look at Little Miss Football. You've certainly changed your tune."

Ella gave him a playful slap on the arm. "I may not be football's best advocate but I'd be foolish if I couldn't see the change it's spawned in my school. If it keeps the kids coming to Hanniford and getting them an education, then I'm all for it."

Jake blinked. He sat up. "You're serious."

Ella sat too, maneuvering herself behind him, her thighs bracketing his as she pressed against the contours of his broad back, her breasts squashed against his hard ribs and spine. "You're a marvelous coach, Jake. If you ever doubted it before, then surely you don't after Tony Winchester."

Jake stared at the sheet. "I never thought about coaching. Not kids anyway."

"Then you've missed your calling."

Jake shut his eyes as her lips pressed kisses along his shoulder blade. "Is this coercion?" he murmured.

Ella smiled against his skin. "Incentive."

"I suppose the pay's lousy?"

Ella nodded. "Yup. But the perks are excellent."

Jake chuckled as her perks beaded against his back. "What about the pub?"

"You're not a publican, Jake. You only bought it because it was something you knew. You're not your father. Pete practically runs it anyway."

Ella let the silence build around them for a while before she prompted, "What do you say, coach?"

Jake grinned, cocking his head back so his lips were almost in line with hers. "I say drop and give me fifty."

# ACKNOWLEDGMENTS

The name on the front of *Holding Out For A Hero* may be mine but all writers know that books are rarely solo endeavours. Sure, putting all those words down is up to you but getting it from the hot steaming mess it always is after you've typed The End to a sparkly masterpiece and into the hands of a reader involves many more people.

Firstly, my ever-faithful beta readers and dear writing friends Robyn Grady, Tina Clark, Rachael Bailey and Anna Cleary. You guys not only helped me make the book better but you've been rooting for HOFAH during all its ups and downs over the years and I know it goes out into the cosmos with lots and lots of love.

My sister, Ros Baxter, who is always my first reader and loves and supports me in ways that go far beyond the literary. She's an outstanding author in her own right and an even more out-standing human being and I count myself lucky every day to have her on my side.

My agent, Clare, whose plot suggestions brought a whole new angle to the book.

To the team at Momentum, particularly Joel Naoum who emailed me to tell me how much he loved the book and wanted to acquire it. He made my year and my Christmas Card list forever!

And finally to everyone who's ever bought one of my books. Thank you. You guys rock!

www.ingramcontent.com/pod-product-compliance
Lightning Source LLC
Chambersburg PA
CBHW030939260626
47169CB00002B/544